Made to be Broken

Rebecca Bradley

Rebecca Bradley

Author's Note

While all attempts have been made to keep this story as factually correct as possible, it has to be remembered that it is in fact, a work of fiction. So, in saying that, I have had to stretch the truth to fit in with how I needed events to work. I am fully aware that toxicology reports from post-mortems take two to four weeks to be returned depending on the level of work that needs to be completed, but that would have slowed down the narrative pace considerably, so in *Made to be Broken*, we have incredibly fast toxicology results from the post-mortems that are conducted. I hope this does not spoil your enjoyment of the book.

1

2 months earlier

It was a Tuesday when she died.

They say the weather reflects these events; rain coming down in droves, slamming into windows like hell unleashed. That's what he thought when he looked out into the weak afternoon sun. Where was hell? Where was the fury? The relentless beating of nature's wrath at one given back too soon?

Instead the sun leaked silently into their desolate world, bleaching the room in swathes of harsh light, lifting the howling sound that came from his wife as she cradled their daughter in her arms. The nurse closed the door behind her as she left them to their grief. A world they would soon become intimate with. There was a sharp but barely perceptible click as the handle lifted back into place, the only evidence the nurse had even been there.

The animal sounds that came from his wife hurt Isaac. It hurt him that their daughter, Em should be subjected, in death, to anything more than the peace she deserved. She'd suffered enough. She hadn't been ready to die. She'd had a life to live. A life filled with promise. Promises of a future career, husband, even children.

Children.

Isaac felt the swell of pain inside him grow. A slow steady uprising from the pit of his stomach. The keening of Connie as she rocked with their baby, intensifying the momentum of his own grief. It rose up and stopped his heart.

He couldn't breathe.

The sun-bleached room gathered its own storm that Tuesday as Isaac's grief and anger overwhelmed him. He dropped to his knees and clutched himself, wracking out great heaving sobs for all he had just lost.

2

There was a heavy quietness to the coroner's court that you didn't get at other courts. A beautiful stone building on the Old Market Square in Nottingham, it held a solemnity you could feel seep into your soul as you stepped through the doors. You were here to discuss the dead and the air was thick with multiple emotions.

My DS, Aaron Stone was waiting for me on a row of padded seats along the corridor. I walked over and he stood to greet me. 'We're in shortly.'

Today was the opening of the inquest into the death of Sally Poynter. She'd been a detective on my unit until last year when she'd been murdered on duty. The coroner would confirm her identity and go over the post-mortem then adjourn until a later date. This was a large inquest, covering a lot of information and would no doubt take some time to account for all the facts.

This was another fragment of a difficult process. We'd been through the trial and conviction of her killer, which would usually mean the inquest wasn't needed, but because she'd been killed on duty, it was going ahead. Something many of us were feeling tense about.

'I know. Thank you.' I sat down next to Aaron. He followed suit and placed the palms of his hands neatly over his knees. I looked at the floor. Aaron's shoes were so polished you could nearly see your face in them. I was grateful he was around, especially today. He was always the level head when I felt emotional.

The remainder of my team would also be here somewhere; my DCs Martin Thacker and Ross Leavy, as would my supervisors DCI Anthony Grey and Detective Superintendent Catherine Walker. Where I ran the investigations on our unit, Grey was my direct supervisor and made sure everything was running smoothly. He attended a lot of the meetings with partner agencies and Catherine oversaw it all. She was responsible for the entire department, for all of us and she worried about how our actions reflected on her.

My phone vibrated in my bag. Ethan.

Thinking of you today. X

I switched vibrate off without responding, left the phone in silent mode and dropped it back in my bag. I had nothing to say. He wouldn't expect me to reply. He knew me better than that after all this time. I needed to get through this. Like I'd managed to get through the past six months. I'd gradually cut him off after Sally's death. I had wanted to feel his arms around me, the familiar warmth and heat of him, to know I was held and safe, but I couldn't allow myself to have that, our careers were too opposed. I'd pushed him away. Yet, he was still there for me. On the day the inquest opened, when he knew I'd feel it more than ever.

Ethan was the crime reporter for Nottingham's main newspaper, the *Nottingham Today* and we'd been in a relationship until Sally was killed, at which point trust had become an issue. I didn't know if I could trust him. I didn't trust myself.

I looked back to Aaron's brogues. I'm not sure how long I stared at the floor, but I picked up the minor twitch in Aaron's body and looked up to find the cause. Tom Poynter. Sally's husband. He stood at the bottom end of the corridor, looking at us. His face ashen and lined. I didn't remember him being so lined, so old looking. I stood. Aaron stood at my side. Tom didn't move. He stood there and he stared.

Not a word was spoken. I couldn't breathe. I had words; I just didn't know how to form them. Not long after Sally had been murdered in the house I had led her in to, as part of a raid on the ringleader of a massive paedophile operation last year, I had visited Tom. I touched his hand and tried so hard to say what needed to be said. The words I felt. Tom couldn't hear anything back then, his grief so consuming. She'd kept a secret from me, I knew there was something bothering her at the time, but I was so absorbed with the task of finding the killers of the children and of finding a missing child, I had been less than a supervisor should be and let Sally's explanations go, rather than pushing for more. I carried that blame with me when I visited Tom and told him of her death, and I felt the weight of blame as he crumbled in front of me while all I could do was stand and watch and feed him the facts as I knew them.

Since that first and only meeting with him, we hadn't talked. Catherine had assigned the case of Sally's murder to another SIO and had told me in no uncertain terms that I was not to have contact with him during the course of the investigation. The circumstances of her murder had also been referred to the IPCC and this investigation was still ongoing. Now Tom was in front of me and once again, words were failing me. Tom took a couple of steps forward. I didn't move. He took another couple of steps; I moved forward away from the seat and went to put my hand out towards him. Just as I did, Tom looked me directly in the eye. My stomach twisted. He turned away and walked past before turning into the coroner's courtroom. I dropped my hand, the thoughts in my head fogged. I felt Aaron's hand on my elbow as he steered me towards the room that would be responsible for bringing light to the facts surrounding Sally's death.

3
2003

Emma was like a beacon of light in his life.

An only child. Though not through choice. He and Connie had spent many years trying for a brother or a sister after Emma had arrived, to make her world more rounded and complete. When nature failed them they turned to the doctors. The doctors also failed to produce the much longed-for second child. The final piece to their jigsaw family. Trying, faith, money nor science would bring the circle round to a whole, so in the end they had to come to terms with what they were and had to make it up to Emma for failing her.

He had failed her. They said Isaac's sperm wasn't strong enough; they died before reaching their destination. It was surprising they managed it the first time.

Emma was a miracle.

So that was it, she was his miracle. He nurtured her. Loved and adored her. Nothing was too much for him.

When she was seven, Em fell off her bike. They lived on a quiet suburban street in Stapleford with little through traffic, mostly just that of the residents, and they drove carefully. Emma was playing with her friends and ended up trying to see if she could go faster than them, beat them to her house after Connie called them in for cupcakes she'd finished icing. Isaac had been at work. From what he'd been told, Emma was so eager to get to the house first, she took a quick look behind her just as she reached the kerb and the front tyre bounced, pushing her right off the saddle and onto the road. She broke her arm.

It took Connie two months to talk him into letting her ride on the bike again. He was so afraid she would do more damage to herself. The sight of her small fragile arm in the heavy plaster cast was nearly too much for him to bear. He wanted to get rid of the bike. To take it down to the dump site while she slept. They argued in hushed tones for days until he let it rest and mulled it over some more, watched Em lug her heavy arm about with pride, like a trophy, asking everyone she met if they wanted to sign it, even complete strangers. She carried a marker pen in her pocket for such occasions.

Isaac relented with unease.

4

The major incident room was just as I'd left it on Friday evening, just as it was every day. Nothing had changed. Nothing ever does. The world keeps turning and life keeps moving forward.

I walked around to the front of my desk. Piles of papers were stacked on each side of the computer monitor. I took off my jacket, wrapped it around the back of my chair and stood facing the single blue folder that lay in front of the keyboard. It held the photographs of Sally's crime scene.

The coroner had adjourned the hearing as expected. It would be several weeks before we'd be back there again. I was drained. My neatly brushed hair felt undone and my barely there make-up was no longer there, rubbed away by the tedium of sitting, waiting, fretting and listening, in that room and in those corridors. In the heat, with the sun blazing through the large oval shape topped windows of the inquest room. We were having a particularly warm spring.

I picked up the folder, pulled open the top drawer of the desk and slid it under the file already in there and left my office.

Walking to the door of the incident room I looked across at Aaron who was rigidly working at his computer, his fingers tapping away, eyes scanning the screen in front of him.

We'd been restructured not long after Sally's murder and as part of the restructuring our base had moved and we were now working out of St Ann's station on St Ann's Well Road, Nottingham. A plain brick building that wasn't open to the public but was simply a base for officers like our unit. I had an actual office in the corridor to the incident room rather than the makeshift goldfish bowl I had at Central police station. I felt a little detached from the team in there, so I often found myself sitting on someone's desk monitoring things from inside the office; but sometimes it proved useful to have that distance.

Instead of having our own Major Crimes Unit, Nottinghamshire had merged our Major Crimes Unit with the major crime units of Leicestershire, Northants, Lincolnshire and Derbyshire to become the East Midlands Special Operations Unit – Major Crime, or EMSOU. The upshot of this new arrangement was that should one of the teams in the other areas be busy with a job, a murder or other serious incident, when another job came in on their area, then one of the other teams could pick it up, regardless of how far away they were. Most of the time it wasn't an issue. There had been occasions however, when officers had been sent miles from home to work a homicide and once it was picked up by the team, it couldn't be handed over at the earliest opportunity to the closest team; the original attending team worked it to the end. So it meant long distance travelling and poor home lives for those who fell foul. We were still Nottinghamshire officers, working from Nottinghamshire in the same team as before, with the same internal set up as before, but now we were part of a larger whole and our patch was potentially a whole lot bigger. We could be sent anywhere in the East Midlands.

I continued to watch Aaron work. We'd gone into the Costa Coffee on the Market Square after the inquest was adjourned and ordered drinks, sitting downstairs; neither of us had much been in the mood for small talk. We'd worked together on Major Crime for the past seven years since I joined the team. Aaron was already on the team before I arrived. He didn't seem to be in a hurry to apply for promotion, but then again, neither did I. We had found our groove with each other and I relied heavily on my detective sergeant. At times he frustrated me, especially when I wanted him to join me in my rants, but he never would, he was always the voice of reason and we worked well that way. I needed that. I knew I could be a little over emotional sometimes.

We'd sat opposite each other in silence for a good ten minutes before I broke through it. Not deliberately. I just needed to say something. The mood of the morning swirling around in my head like a fog wrapping itself around cars travelling on a dark road.

'She's good,' I said.

'Who?' he'd asked.

'Elliott. The coroner. She'll do a good job. For Sally.'

'Yes. She will.' Aaron straightened his tie, pulled at it a little, tightening it up around his throat. He swallowed and silence enveloped us again. I had nothing in me to break the spell it was weaving. I let it lie and drank the rest of my drink in silence, taking a couple of painkillers to ease the pain that had gathered in my arm through the day.

Now we were back in the office, Aaron was throwing himself into the work on his desk, his shoulders starting to hunch up and his fingers slowing as he read the words across his screen. I walked away, leaving him to work through his own feelings, however he needed to.

5

Ross Leavy sat at his desk, staring at the blinking cursor as though it would hold the answer. It was the day from hell, going to the inquest, dredging it all up again, but having it pulled out into the open, pored over and studied like a specimen, didn't feel right. It had unsettled him – and now he was back here in front of a screen again.

He hated this part of the job with a passion. The endless amount of sitting about and typing. Typing for the sake of fucking typing half the time. The phrase dotting i's and crossing t's annoyed the hell out of him. He wanted to police. Catch the bad guys. Not sit on his arse and do nothing. The red tape was bureaucracy gone mad. Court cases were nothing but a game to the playing barristers and everyone else was just a pawn waiting to see if they could make it to the other side or if they would be taken off the board. He was sick of it. The cursor blinked some more. Ross looked back. At the night he picked up that job. The night he became the OIC, Officer In Case, for a Category C murder.

He'd walked up to the small two-up two-down semi on The Markhams, in Ollerton. Martin by his side. One patrol car parked on the road. An old-timer cop stood on the pavement waiting to update them and a cop he recognised as a probationer because of his collar number, stood at the doorway looking green under the sodium street lights that had only just come on. His back ramrod straight and his fists clenched tightly at his sides. His whole body; tense and rigid. His throat swallowing hard. This must have been his first murder. Maybe even his first dead body.

Steve Lynde, the old timer, approached them. 'Husband and wife, no kids. Wife is on the kitchen floor; bloodied stomach and chest with a couple of wounds visible. Husband was still stood over her with the knife in his hand when we turned up. Just stood there. Looking down at her.' He rubbed his wide forehead. 'Strangest thing.' He looked at Martin, the older of the two detectives. 'He stayed looking down for a few seconds while we shouted at him to put the knife down, then handed us the knife and continued looking at her. We called for another car and arrested him. He didn't say a word. Just kept looking at her. He's down at the Bridewell custody suite now. Newark custody block is closed. Apparently they have a lack of custody sergeants so it's down to the city. Better for you guys I suppose. It's a bit of trek up here for you. Get a nose bleed on the way up did you?' It was the usual joke when you went further north in the county. It seemed Lynde just didn't want to stop talking.

Martin thanked him. Always polite. Ross blanked him.

Her knees were bent underneath her where she fell, blood congealed in her hair from an open wound on her temple. It glistened, reflecting in the two strip lights overhead. Her head close to the set of drawers, each with its own square metal handle. Below her head were a couple of darkening red patches on shredded clothing and blood around her pooling on black and white kitchen tiles.

Ross stared at the screen, thinking about that night. All that blood. The knife wounds.

The cursor blinked back at him.

6

Ross walked out of the house. He needed to wait for the CSIs to do their stuff. The woman's blood red blinding him as he walked. She had a familiarity about her. Her colouring. Her build. Ross suddenly felt unsteady and he knocked into the hallway table, which was covered in mail, leaflets for county days out, a pen pot. Blinded by the blood.

He knew where the familiarity came from.

Martin pulled him by his elbow as he exited the door. 'What the hell, Ross?'

Ross blinked.

'No Tyvek suit?' he clarified.

'Shit. Sorry Martin. I didn't touch anything. It's just as Lynde said. Looks straightforward. Wait for the CSIs, interview the guy at the Bridewell and go from there.'

Martin didn't answer. He waited a beat. The air cool and darkness starting to fall. Lights being switched on down the street as people settled in for a night in front of the TV. Life.

'I know.' Ross ran his hand through his already tousled hair. 'Mate. I know. I wasn't thinking. I'm distracted. You know that.'

'Talk to me is all. We're all feeling it. But we still have to do the job. Bottling it up won't help her, you or anyone else we deal with. I'm here.' Another look. 'Okay?'

'Yeah. Okay. The scene is intact. CSIs will show that. I'll do better. I'd appreciate if the boss isn't made aware.'

7

Bill's restaurant on Queen's Street used to be a bank; it had high ceilings and was just beautiful. One of my favourite places to eat and I needed something substantial inside me after the day I'd had.

We sat on the mezzanine, the table between us, our silence speaking volumes. Telling more than our words would ever say. I sipped on the wine I'd ordered and observed him over the top of my glass. Ethan hadn't changed. He was looking after himself. He was obviously still using the gym, his clothes fitted well and he took care of himself in a relaxed, *I'm-not-really-trying* kind of way. He smiled.

'What?'

'You think I can't see you because you're drinking?'

'Okay.' I put my drink down.

'How are you? I was surprised to hear from you.'

'You did text me.'

'I texted you many times. And called you. It never stopped you from ignoring them. Why now, Hannah?'

I looked around the restaurant. A couple of women opposite us were leaning over the table peering into a mobile phone and laughing at whatever it was they were seeing. An easy evening out for them.

I sighed. 'It was a tough day. You texted me. I thought you might want to eat.' And at that point the waitress arrived with our meals. I leaned away from the table and let her place our food down before speaking again. 'Was I wrong to call you?'

'I text you because I care. I cared back then, Han.' He rubbed his hands over his face and silence enveloped us again. I looked down at my plate. The food looked good. Grilled seabass fillets, avocado and caper salsa with pan-fried potato rösti. I picked up my fork and started picking at it.

I let the silence lay while I ate, until he asked again, 'So?'

'What?'

'How are you?'

'I'm tired, Ethan. I'm tired of everyone looking for someone to blame when I know where it lies.'

'Where's that?' His fork went up to his mouth.

'Squarely with me.'

'And that's why we imploded.'

'What do you mean?'

'Look at yourself, Han; you can't take the blame for everything. The world doesn't revolve around you. Other people were involved back then, they took actions and their actions have consequences.'

'Yes, my inactions had consequences as well.'

'For fuck's sake.' His voice raised and a couple of heads turned our way. He put his fork down and lowered his voice. 'You need to look in the mirror and take some responsibility for yourself, Hannah, regardless of what others are doing. You will be so much happier if you can live your own life before you try and mend everyone else's.'

'But—'

'No buts, mend yourself. Before you destroy yourself.' He looked me in the eyes and smiled, a smile I knew so well. He was making me angry but at the same time I wanted to talk some more, to figure this out with him.

'So what now?' I asked.

'That's up to you.'

'My place? We can talk about it. I can tell you how far wide of the mark you are.'

A strange look crossed his face. My stomach twisted.

'Hannah, it's been six months. I want to see you happy. To heal and move forward … but what did you think I'd been doing in that time?'

8

Lianne steadied herself against the kitchen worktop, the feeling of unsteadiness taking her off guard. She didn't need this today. She had to take Megan to dance practice and that useless ex-husband of hers wouldn't lift a finger to help. Since the divorce he had become even more of a bastard than before. His parental duties came below work, drinking, and the golf course. Megan handled it well for a six-year-old. She was a calm and patient child.

Nausea swept over her again and the motion of the solid kitchen floor buoyed again. Her fingers whitened as she held her grip. Where was Megan? She tried to recall. She didn't want her daughter to see her this way. Recent moments filtered through her mind. Snapshots. Bags of shopping. That was this morning. She looked at the clock. But it was nearly 12.30 in the afternoon. What had happened? Where was Megan?

'Meg?' Her voice didn't sound right. It was weak and slurred. What had happened? She looked down at herself, palms pushing on the edge of the worktop, arms outstretched, elbows locked.

Faded blue jeans and grey T-shirt, just as she remembered dressing in this morning. Flat-heeled ballerina style pumps scuffed around the toes. Her right elbow unlocked, her arm sagged and she slipped sideways. Her body slammed down hard onto the counter top, fingers scratching at the shiny laminate in an attempt to regain her balance. She felt the rolled edge of the worktop dig hard into her ribs and she yelped, trying to keep the sound low as it escaped. She didn't yet know where Megan was and she didn't want to scare her. As she rested on the worktop, a wave of nausea hit, she had no choice but to fall to her knees, lean forward and retch hard. With her palms open either side of her on the cool floor, back arched, a low moan escaped as the yellow contents of her stomach, watery and sour, flooded on to the white gloss tiles. Her hair hanging down the sides of her face caught up some of the splatter and the stench clung to the insides of her nose. She heaved again, her face contorting in pain, each spasm of her body bringing her face unbearably close to the floor. Lianne didn't understand what was happening.

She knew she had been unconscious where she fell. She could feel sticky wet fluid under her cheek, chest and hands. She moved a couple of fingers and disturbing the rank yellow stomach contents, felt a heady rush as the acidity hit her brain. She pushed at her eyelids, but they didn't seem to be working. She had no idea how long she had been on the floor. It was still light, but the days were long now so daylight gave little indication. She felt weak. There was no fight in her.

Suddenly she stopped worrying about the situation as her body went into convulsions. Her arms and legs thrashed out independently and her right ankle slammed hard into the leg of the breakfast bar chair, bringing it down on top of her as her body heaved back and forth. The chrome back of the chair landed on Lianne's head, causing her face to smash into the tiles, bright red blood from her nose and mouth and cuts on her face mingling in with the yellow of the vomit. The chair bounced wildly, her leg hooked through the spindle that crossed between two of its legs. With each convulsion the chair came down on the backs of her legs, lower back and head. Bruising and swelling appeared rapidly. Lianne stayed in this freakishly odd dance on the floor for several minutes before it ebbed away; the energy of her body slipping from her and leaving her helpless and broken. Only ten minutes later, she slipped into a coma.

9

2000

'Stay in bed, Daddy,' she'd said in her soft lilting four-year-old voice as she jumped up and down on her toes at the side of him, tugging at Connie's hand as she did so. Connie was smiling, her eyes shining brightly at her daughter.

'It looks like I have to get up,' she said, 'and you have to stay where you are,' she winked at him.

'Come on, Mummy!' Emma tugged harder on Connie's hand.

'Okay. Okay.' Connie pushed the bedclothes to the side, got out of bed and walked out of the bedroom with Emma leading the way, leaving Isaac in bed with a feeling of warmth, love and total contentment. He lay back on the pillows and let out a deep sigh relaxing in the early June morning sunlight that was filtering through the curtains. He wasn't sure how long he'd lain there before he heard Emma's voice again, this time behind the door, whispering.

'I can carry it, Mummy. I'm a big girl now.' Connie murmured something and then Emma again, 'I can!'

The door was pushed open a little bit further and Emma very slowly and very carefully made her way into the bedroom with a tray in her hands, balanced on which was a plate of toast, a glass of orange, a card and a box in wrapping paper. Isaac pushed himself up in the bed until he was sat upright and could see her properly. Her steps were slow and tentative but her smile was as bright as a lighthouse shining to ships in the night. Eventually she made it to the bed and Isaac took the tray from her.

'Happy Father's Day, Daddy.' She couldn't stop beaming and it was contagious, Connie stood behind her glowing and he could feel his heart bursting with pride as his face mirrored hers. He put the tray on his bedside table, then scooped her up onto the bed where she wrapped her short arms around his neck.

'Thank you, sweetie. This looks delicious.'

She pulled away from him and put on her most serious face. 'Daddy you haven't opened your card or present yet.'

He looked at her seriousness and tried to straighten his own face a little to match. 'No, you're right I haven't. I'll do that right now.' He picked up the gift-wrapped box and looked at Connie who was now on the edge of the bed watching them both, a gentle smile on her face. How he adored this woman.

Emma was bouncing up and down on her knees with excitement. He took the wrapping paper off, opened the box and pulled out the mug – *World's Best Dad*. 'Oh honey, this is just brilliant. My own mug to drink my coffee from. Thank you.' He gave another hug as she bounced with excitement.

'Now your card, Daddy.'

He put the mug on the bedside table and opened the card. Now he could see why she was so excited. He looked at Connie who was smiling widely then at Em, who could barely contain herself. Inside the card, for the very first time in her own handwriting, Em had written – *love from Emma X.*

10

DC Martin Thacker sat in front of me. I'd asked him to go out to a job that had been called in and now I needed an update. From what he was saying it seemed to be straightforward and Martin was reliable enough to have everything in hand.

'The school couldn't get in touch with Mum. Dad wasn't answering his phone and they had no other contact details. The teachers couldn't wait any longer so they phoned the police.' I rummaged through the paperwork on my desk for my notepad and pen, and made notes under the date as he talked.

'Then what?'

'Bramcote uniform don't get a reply when they knock but see Mum on the floor when they look through the kitchen window. They force entry and in their words, she's obviously dead; a bit of a mess, vomit and some bruising, so they call it in as suspicious, just to be careful.'

Aaron grabbed a chair at the side of Martin.

Martin continued. 'I attended. It was a weird one to be honest, boss. Other than some minor bruising, I couldn't see anything suspicious. She was lying in a pool of her own vomit, which was an odd colour if you ask me, but all the same, she'd thrown up. One of those tall legged stools that are needed with those breakfast bar things was on top of her, as if she had fallen off it or pulled it down, which could account for the bruising. There was no other sign of a struggle. No sign of forced entry. Nothing obvious stolen. I found her bag and purse with bank cards and some cash and all major electrical items accounted for; TV, laptop, Sky, DVD player, etc. Even her car was still on the drive and the keys were on breakfast bar.'

'So, what did you do?'

'CSIs and body off for PM. The neighbours weren't much help in identifying anyone who may have been next of kin for her other than the ex-husband, so I don't as yet have an official ID sorted.'

'And the child?' Aaron asked.

'Dad's current wife is picking her up. Social care has her at the moment, but is happy that Dad and wife take her and can't wait for them to take her off their hands. You know how they are. One less child to find a bed for the night.'

I nodded. It all sounded in order. 'I take it Dad is coming in here so we can talk to him, get some details?'

'Yes. I told him we needed to get that done then it was out the way and he could concentrate on his daughter for the rest of the night, that's why his wife is collecting her.'

'And is Ross helping you out with it?'

Martin shifted in his seat. 'He's busy prepping and stressing about the case he's got in crown in a couple of weeks. I told him I'd talk to Dad alone.'

'He's got nothing to stress about. It's an open and shut case.' Aaron spoke. I watched them both for a minute. It had been a hard six months and we were running a team member down.

I looked pointedly at him. 'Thanks, Martin.' He took the hint and left the office.

I then directed my gaze to Aaron. 'Ross seems a bit stressed lately, Aaron. He's persistently late, where he used to be here at least half an hour before the start of the shift. He's letting himself go and he seems to be running on a short fuse. He used to be the most laid back person I knew.' I took a breath, 'I know we are all still feeling the strain, but I think we need to keep an eye on him. He was close to Sally. He looked up to her on the department and there's probably some unresolved guilt as he was with her just before her death. He's still going to the mandatory counselling, right?'

'We're all on it, Hannah.'

'I know, but you've not been informed that he isn't attending?'

'No.'

'Okay. And that case he's got in a couple of weeks, it's open and shut?'

'Yes. Shut tight.'

11

Sean Beers was a slim man with a shock of brown hair, which seemed to have a mind of its own. He wore jeans, T-shirt and trainers as though he had dressed in a hurry and thrown on the first thing to hand, but he wore them with a silent confidence. His face was solemn as he seated himself in the witness interview room. I'd been watching him since we introduced ourselves at the front counter. His display of grief was contained for his ex-wife; there were no tears, not one shed for the mother of his daughter. And his worry was verbal for Megan. He wanted to know where she was, who had her and if she had been with her mother when she had died. We reassured him that Megan was safe but left further details for our intended discussion. He had not once called Lianne by her name, but insisted on referring to her as Megan's mother. Martin left to make him a drink as I continued to watch, all the while monitoring his face and non-verbal communications. He was closed off, legs crossed and facing away from me. Arms tight across his body. His arms toned. A man who took care of himself. Maybe he was self-restrained. Maybe there was something to hide.

Since asking uniform cops to pick him up, we had found out that the school had been informed by Lianne that in case of emergency, she was the only available parent, as he was out of the country, when in fact he was at home with his new wife and baby. Why the dishonesty? He still saw Megan on a semi-regular basis. Beers had some questions to answer but we had to tread lightly at this point. His daughter had lost her mother. We had no cause of death. For all we knew Lianne Beers had died of natural causes, though for someone so young to die so suddenly did give rise to some suspicion so it was better to keep an eye on what was happening than find out too late that there was nothing natural about her death at all. But, who was I to judge marriage and the breakdown of one? I hadn't been there. I hadn't felt the poison seep in as the cement holding it all together crumbled around their feet. I could only judge a man with an uncomfortable attitude in a police station and that's what we had here.

With drinks in place, I sat down. Close to Beers. No table between us. No distractions. I was the concerned DI wanting to reassure him of our best intentions. 'We have Lianne,' there was a look from Beers I couldn't fathom, 'Megan's mum, at the mortuary where a post-mortem will be carried out tomorrow. It's usual in cases like this where the death is sudden and she hasn't seen her doctor recently.' He cradled his cup, looking into its hot contents. 'Megan hasn't been told.' His head jerked up like a string had been pulled from his head skywards. 'We thought it best for her to be taken home by you, be somewhere she is comfortable and with someone she loves.' The string slackened and his head bounced a couple of times. 'Can I ask why the school thought you were out of the country?' Beers straightened his back, shifted slightly in his seat and crossed his legs the opposite way before answering.

'My wife. My current wife. Janine. She doesn't like the demands and interruptions Lianne makes on our life.' He put his drink on the floor and crossed his arms. 'I mean, *made*, made on our lives,' he corrected himself.

'So, sometimes. Sometimes, we say I'm out of the country on business. It's feasible and it means Lianne won't call about anything as she won't talk to Janine about it, only me. It's easier on our family that way.' His arms tightened across his chest.

'So you weren't out the country this past two days?'

'No. No I wasn't. I've been at work. Here. And at home with Janine and Sofia. Our little girl.' He relaxed, uncrossed his arms, opening them as he explained, 'She's eighteen months, a real daddy's little girl.'

'Did Lianne have any medical conditions or allergies?'

'Not that I'm aware of. But we haven't been together for over two and a half years so anything could have happened.'

'What about family we can contact and inform? Parents? Siblings? New husband or partner?'

'No, it was just Lianne and Megan. She pretty much kept to herself. Doted on that child. It's what drove us apart, if I'm honest. She cared more for her than she did for me.'

'In that case, we need to ask you to officially identify Lianne for us at the hospital. It won't take long. You'll be in a separate room to her and then you can go and take care of your daughter.' He nodded.

I gave Sean Beers our contact details and that of the coroner's office. Martin would get the official ID sorted and return Sean to the station to collect his car so he could go and be with his daughter and wife. Sean Beers had the look of a worried man as he left the building, which left me wondering if this was simply due to the shock of the day, the speed of the adjustments he would have to make, or if being here, in the confines of the police station, had made him nervous. If Lianne hadn't died naturally, Sean had gained by her death and we always looked at the spouse first, even if it was the ex-spouse in this case, the circumstances fitted. Sean Beers was now free from a nagging ex and didn't have to ask permission to see his daughter. What better motive?

12
1996

As time drifted by, they became a secure and happy family. Secure in who they were and in what they had. Em was everything he could ever want in a child. She was bright and she was beautiful. She shone. And not just when her face lit up as she smiled, but from within. A real genuine spark of pure, clean humanity at its best. He did everything in his power to give her the best start in life, the best experiences he could afford to give her. They travelled to see and to explore. Her mind was sharp, but the constant questions of *why* that so many parents complained about never got to him. He was happy to share what he knew and find out what he didn't, so he could let her know later. Emma was so inquisitive. He felt that he was on a journey as much as she was. They weren't well off; he worked hard for what they had, so being able to visit the museums in London for free was wonderful, for both him and Connie, financially, and for the joy they brought Em as she could spend a full day in each museum. They'd travel and visit the Natural History Museum, Science Museum and the British Museum. They'd also visited the local Nottinghamshire culture including Nottingham Castle, The Caves, the Galleries of Justice and the D. H. Lawrence Heritage Centre. He adored that curious time of her life.

He and Connie were happy. Connie worked part-time as she wanted to be at home as much as she could for Emma but finances dictated that they both go out to work, so she did it on a part-time basis to suit her. She liked to have dinner on the table when he got home so they could all eat together every night and she and Em baked each weekend. Isaac would be their taste tester, though of course, he was never one to pass a negative comment. Everything passed muster and much delight was had in polishing off each batch of baked goodies.

Life was good.

Until it wasn't.

13

Ross watched Sean Beers go with Martin and Hannah through to the witness interview room. In that brief instance of seeing him walk past he held an immediate dislike for the man. No reason for it. Something about him, a vibe that said *I really don't give a damn what you think.*

Then he went back to the statement he was typing and the fucking blinking cursor, like a silent judgment before he could even get a word out. He put his fingers to the keys and his mind back to the incident.

It was a Friday night. He didn't know what he had expected other than holy hell in the Bridewell custody suite. Martin had parked the car in the custody yard and they'd walked in through the solid metal rear doors, past the fingerprint and photograph room where a woman with lipstick smeared across her face like a clown was yawping that it wasn't her fault her neighbour was a twat and couldn't take a joke when she'd been caught kissing her husband in the pub. He wasn't worth the hassle anyway, so why was she going to take that shit from her. Of course she was going to lamp her one. Stupid slut.

The smell of alcohol, vomit and cleaning materials was strong that night and Ross thanked his lucky stars he hadn't gone for promotion and been landed down there day in night out, with no natural light and nothing but complaining prisoners and uptight solicitors. Though if he were working in custody then he wouldn't be able to let any of his colleagues down again. They might be safer if he was here.

Then they were at the narrow custody booking-in desk area where cops queued with their offenders waiting to be booked in to the system, but at this time on a Friday, the mood wasn't great and three strapping custody staff dragged a cuffed bloke past them and towards the cells as he screamed he was going to kill them all as soon as his hands were freed. Ross saw saucers where his eyes should have been. A good job there was medical personnel on the premises, he noted when he saw the blue tunic of Sherry the MEDAC nurse behind the high custody desk. He caught her eye from where he and Martin stood after letting the staff pass and he smiled. She grinned back and gestured with her chin that the next floor up might be the place he needed to be. She was right. Robert Pine, thirty-six years old, booked in on suspicion of murder, was currently being held in one of the cells on the first floor of the building. It was moderately quieter here, though waiting times at the desk could be significant.

The custody sergeant had requested Pine be examined by the doctor for fitness to be interviewed and after being signed fit he was interviewed without a solicitor at his own request. During the interview he admitted the knife in his hand was the one that had caused the fatal wound to his wife. The words and images of blades and blood flowed through Ross's head. The admission was quick. The interview, short. The custody sergeant, John Blake authorised further detention while Ross and Martin continued their enquiries.

Pine went back to his cell. By now the custody block had calmed considerably and night-time settled over them like a thick blanket, bringing a stillness and quiet in the windowless, grey block.

Ross leaned back in his chair. He couldn't believe how much was still being done this close to the court date. Paperwork; he hated it. He stretched back, arms behind his head, fingers intertwined, pulling out all his tensed up muscles. Fucking Christ, he'd be glad when this job was over and he could get back to working with the rest of the team. Ross wanted this case over.

14

After another full day at work, keeping an eye on the sudden death that had come into the office the previous day, that Martin seemed to have a handle on, and organising the necessary media holding statement, I stopped off at the newsagents, on the way home, to pick up some chocolate, a copy of the *Nottingham Today* and a fresh pint of milk – as I was sure the stuff I'd drank that morning had probably been at least two days out of date.

Home was an apartment at the base of Nottingham castle, which had a great view of the cave entrances, caves that ran underneath a great portion of the city. With the door bolted behind me I kicked off my shoes, leaving them where they landed and padded to the kitchen. The milk and one bar of chocolate went in the fridge and I tore open the wrapper of the second with my teeth as I reached for a glass and poured myself a red wine. The long day had taken its toll on my still healing body so I shoved a couple of painkillers down with the wine. The chocolate was half eaten as I slugged back the deep red liquid. Soothing and relaxing. I turned to the counter and opened up the paper. I found the small article on the death of Lianne Beers that our media liaison, Claire Betts, had released, reporting that police were dealing with an incident at Bramcote, which at this time was being treated as suspicious. Arrangements had been made for a PM etc. However, it was the featured headline I was interested in:

Inquest Opened into murdered Detective Sally Poynter

The byline was Ethan Gale's.

I shoved the rest of the chocolate into my mouth, grabbed the glass, bottle and the paper and carried them into the living room.

Cross-legged on the sofa, I read the article.

Detective Constable Sally Poynter, 32, was murdered in the course of her duty on 4 November 2013. The inquest into her death was opened at Nottingham Coroner's court yesterday.

The inquest will look at the facts of the case including DC Poynter's involvement in the homicide investigation that was running at the time, the management of the investigation and staff and the risk assessment that was made of the premises where she was killed prior to a forced and rapid entry.

Her supervisors at the time were Detective Sergeant Aaron Stone and Detective Inspector Hannah Robbins. Neither of whom have been willing to speak to the Today *on this matter.*

Nottinghamshire police have instigated an IPCC investigation into the murder of DC Poynter and state they will not comment until that investigation is complete.

A colleague who joined Nottinghamshire police on the

same intake with Sally Poynter said, 'Sally was a great cop. She loved her job and was always smiling. I can't believe this has happened. She will be sorely missed and always remembered.'

DC Sally Poynter leaves behind husband, Tom Poynter.

I slugged back the wine and stared at the article that was now shaking in my hand. Ethan Gale. My ex-lover. A relationship that had been growing and could maybe have gone somewhere, but when everything had blown up in my face that night it had been the start of a very rapid ending. He had, of course, been there for me when he heard of my own injury, the knife wound to my right bicep, which had needed surgery and still gave me problems, but his job conflicted with mine to such an extent it was just untenable. Every time he had wanted to talk I had never known if it was to help and support me or to feed his growing byline portfolio. It had been a high profile case, my emotions were a mess and his career possibilities grew as each day passed and the force tried to pick up the pieces from the incident.

Now, reading his report I felt … hurt. Especially after our meal out, where he had offered support, again. But within this article, was he blaming me for Sally's death? Subliminally? Was the paper going to cause a public outcry and demand further blood be spilled? I wondered how he felt in the writing of it. Did he need to dull the pain of loss with a glass of wine to write it, just as I did to read it?

I refilled my glass and read it again.

15

The office space we were sitting in with Home Office forensic pathologist Jack Kidner at the Queen's Medical Centre on Derby Road was neat and clinical and smelled strongly of antiseptic. The sharp clean smell made me want to sneeze and I kept wrinkling up my nose.

Jack worked an on-call system with several of his colleagues over a five-force area that mirrored the EMSOU force structure.

Jack sat behind a desk that had one in-tray on one side and one out-tray on the other, with a laptop sat neatly between. A desk I could only dream of. I picked up my green tea, which Jack brought in especially for my visits and swallowed the soothing drink. DC Martin Thacker sat on my right. I'd asked him to attend Lianne's post-mortem on a just-in-case basis and now, several days later, as we'd been called in by Jack, I knew it had been the right decision, though at the time he'd had nothing to report from the PM other than a fairly healthy woman with no obvious signs of illness or foul play. Something was obviously amiss.

I put my cup back down on Jack's desk and looked at him. He cleared his throat and opened a file; the contents I could see upside down contained reports from the PM.

'So, young Hannah,' he looked back up at me, 'this was a difficult one to deal with. Initially this was a negative post-mortem as I'm imagining Martin told you.'

Martin nodded.

'But with such a young and healthy young woman we couldn't leave it there. I obtained bloods and a stomach sample for toxicology but they came back with a negative result.'

'So, what are you telling me Jack, that this really is a natural death?' Had he really called us down here for this? It wasn't like him.

He frowned at me, peering over the top of his reading glasses. I felt the weight of his disapproval. 'No, Hannah, I'm not telling you this is a natural death; do stop getting ahead of yourself, dear girl.'

I crossed my legs and waited for him to continue.

'It would seem that we have a suspicious death on our hands.'

I looked across at Martin who knitted his eyebrows together and shrugged.

'Everything is in order so far, Ma'am. We haven't missed any opportunity at evidence gathering.'

'But, you just said …' I returned my gaze to Jack.

'Let's start from the beginning, shall we? The bruising we saw corresponds to the crime scene photographs of the location of the body with the kitchen counter top, floor and stool falling on her. None of the injuries would have been likely to be cause of death. They weren't significant enough.' He referred to his report again before continuing. I knew better than to interrupt him. This was his field of expertise and I needed his answers.

'The toxicology, as I say, came back negative, but I wasn't happy, I really don't like negative post-mortems, especially in people so young, so I sent it off again for a new set of tests, which is why it's taken this long to come back to you with the results – but this is where it gets interesting.' I'm sure I nearly saw Jack smile, though he was very aware of being professional about his patients. 'Lianne Beers had digoxin in her system and enough to kill her.'

Ah, this is why we were here. 'Was she on di—?'

'Digoxin. It's derived from the Foxglove plant, *digitalis lanata*. Agatha Christie used Digitalis as a weapon of choice once you know. *Appointment With Death.*'

For a man dealing with death day in, day out, Jack had a love of all things crime fiction. It was fascinating to see.

Sometimes.

I nodded. Sipped my tea again. Out of the corner of my eye I could see Martin smile.

'It's usually given to patients with atrial fibrillation, atrial flutter and heart failure and after doing her PM and reading her doctor's notes and seeing all the drugs you seized from her home, I can tell you she didn't have any problems with her heart. There was no reason for me to find digoxin in her system. She was in a reasonably good state of health.'

I didn't like where this was going. 'So what are we saying then?'

'I'm saying,' and he did smile at me now, 'that she was killed by digoxin toxicity, of which there was no medical need for her to be using and it was not listed in the drug contents at her home ... so it would appear you have a suspicious death on your hands, Hannah.'

Martin leaned forward now. 'Any idea how it got into her system? Were there any needle marks on her body that you found?'

'Ah, now then, there were no needle marks on her body, so that question is one for you to answer.'

16

'So what are we looking for?' Anthony Grey, my chief inspector, asked. He steepled his hands, contemplating the new information I had just given him.

'I'm not sure.'

'So we're going back into Lianne Beers' house to look for something, but you don't know what. I presume you're taking a team of CSIs with you?' He rested his chin on his hands as he thought through what I was saying. I could feel the pressure building around me. Since Sally's murder last year, I could see our team had only been picking up the jobs that looked cut and dried. Nothing too taxing to wear us out or for us to screw up while the force assessed the emotional damage to the team, emotionally, but more importantly to them, reputedly and accountably. This had looked to be one of those steady jobs when it first came in and now here I was telling him that it was bigger than first thought. That rather than a nice, medical justification like a blown aneurysm or some other such reason, Lianne Beers' death was more likely to be something sinister that we had to look into and deal with seriously. Grey had aged at least another couple of years in the last six months. He was obviously feeling the stress and wouldn't want this right now.

'Do what you need to do, Hannah. Talk everything through as you do it with Jack, as he knows what's possible and what's not, and talk each step through as you do it, with the senior CSI on duty.' He sighed and pulled his hands apart, leaning back in his chair.

Leaning away from the job.

17
2010

The teenage years and alcohol experimentation was a difficult time. At fourteen years of age he nearly had a meltdown. All he had taught her, and her peers had undone all that hard and loving work in no time at all. Now every time she was out of the house in the evening Emma was managing to get hold of some kind of alcoholic product and it didn't really matter what kind it was. Though Blue WKD was a favourite, cheap old cider would do. She would say she was going out to a mate's house but he would find out she'd been hanging out with her friends on the shop fronts on Derby Road. A large group, which was intimidating to many who passed them.

Isaac spent many sleepless nights trying to resolve the problem. He'd start by grounding her for a few days. It made the atmosphere in the house electric. Tight and fierce. An angry burst of energy about to be fired off at any opportunity. He had never experienced anything like it. He stood his ground and hoped that she would learn her lesson, that drinking this stuff outside on the street was both dangerous and unhealthy. When the time for her to be allowed out of the house came, it was only a week before Connie came to him after noticing alcohol on her breath again and a bottle under her bed.

The second time around, Emma was grounded for two weeks. She voluntarily cloistered herself into her bedroom. She wanted nothing to do with him. To her, Isaac was evil and knew nothing of what life was really like. She was capable of taking care of herself and there was nothing wrong with drinking on the street on a school night. Isaac paced around the house. Tried to speak to her at the dinner table. But on the whole he left Connie to try and talk to her about her safety. When she was drunk anyone could take advantage of her and she could be hurt in any number of ways. To have these discussions going on in his house made his skin itch and his fingers crawled their way up his sleeves and clawed away at the skin on his arms. He hoped she would pass through this phase soon.

She came home from town one Saturday with the tragus piercing; to him it was just the bobbly bit at the front of her ear that should not be pierced. He ranted at her. Towering, using his height to full advantage to show his rage at what she had done to her body, how she had mutilated herself. He was livid. She was perfect. Flawless. Born pure and clean and she had taken a choice to do this to herself. This didn't matter to Emma. She stood mute. Listening to him, her father. Watching until he burnt himself out with his tirade. Refusing to provide the information of where she'd had it done. She also refused to take it out and he wasn't going to do it forcibly for fear of injuring her, causing even more permanent damage. So they stood at an impasse. He couldn't believe how stubborn and rigid she was.

It continued like this and he thought he had lost her. His only beloved child. Lost to the jungle that was teenage hormones and peers and environment. Parenting had never been so hard. Sleepless nights and dirty nappies had nothing on these years. He just wanted his Em back. The sweet Em. The Em who loved and adored him. The Em who had a future and who wanted that future. Not the Em who didn't care what the world held as long as it was with her mates in Stapleford.

This Em didn't care if she had a future of any kind or not ... and it broke his heart.

18

Ross saw the activity happening around him. Like a hive of bees humming in his ears. Excitement he hadn't heard in a while. A slow, but steady and constant hum – not the normal drone of a working office with voices talking, fingers tapping on keyboards and drinks being slurped at desks – a higher level buzz that meant something was in the air was holding interest. The day-to-day goings on were virtually abandoned as they hummed about the office spreading words of doom from another person's life. Ross couldn't stand it. The excitement and glee were horrific. Jobs in here only meant another person, another family was ruined and it wasn't just what you saw at the immediate scene. These people had extended family. They had friends and work colleagues. They had book groups or sports activity groups. The ripple effect of someone, one person, being savagely taken, was felt wide and far and Ross understood that, he felt it.

Working in an office like this turned you into a person whose vision was skewed. It became warped to society and societal values in general, but also narrowed. Sharpened to a point. A darted implement with only one target. To solve the crime, gather the evidence, do it forensically and securely and pass it to the CPS for a decision on prosecution. That's as far as this office, this job could take you.

Ross knew he had become that person. That dedicated detective. The love of the job had driven him forward every day. He'd always woken before his alarm, eager to get into the office. Always on top of his work, waiting for the next job to come in, for the next thrill of being involved in such an important investigation as a murder; methodically chasing down the leads to catch the killer. That sweet moment when you had them in your sights, when you knew who they were and you zoned in on them and they didn't know you were coming. So, so sweet.

And working within the team, he adored them. They took him in and immediately made him feel at home. He thrived. He had loved it.

But what about the people? Actual people involved or not involved at all but affected beyond all imagination by the incident. Justice is all well and good, but what about the people left behind?

Ross started to feel sick to his stomach with the heightened noise around him. He clenched his teeth, the muscle in his jawline twitching with the pressure. His fingers hovered over his keyboard. He had work to do, final bits for the trial, but he couldn't think straight. He just couldn't. He pushed back hard on his chair as he stood and stalked out of the incident room. Fists clenched at his side.

Martin leaned back in his own chair and watched Ross leave.

19

So far, our team was still small, meaning we had the space to move and do what we needed to here. More space than we'd had at Central police station, but it felt as though we were rattling around an abandoned house. There were desks with empty chairs and unused computer terminals. The building was newer and not falling to bits like it was at Central, but I'd loved that place. I'd felt comfortable and we'd been torn out of it just when we needed to stay. Not long after Sally's death, when we needed to keep our working lives looking like a version of normal, but we'd had to adjust.

And now we had a suspicious death to look at. We had a cause of death, but we didn't know much else, so Walker hadn't drafted any more staff in. The briefing was succinct as I provided the facts, as we knew them.

'Lianne Beers died from digoxin toxicity. At this point we don't know if it was suicide, accident or murder.' Blank faces stared back at me. Working with the unknown for something that could turn out to be an accident wasn't what they thought of as a conducive day's work. 'For now we need to be looking into Lianne's life. Her family, her friends, and we need to look closely at her ex-husband Sean and his new wife. Aaron and I will speak with them, today if we can. He seems to have the most to gain if this does turn out to be a murder. We'll ask both him and his wife about illness and if they're taking any medication; if so, what? We'll see if they'll sign medical consent forms while we're there. I need you to find out what he does for a living. Who does he have contact with that could get hold of digoxin? Find out how easy it is to get hold of if it's not prescribed.' Aaron's head was down, his pen moving rapidly over his major incident notebook.

'Look at his new wife. Check PNC for both of them. Where does she work?' I paused, as a thought came to me. 'Also check both addresses – Lianne's and Sean's – for reported domestic incidents, see if there were any acrimonious issues that Sean isn't telling us about. Even if attending cops got the bums' rush while there, maybe it was a neighbour who called it in, if so, the details will be in the log. Canvass both sets of neighbours.' I paused again, looking at the team. *Team.* It wasn't a word that really fit us at the minute. We were running short staffed and Ross was still doing last-minute paperwork for his trial. He was great at doing the legwork that needed doing, always eager to get out of the office and get things done. He'd been enthusiastic for the job since joining the unit. I knew I could pull him in for a few small enquiries if he thought he had the time. He'd help out if he could.

Then I had Martin, the oldest and most experienced DC who was calm and got on with whatever needed doing, which left Aaron and me. Okay, so basically unless we had Ross, there was Martin, Aaron and me to do the legwork. I hoped this turned out to be accident or suicide. I faced Martin. 'If I can leave you to do the intelligence enquiries when Aaron and I go, give Ross a shout if you really need a dig out, Okay?'

'No worries, boss.' He leaned back in his chair; his shirt buttons straining over his stomach. Not a lot fazed him.

'Don't get too comfortable yet though, first we have to go and do a search of Lianne's address with the CSIs to see if we can find the source of the digoxin.'

The house was a two-bedroomed semi on a narrow idyllic-looking back road in Bramcote. It was clean and tidy, considering a young child had lived here. There was a box in the corner of the living room that was stacked with children's toys and a bookshelf that was home to adult novels of eclectic taste; romance, crime, fantasy and non-fiction, which were all filed on the higher shelves, and children's books on the bottom two shelves. The open plan layout into the kitchen showed items as they had been left. The stool on the floor and half unpacked shopping on the worktop. No one had been in to clean up and the stench of the excreted bodily fluids was strong, the green stomach contents now dried hard on the tiles. Lianne obviously had no one close to come in and take care of things for her. I'd sort something out when I got back into the office. I didn't want Megan to come here, to collect her clothes or books and toys and walk into this.

The CSIs filed in, all suited up, as we were, but carrying boxes containing evidence gathering kits to collect various samples, including food, drinks, medicines and anything else a search would throw up that may have been a mode of contamination. Jack hadn't found any injection sites so it was likely that Lianne had ingested the digoxin. But if it had been in the home, why hadn't it killed Megan? So what had Lianne had access to that Megan hadn't? If we had a killer on our hands, would they have known that only Lianne would die or were they careless in whether a young child was caught up in their long distance killing? I was just grateful that local cops had gained access to the house and had found her, rather than her daughter finding her that way. It was hard enough for a child to lose a parent without having to process seeing their body contorted in agony on the floor as Lianne's had been. How long would that image take to dissipate – if ever? And what kind of life-limiting effect would it have had on her?

We also needed to look through Lianne's life with a fine-tooth comb so her computer and phone would be coming with us, as well as diaries, calendars, notebooks, anything that could give us a clue as to where she had been and who she had been with in recent weeks. Now we knew what had killed her, we would also be looking closely at Sean. He had gained full custody of his daughter with the death of his ex-wife. His family was now complete and argument free.

20
2012

Prom night was one of the proudest nights of his life, though he didn't quite understand what it was. Some fancy and very expensive idea that seemed to have come over from America. Em had insisted on the whole lot if she was not to be laughed out of the event. Dress, clutch bag, shoes, necklace, hairdresser appointment for some fancy hair-do, fake tan appointment at the beauticians. All this on top of that very expensive dress. It was just a dress for heaven's sake.

She had turned things around a lot and had worked hard for her exams. They had not seen signs of her drinking. There had been a marked change in attitude towards them as well. That couldn't-care-less had vanished and instead a head-down-and-study attitude replaced it. Friends who both he and Connie had been uncomfortable with drifted off and more studious and level-headed girls were coming around and hitting the books before going out and doing normal teenaged girl things. Activities that didn't include drinking on the streets and causing them both huge amounts of stress.

But still. This wasn't Emma's wedding day. It was her Prom. She was sixteen years old and it felt as though they were preparing her for marriage. She had behaved as though it was as important. The preparation went on for nearly as long. He had never seen her as excited about anything and he didn't begrudge her the money they spent as she had turned her life around. It could have so easily spiralled the other way. Her exam results wouldn't be back until after the Prom but he knew she had worked hard and that was why he was so proud of her. The significance that was placed on this one evening was beyond his comprehension though.

He would remind her of all of this when she did get married. When she was making a commitment of a lifetime to the person of her dreams.

He paced about in the small kitchen, with its newly fitted units and appliances. It gleamed. But he needed to have a table in the centre so he could still sit and still read his paper and still chat to Connie. The woman of his dreams.

His daughter walked in and though she might still have a wedding in her future, at this moment, she looked more beautiful than she ever had in her life.

It was her first big night and Isaac felt anxious, yet he couldn't say why. He felt troubled as she stood there, looking beautiful in a simple flowing gown, more adult, and more serene than he had ever seen here. He wanted to capture this moment forever, but forever had a diaphanous feel, like if he tried to reach out and imagine it, it would float away from him. Instead he took out his camera, watched as Emma posed, and snapped the moment in time.

21

Sean Beers answered the door on the second set of knocks. His unruly brown hair appeared to have grown more ruffled. The sun behind us lit up his face, which was looking pale and lacklustre. Dark circles under his eyes stood out like purple crescent moons. He looked from Aaron to me and back again. Not a flicker of recognition crossed his face. His hand rested on the door handle as his mind fought to place the two people in front of him.

'Mr Beers,' I went in to help him. 'DI Robbins from last week at the police station and my colleague, DS Stone.' His lips parted in an O shape. 'If we can just come in for another chat.' I didn't want to phrase it like a question. I didn't want to give him the opportunity to come up with an excuse to turn us away. At the minute we were keeping in touch with the family of a suspicious death victim. How this played out remained to be seen. Would he be grieving, a supportive father or something else altogether?

'Honey, who is it?' A slender woman with bright auburn hair popped up from under his arm somewhere. A bright smile that went all the way to her eyes. Beautiful, even without a trace of make-up on her face.

'It's the police.' He found his voice and looked at her. 'About Lianne.'

'Well, let them in.' She backed up a couple of steps, forcing Sean to back up with her. 'Come in. Come in.' She ushered as we all moved at once. 'I'm sorry, he's not quite with it at the minute.' The woman apologised as we all continued moving in unison away from the doorstep and any prying eyes that might be there. We took a right turn through a doorway following her into a large square-shaped living area. Two three-seater sofas at right angles to each other kept the room in a box shape, but were softened with extra cushions thrown about them in a multitude of colours. Smiling faces in a mishmash of frames shone out from the walls and an overweight, golden retriever lay on a rug on the floor, lifting its head in acknowledgment before dropping to the floor again. 'Sit, please.' The woman waved her arm in front of the two sofas, indicating we could take either. Aaron looked down at the dog and sat in the furthest seat facing back into the room. A large oak bookcase loomed behind him. I followed, sitting next to him I sank deeper into the plush cushions than I expected to and put my hands down to steady myself. The woman smiled at me. Sean and the woman, I presumed to be his wife, seated themselves on the other sofa.

'I'm sorry,' she said. 'I haven't introduced myself. I'm Sean's wife, Janine.'

I smiled. 'I'm Detective Inspector Hannah Robbins and this is Detective Sergeant Aaron Stone.' I paused and looked around, not wanting to say too much if a child was going to walk into the room. 'Can I ask where the children are before we go on?'

'Yes, Sofia is with my mum,' Janine spoke again. Sean kept his face turned down towards the floor.

'And Megan?'

At this Sean looked up but still didn't speak. His wife was doing it all for him. 'She's upstairs, resting. We were up most of the night with her again and she's worn herself out now. We'll hear her if she starts to come down the stairs though, so we're okay to talk.'

'Why is Sofia with your mum?' asked Aaron.

'It's a tough transitional time and we thought it best that she be in a stable place as we get through this initial grieving period with Megan. She's so young.' I nodded. 'We'll get the two girls together more often on a gradual basis as and when we feel they will both be able to deal with the emotional implications of what it means – that they are sisters, on a permanent basis. For Megan that is going to be traumatic and could have some massive knock-on effect towards Sofia, maybe without her even realising it.'

This woman seemed to have her head screwed on. She wasn't the woman I was expecting and certainly not quite the woman Sean had drawn her to be.

'How have you explained it to her, Sean?' His head popped up at the same time Janine's eyebrows lifted away from bright eyes.

'I … erm, we … erm, said … We told her that her mummy was in heaven, obviously.' I waited.

'We told her it was an accident and she was going to be living with us in her room here.' I waited some more.

'How the hell do you think she took it?' Aah. The response. I felt Aaron shift forward, balancing his elbows on his knees.

Janine stood. 'Can I get anyone a tea? Coffee? Water?'

It was another warm day. 'I'll just have water, please.'

She looked at Aaron.

'I don't drink in people's houses.' She brushed down her jeans and walked out of the room. I took a deep breath, closing my eyes for a moment, then looked back at Sean. He continued to look down at the floor.

'How are you doing, Sean?' He looked up, as though only just remembering we were still there.

'Shocked. I'm shocked. It's all hard to take in you know, and then to deal with the girl's pain, well, it's … I never thought anything could be this hard.'

'I can only imagine. You have strong support with Janine by the look of it.'

'Yes. She's been wonderful. I don't know what I would have done without her.' He lifted his face to the display of images on the wall and a smile flitted across his lips.

'We need to ask you about medications, Sean.' At that point Janine walked in carrying a tray with two cups and a glass of water. I waited for her to put it down on the coffee table before continuing.

'Medications?' she asked. I could see who was more aware in this relationship right now.

'Yes. Is anyone in the family on any heart medication?'

'No. No one. I'm presuming this has something to do with Lianne's death?'

I didn't want to give too much away but I needed to have my questions answered. 'It's something that has been identified during the post-mortem but we couldn't find any in her home.'

'That's strange. Lianne wasn't ill, as far as we knew. She would have told us if there was something wrong. She liked to keep in contact with Sean. Too often, if I'm honest. There was no need for the amount of contact she wanted when a schedule was set up for Megan, but every time Megan had a sniffle she let Sean know, she grazed her knee, she let Sean know.' She paused. I let the silence play. 'Listen to me. I'm sorry.' Janine put her hand to her chest. 'Like I said, no one in our family is ill. We don't have any of that kind of medication in the house. In fact we don't have anything other than a basic first aid kit stored.'

'Do you know why she might have some, Sean?' Aaron asked. Again, it took a moment for him to answer.

'No. No idea. I have to look after my family now though, don't I? This is my family now.'

We had no other questions at the point and left without touching the drink Janine had made.

22
2015

The day she came into the house to tell them was a day of sunshine and warmth.

It was wrong. A contradiction. There was no way the sun should have been shining, the flowers showing their faces upwards in joy or birds singing. The sky should have clouded over in the darkest cloud cover seen. As black as night and as thick as Beijing smog.

Connie was washing the dishes and he was at the dining table, the two of them making small talk. Connie was chattering about Beryl Kingston down the road who had just had her second hip replacement, a cup circling in her hands, soap suds exploding out of the inner cup as she cleaned, paying little attention. Isaac himself paid even less attention to Mrs Kingston's medical issues, instead choosing to alternate between reading the sport's pages and listening to his wife's soft lilting tones rather than the actual words.

Then it happened.

Emma walked in. It was a Wednesday afternoon. She wasn't expected. She should have been at work, at the chemist. But she walked in looking pallid and drawn. Her lips thin and as pale as her face. Her eyes blinking rapidly, her breath quick. Connie turned to see who the visitor was and as soon as she saw Em the cup that was still circling in her hands slipped. It bounced once on the edge of the sink, the handle splitting off before it dropped hard on the tiled floor, smashing in the otherwise now silent kitchen. Connie ignored the mess that was at her feet and in seconds crossed the space between herself and her only child, taking her up in her arms. At once Em broke down. Her handbag dropped to the floor, her arms circling her mother's waist as great heaving sobs wracked her body. Connie's arms had, like a reflex, wrapped themselves tightly around her daughter and dropped her face into her hair, one hand gently circling her back to let her know she was there and supported. There were no words uttered, yet the kitchen was filled with a sound that tore open Isaac's soul. He faltered as he stood. She was his beautiful child, but now an adult crumbling in front of his eyes in her mother's arms and he felt impotent. Helpless, his daughter breaking before his very eyes and he didn't understand why. He knew not what he could offer. Knew not what he could do.

He knew he would do anything.

23
2015

They say the world stops spinning or time stands still when grief this profound hits you. Yet if his world did, stop spinning or stand still, then Em would have no future and he couldn't recognise a world where she didn't have a future. It just didn't exist for him. She had the whole world at her feet so it had to be spinning, it had to keep going. She had plans. She wanted to finish university and train to be a barrister. And Em, Em bless her, he knew, she also wanted the family. Husband and 2.4 kids. She wanted the white picket fence, though she'd only ever seen those in American movies, she was a romantic at heart and thought she could have it all, if she worked hard enough. And she *had* been working hard enough.

They had been worried about her of late. She had looked peaky on recent visits but they put it down to studying hard, partying hard and working a part-time job in a chemist on top of that. They'd told her to take things easier. To get some rest. He'd bet his money Connie had told her to get a check-up at the doctors, although he would never have considered it. He knew students burned the candle at both ends. Though how he knew that was through watching movies and documentaries and none too flattering news items, as he'd never been inside a university until the day they started 'shopping around' for Em. He'd barely got through school but had managed to get an apprenticeship in one of the local factories in

Stapleford. He'd put many good years into it. Times were hard on the businesses in the town and many closed. He'd watched and held his breath as factory after factory closed their doors but they'd been lucky and held on. He'd wanted a better life for Em and she'd gone off and started it. They visited three universities before she settled on Sheffield. It wasn't too close, but neither was it too far away that she couldn't come home and visit or get her washing done should she need to. They'd bought her an old run-around Fiesta to take with her so she could make the journey home when she needed to. Though they missed her, they received weekly email updates from her including photographs where she had any of interest to include. Or as he assumed, if there were any she was okay with her parents seeing. Law was a tough subject, so he knew she would be spending a sensible amount of time studying and not just drinking in the students' bar.

Until now.

24

Finlay watched the brick houses pass. The shops. The takeaways and restaurants. All that made up his hometown of Beeston, with nothing but a barely perceptible interest as Imagine Dragons thumped a beat out into his ears. His slender fingers, nails bitten to the quick, tapping along in time on his rucksack on his lap. The seat beside him empty as it often was. People were nervous when it came to sitting next to him. Snap judgements were made in that split second it took to choose a seat on a bus, even that early time in a morning when they were heading into work and space was tight. They saw a lanky white youth with earrings you could actually see through, bigger than his earlobes and a piercing through his eyebrow and made a decision to not sit next to him. He always laughed to himself. It gave him room to himself and it made his mum howl. She thought they were 'uneducated judgmental pricks' – her words. And he loved her for it. She loved to rub his head and try for a cuddle as often as she could, even if it was in front of his mates, much to his embarrassment.

The thing was, he was nothing like the person others perceived him to be. And he knew what that was. He was actually the boy who would help his mum around the house. Do his nan's garden on a weekend when it needed it and the boy who pined over April Lacey in class 10C, though he wouldn't have the guts to tell her.

His thoughts of April were interrupted as he felt a weight drop down at the side of him. He turned from his view out the window to look at his brave companion and saw the reason he had company was that the bus had filled up while he had been caught up in his own thoughts. His companion was sitting as close to the edge of the seat as they possibly could without falling off the end. A man in a pair of old grey trousers, which matched his hair and a navy bomber style jacket. No accounting for taste.

Finlay started to feel hot. He leaned his head onto the cold glass to get some relief and closed his eyes. Time slipped by. His eyes snapped open as his chest tightened hard. He pulled his fists up quickly and gasped. As he opened his mouth, he vomited. He couldn't stop and he was trapped in his window seat. His chest was being squeezed, his insides being torn apart. His body was betraying him. The pain across his chest and the feeling that he was being shredded from inside confused him. He had never felt so bad. He hoped someone could see and would assist. Through the music still ongoing in his ears he could hear shouting and feel movement. He pulled on his earphones and tried to ask for help but could hear someone yelling at him. Calling him a druggie? He needed help. *Someone, help.* Pain clenched its grip around his chest again and in its fury Finlay jerked forward, banging his head hard on the metal bar of the seat in front. The pain stopped as the world passing by suddenly went black.

25

His position in the seat could suggest he couldn't be arsed; head at rest on the bar in front, his hands in his lap. If it wasn't for the vile-smelling puddle of puke on his lap covering his hands and trailing down over his black skinny jean-clad knees, onto the rucksack that was partway to the floor between them, you would never have known. Most people would probably have ignored him and left him here for heavens knew how long. Male youths asleep or in distress on public transport wasn't uncommon and they didn't engender support or sympathy. This boy however had made his death loud and ungainly, which made it difficult for his fellow passengers to ignore and in turn made it difficult for the driver to not call it in. So here we were, Aaron and me, stood side by side in the narrow walkway of the bus, looking down at the boy on the bus. A sad, early start to Friday morning.

All the passengers who were still around when we got there and hadn't rushed off to work before police arrival were now off the bus and had been herded into a local coffee shop by Martin so he could contain them. He needed to obtain details and accounts of what they saw, regardless of which level of the bus they were on. The boy was on the top deck and even lower deck passengers were needed, as they might have seen him getting on or seen someone else that we needed to talk to.

If it wasn't for the gang shooting in Bestwood last night, another team would have been drafted in to deal with this, but as our only current job – Lianne Beers – wasn't yet identified as a homicide, we were told in no uncertain terms that this one was ours as well. Budget cuts were eating away at staffing and that meant we all had to take on more to provide the same service – or not the same service but a better service, because that's what the government was promising, while at the same time it cut millions from public services.

A couple of uniforms were helping Martin keep the unhappy witnesses in one place and the gawking non-witnesses in another – which was further away from the bus and from us.

'So suicide, accident or murder?' I asked Aaron.

'I don't think we can tell just from looking at him, can you?'

I looked from the boy, to Aaron. 'No, I suppose not.' And at that moment, Jack made a timely appearance.

'Well, if it isn't my favourite Detective Inspector and Detective Sergeant. How the jolly well are you today? Made any headway with our digoxin toxicity job yet?' he asked as he dropped his medical briefcase to the floor of the bus, making, I imagine, anyone downstairs think the ceiling was about to cave in.

'Hey, Jack.' I smiled. Aaron nodded and moved up the bus slightly to allow Jack better access to the boy, his Tyvek suit rustling as he moved. 'Slow going on Beers so far, but we'll let you know if anything significant comes up. Today we seem to have another odd one. No obvious external signs of trauma, and witnesses said it was pretty sudden, so I thought we'd better bring you down to the scene to have a look in situ.'

Jack pulled on his blue medical gloves, hitched his white paper trousers up at his knees, providing a flash of his striped orange and pink socks, and crouched down in the walkway to the side of the boy and peered up at him from his lower vantage point without touching anything.

'He's got a nasty bruise to his forehead, but from how he's resting. I imagine that will be corroborative with witness statements of him bashing his head against this bar he's up against.'

I looked out the window. To my side, I could see a woman waving her arms around wildly at Martin, her face turning a shade of puce I hadn't seen on a live person before. Martin stood stock still, his hands resting low and relaxed on his belt buckle with his pocket book and pen in his hands. I tuned back to Jack who was talking about vomit colouring and smell. I looked at Aaron who was paying rapt attention. I could rely on him to catch me up.

'So,' Jack said, rubbing his knees as he unfurled himself from his crouched position, 'we'll transfer the young man to the QMC and see what is going on. I must say, Hannah; I don't like the look of this. I do not like it at all.'

26

I paid for a tea and thanked the owner of the coffee shop for allowing us to commandeer his space. He nodded continually as he spoke, enthusiastic about helping out the police, especially when it involved a death. Yet again I envisaged a tall story that someone could go home and tell their family. But if that's what it took for people to help us, then that's what it took. Many more people were a lot less willing to help out and would rather spit in our faces than give us the time of day.

I placed my drink on the table and seated myself next to the man who was already there nursing a hot chocolate.

'Thank you so much for talking to us. For stopping and giving us your time.'

He looked up. Strong lines etched on his face deepened as he smiled at me. 'My pleasure, young lady.'

I smiled back at him. 'I'm always happy to be called young.'

'Ah, you're a babe in arms, girl. It's when you get to my age, you know what real age is and you wish you could do it all again. It disappears so fast.' He sighed. 'Just look at that youngster today. Not a chance to live his life before it's gone. Make sure you enjoy yours, won't you?'

I put my hand on top of his, where it was resting on top of the table. His skin felt thin, papery to the touch. I feared I could tear it if I wasn't gentle enough. 'I certainly will, Mr Cleaver.' Martin had told me his name before I came over to see him. He was eighty-two years old and looked every day of it. I hoped he'd lived it, that the lines and tiredness had been hard earned. I took my hand away.

'What can you tell me about this morning?'

His eyes held a deep sadness. 'I can't tell you anything I'm afraid. I was sitting on the lower deck, I'm too old to get up those winding stairs, you see. But I see the young lad every day. Same bus every morning, without fail. I hear people tut as he gets on. I know why, the way he looks, but he's young. He can do what he wants while he's young.' He paused and looked hard at me. 'They tut at you when you're old as well, you know.'

'I'm so sorry to hear that.' And I was. Why were people so frustrated with our elderly? Did they not expect to age? And had they forgotten what it was like to be young? Both ends of our lifespan seemed to annoy the average person living life in between.

'He'd not been up there long when I heard a commotion. I have my hearing aid in and it's bloody good. There were people shouting. I heard the word *druggie*. I knew they'd be shouting at him. I like to people watch and at this time of day there really aren't any druggies getting on the bus. I felt for him but I couldn't do anything because I can't get up those stairs. And then someone screamed. And all hell broke loose.'

He stopped speaking then. Looked down into his hot chocolate. I waited for him in case he had anything else to add.

'Then the bus driver tutted.' Mr Cleaver shook his head slow, his eyes holding a deep sadness. 'He tutted and all the while the boy was up there needing his help, dying.' He looked at me, white ringed pensioner eyes taking me in. 'And who knew if someone had done something, if he could have survived.'

27

Finlay McDonnell. Sixteen years of age. Mum, Dad, one older brother, three younger sisters. In his last year at school and wanting to stay on to do his A levels in Chemistry, Physics and Maths and then go on to university. Not one person had seen anything. They didn't even want to have seen the boy. Though with the way he was dressed and his body adornments I knew damn well they had not only seen him, they had gawked at him, from a safe distance. I wondered how quickly someone had got up from their seat to help him or if he had died alone and scared. The thought made my blood boil.

'How many names are there, Martin?'

He flipped open his pocket book, thumbed through a few pages and read down the list he'd made. I could see him counting in his head, his lips moving silently in sync with his mind. 'Thirteen.'

'An eight a.m. bus and only thirteen people on it? I suppose we're lucky that thirteen people were nosy enough to stick around.' I sighed. 'I'm being disingenuous; I know there were some good people there. I talked to a couple. Tell us what the overall picture is from witnesses.'

'It's not a lot really. The lad was on the bus. Staring out the window with his earphones in, when all of a sudden he threw up in his lap and it was over.'

'Anyone know him? See him with anyone before he threw up in his lap?'

'A couple of people recognised him as travelling on the same bus daily. Said he kept to himself and though he might look weird,' Martin looked at me quickly, 'their words,'

'You're okay. Go on.'

'Though he might look weird, he was actually just a quiet lad who didn't bother anyone and it was a really awful thing to have happened.'

'And as far as anyone being with him?'

'No. He's always alone.'

'So what happened?'

'Beats me, boss. I think it's one Jack's going to answer for us.'

'Any initial thoughts from the Crime Scene Unit, Aaron?'

'They've seized the bus—'

Martin started to laugh, deep from his belly and I couldn't help but smile with him. Aaron frowned at the interruption. I clenched my teeth to stop myself from laughing with Martin. I could see Ross's shoulders shuddering as he listened in from his desk.

'They've seized the bus—'

'Oh my God, that's classic.'

'Martin, do you want to know about CSU or not?' Aaron asked him.

I stopped smiling.

'Yes. Sorry, Aaron.'

Aaron told us about the seizure and examination that the CSU were going to do of the bus that Finlay had been found on. I'm sure the bus company would be calling very soon about that one. I might refer the call through to the Crime Scene Unit to deal with.

'Guys, we need to find a connection between McDonnell and Lianne Beers. Jack is already getting an uneasy feeling about this and that's before he has any results back. You've got the signed medical consent forms we obtained from Sean and Janine Beers to check their medical records as well.' I started running through a list of actions on my fingers, starting with my thumb.

'We need to visit the school and speak to all his classmates to see if Finlay was using any drugs or medications his parents weren't aware of, or if he was in real trouble with anyone.'

Another finger. 'We need to speak to his teachers with the same questions because they'll see it from a different perspective.'

Middle finger. 'Our thirteen witnesses need interviewing properly in an interview suite, because in quiet surroundings with a correct interview model, they could and probably will, remember things they haven't yet said. You never know, someone of investigative importance could have been close by. Someone who wanted to see Finlay die on that bus.'

Ring finger. I was getting incredulous looks now. The amount of work that needed doing was long and time consuming and we didn't have the staff. I knew this but it didn't mean we could get away with doing half a job.

'Ma'am?' It was Martin.

'Yes?'

'Can you confirm you want us to start all this before the PM results are in?'

'Actually, Martin, you jumped in, as my next action is to attend the PM. I know it's a lot of work when the results aren't in, but if Jack is already saying he's not happy and we have a dead child, I think it's safe to say we're more than likely going to have a suspicious death than a death by natural causes and I'd rather get out in front of it than be trying to catch it up.'

'Yeah, okay. I'll do the PM if you want?'

'Sounds good, thank you.'

'I'm going to need everyone to work through the weekend as well, as with any other murder investigation. Though this is tentative at the minute, it doesn't feel right. We can't just knock off and go and relax for a couple of days when we have two bodies in the morgue and two families wanting to know what happened.'

Aaron and Martin nodded.

'Also,' I looked back at Martin, 'the enquiries I had you doing on the Beers, where did you get to with them?'

'Nowhere. As in, there was nothing we can really pick up. Yeah, they got divorced but there were no recorded domestics. Neighbours haven't heard anything out of the ordinary. She kept to herself. As far as jobs, there's nothing that would give the ex or his wife access to drugs of any description. I came up cold, I'm afraid.'

I nodded slowly as I took it in.

'Okay. Ross, are you ready for court? Can you give us a dig out today with the list of enquiries we've now got running over the weekend?'

He looked up in surprise. 'Er, yes Ma'am, I'll finish off these few bits and pieces and I'm all yours.'

'Great. I need a link between the two cases, everyone. It'll help nail it all down. Find me that link please.'

I stalked out of the incident room and headed straight for the Ladies. One of the stalls was occupied so I went into the other one. I didn't need to go, but I wanted the space to myself. Once I heard the outer door close I opened my stall door, washed my hands and scooped up cold water into my hands and then over my face, feeling my shoulders relax. I had to keep going, to show the team I was back and okay, and importantly, to show Grey and Walker I was still capable of leading them.

The mirror in front of me reflected back a pasty face with dark shadows smudged under each eye. It was to be expected. None of us were fully up to speed yet. How could we be? The pain in my upper arm nagged where the knife had sliced into me. I held onto my arm as the dragging pain deepened and dropped down to my elbows and rested on the counter. I could do this. I could.

My team were relying on me and I wouldn't let them down again.

28

The room was small and narrow, but was carpeted and furnished with a couple of two seater sofas and an armchair. The walls were papered with tiny floral patterned wallpaper. It was a room that was trying to lend itself to being a place of comfort. There was nothing comfortable about being stood in there, the four of us together, too close with no escape. Aaron was pushing his back up hard against the furthest wall. He didn't want to be here but if he were needed he would be within arm's reach. The McDonnells were staring wide eyed at the vast window filling the long wall in front of us where a pair of dark blue curtains obscured their view. Their hands clung together, each taking from the other. Hoping, I expected, that we were somehow wrong and that this would confirm that for them and to us. Hope that their youngest son was not in fact dead. Hope that they had their lives to walk back home to.

I touched Miriam McDonnell gently on her arm. It quivered beneath my hand. 'Are you ready?'

She jumped, forgetting I was there, in this room. Her face looked upwards to her husband. He nodded, his eyes still holding that vacant stare. I pushed the intercom button on the wall and simply said, 'Okay.' The curtains on the other side of the glass started to roll back, parting from the centre. A small sound escaped from Mrs McDonnell's lips, her husband put his arm around her waist and pulled her closer, his other hand keeping a tight grip of hers. Out of the corner of my eye I saw Aaron push his shoulders further up the wall in an attempt to become invisible. The opening provided by the curtains showed a body covered by a clean white sheet. Eventually they were fully open and the face of the young boy was there for the couple to see. Mrs McDonnell threw herself at the glass. Both her hands open palmed as though pushing to get through.

'Noooooooo.' Her knees started to buckle but her hands clung onto the glass.

'No. No. No. Please. No,' she begged.

My eyes welled and I swallowed hard, trying to stay professional.

Mr McDonnell, still close to his wife, had one hand covering his mouth now. Both of them as close to the glass partition as they could be. 'My baby boy. My poor baby boy.' She turned to me. 'I want to go to him. Please. Let me go to him.'

I swallowed again before I spoke. 'I'm sorry. We need to do a post-mortem on Finlay because we don't know the cause of his death and in case there is any possibility that this is suspicious then we need to keep him away from anyone for the moment. But as soon as it has been done, then you can come back and spend as long as you need to with him.'

She turned back to the glass partition and a heart-wrenching wail sliced through the room.

29
2015

Her heart was failing. That's what the doctor had told her. He sat there in numbed silence. The chair hard, beneath him. He could remember that. The feel of the kitchen chair.

Solid. Unforgiving.

They hadn't even taken her into the living room. She had stayed in the kitchen with them and explained the medical terms to them once Connie had calmed and soothed her. All he had done was sit his behind on the hard wooden chair. A voice somewhere inside his head, screaming at him to move. To speak. To hug. To love. But he sat there. Listening to his beautiful daughter explain how weak her heart muscle was. That it had been a problem for some time but she had put off seeing the doctor, thinking she was just burning the candle at both ends and needed to get some rest, but when that hadn't worked, she had gone to see her GP.

Her eyes dried. Her voice levelled. She stared off into a corner of the room as she spoke. Focusing on a point just past Connie, whose hands were wringing. Her gentle soft white hands were wrapping and clawing at themselves as she tried to remain strong for her child. He could see it from his distant point.

He viewed the surreal scene in that kitchen. His kitchen. His daughter, his child, his very soul, and it was in the process of being ripped out of him, slowly but surely, piece by tiny piece.

He saw blood. Connie's hand. She had scratched herself in her effort to remain still and strong. The blood sat there, vivid red against her pale skin. A streak of life. Just breaking the surface.

Emma talked on. For now she was being prescribed a drug. Diji-something. It wasn't going in. His mind was deserting him.

She wanted to come home.

Of course he wanted this. This was her home and always would be. If that was the only thing he could do, then it was hers. No question. But it felt so ineffectual, in the grand scheme of what she was going through, saying she could return to the home that was already hers didn't feel enough.

He wanted to do something of substance for her.

He wanted to do what he'd do when she was little and protect her from the world. Protect her from what she was facing. He wanted to rub the scrape better and stop it hurting, put some magic cream on the cut, turn the light on when a nightmare invaded the dark, but none of that applied here and all he had was a home, her home and he could continue to be her father.

And he'd do that with everything he had in him.

30

Grey's office door was closed. His PA was outside. I couldn't for the life of me remember her name but I liked her. She always had a smile and a bag of sweets on her desk.

'Has he gone out?'

'Oh no, he's in, he asked that you go straight through.'

She proffered the bag from the desk at me. I peered inside and saw Murray Mints.

I smiled. 'I'd better not, thank you. Can you imagine if I took one and was busy sucking on it while trying to talk to him? I wouldn't be able to speak!'

'Why do you think I eat them? It stops me interrupting him when he's speaking to me.' She winked. I couldn't help but smile again. Such a stressful day but I was smiling again.

'Here,' she picked one out and held it up, 'take it for later. You never know when it might come in useful.'

'Thank you,' I whispered to his adorable PA as I moved past her into his office.

She smiled in response and put her head back down.

Grey's office was neat and sparse. *Grey* was neat and sparse. Saturday morning and I was sitting in front of him, having come into work because the job demanded that extra push of senior investigating officers. We didn't have set hours. If a case was running, then we were running as well. With no extra pay. It was just the way it was. However, lower-ranking officers who came in were on overtime when a murder was being investigated. At the minute we didn't know what we had, but it was suspicious so we were all working.

There was too much to do. Too much of a coincidence. Even if it didn't turn out to be murder, people were dying. We couldn't speak to the school this weekend, but we could interview the witnesses from the bus and we could access Finlay's friends while they were out of school and their parents were off work. Better for them that they had parents around to support them at this time.

I waited for Grey to finish the email he was typing out, the concentration making his face frown. He was a man I rarely saw smile. At his level of command there was a lot more paperwork and meetings, more log keepings and oversight. It was a reason I didn't want to go for promotion again. I would rather get my hands dirty and get out of the building with my team and get involved. Shuffling papers suited Grey. I couldn't imagine him meeting members of the public in times of crisis. He'd be one step ahead wondering what papers needed filling in and wouldn't have his full focus on the person he was speaking with. Pretty much like he was with his colleagues.

He dropped his finger to his keyboard with a flourish, which I took to mean he had sent whatever he was doing and he sat back and looked at me. 'What is it, Hannah?'

'I've had an uncomfortable phone conversation with Jack not ten minutes ago and now have the report we discussed printed out from the email he sent me. It's the PM on the young lad, Finlay McDonnell.'

Silence.

'The blood work came back from the toxicology screening. He pushed it through as urgent and with specific requests attached.'

Still nothing.

'Sir, Finlay McDonnell died from digoxin toxicity.'

Grey leaned forward in his seat. 'What are you saying, Hannah?'

He really wanted this spelling out to him. 'I'm saying that we now have two people who have died of digoxin poisoning, neither of whom were on digoxin and neither of whom, it seems, had family on the drug either. Sir, we have two suspicious deaths by the same MO.'

'So, other than the digoxin toxicity, how are the people linked?'

'As far as we can see at this time, they're not. We've a lot of work to do to try and find that connection. With Lianne Beers we had at least had her ex-husband with a motive to kill her because he gained custody of their daughter and his new family was complete, with his annoying ex-wife no longer in the picture. Now with a young boy dead by the same MO we have a problem, because we don't have anyone immediately obvious who would want him dead. I mean, a lad of his age, who does?'

Grey studied me as I continued to lay it out for him.

'With Lianne we didn't even know if it was suspicious or if it was an accident or suicide, though we haven't found any obvious ways she could have done it to herself and there's nothing of concern on her computer or diaries. But now that Finlay is dead we can at least rule out suicide – even if we can't rule out some kind of accidental poisoning.'

'But accident how?'

'That, I don't know. Industrial accident of some description?'

'So, how do you progress this?'

'We look at who has access to digoxin. There will be pharmacies, distribution centres, hospitals and other places, I'm presuming. Maybe there was an accident at one of these places that managed to affect both Lianne and Finlay so we also try to find that link between them both.'

I paused for breath.

'I also think we need to come up with a media strategy. We need to get ahead of this if we can.'

'You're right. We don't have a good track record with the *Today*. See Claire and set up a press conference for later this afternoon, get out there and show the public we're in front of it. Ask them for their help; see if they can link the two victims as well as asking for witnesses to the offences.'

'Me?'

'Yes. Who did you think was going to do it?'

I ran my fingers through my fringe. 'I hadn't.'

'Okay. You'll be fine.'

'What are we doing about disclosing the digoxin?'

'Thoughts?'

'We keep it to ourselves. If we disclose the information we risk copycats and we won't know one offender from the other. Plus, if we withhold it we have that information to confirm the truth if anyone walks in wanting to make admissions. You know how weird people can be on high profile cases. It's documented well enough.'

'Right again. You know what you're doing, Hannah, which is why I said you'd be fine with the press conference, you're the obvious person for the job.'

'If you think so.'

I didn't want to do this. Ethan would be there. Mixing the personal with the professional again. But I knew I had to get a grip.

31

The nerves danced through me like small bolts of electricity having a party at my expense. I was sure I could probably make a lightbulb glow if anyone chose to attach one to me at this point. I didn't join the job to get myself in front of a bunch of cameras or a crowd of journalists. Including Ethan. I wasn't sure if it was the fact that I was doing the press conference that was making me so jittery or that Ethan was out there in a chair waiting to throw a question at me at the earliest opportunity. We hadn't talked since the evening of the inquest. Seeing him again had dredged up all the old feelings I had for him but it had also thrown me into a tailspin. Could I really have expected him to wait for me when it was an impossibility that we could maintain a relationship in the roles we held? It had still knocked me for six when he told me he'd been seeing other people, but I'd done my best to look pleased; was that the right word? Comfortable with it, may be a better way of phrasing it. He'd gone on to clarify that he wasn't in a relationship but that he'd been dating, he wanted to be open and for me to know.

Well, now I knew.

Could I keep my cool and react to him as I would any of the other journalists or would I glow with this electricity gathering inside me?

On the whole, EMSOU didn't do many press conferences unless they were a necessity, so the fact that we had called one had sparked interest. The room was full and it was noisy, the journalists and their photographers and cameramen talking among themselves as they waited for someone to appear. Like a pride of lions waiting for its kill.

And I was the gazelle, soon to be caught with nowhere to go.

'All set?' asked Claire, looking far too happy. But I couldn't fault her, it was her default setting and this was her world anyway. She revelled in it, it made her buzz and gave her a permanent smile.

'Do I have a choice?'

'Of course you do. We can send them all home and they can make up their own stories.'

'Okay, okay. I'm just saying.'

'You'll be fine. Think of them as a bunch of schoolchildren who are trying to get their teacher's attention and approval.'

I grinned at her. 'You're good.'

'I know. Now get your arse out there.'

I looked at her.

'Inspector.'

I smiled again and she winked. I walked out to the single table and chair placed in front of three blue felt boards – the Nottinghamshire police logo prominently displayed, along with the helpline number – to a barrage of flashes and a crescendo of noise. I took a breath and seated myself. The flashes continued. I waited until the noise died down before I spoke.

'I'm going to read a statement out and will then take questions. I'd ask that you please let me answer them before shouting out any more or we're just going to have pandemonium.'

The room went quiet other than the continued clicking of cameras. I took a sip of the water from the glass that had been placed on the table.

'Last week a woman, Lianne Beers, was found dead in her home in Bramcote. Post-mortem evidence has identified cause of death to be a drug overdose. Two days ago a young boy, Finlay McDonnell, died on a bus on the way to school. A post-mortem also found that he had the same drug in his system.'

Camera flashes became louder and seemed brighter in my face.

'At this present time, we are treating these deaths as suspicious. We don't know how the poison got into their systems. We don't know how or if the two victims knew each other. If anyone knows of any link or knows any information that can assist police with our enquiry can they please contact us on the helpline number provided? Thank you.'

I looked out at the shocked but eager faces. I was about to face a barrage of questions.

'I'll take some questions now.'

The whole room seemed to be made of arms as a cacophony of noise and arms went up in unison. I didn't know where to look first. There was no order. Just chaos. Chaos I wasn't used to handling. I looked to my right and sought out Claire who mouthed *children* at me. I smiled and turned back to the gaggle of *children* in front of me and pointed to the front row.

'Are you going to tell us what the drug used was?' A woman I recognised. Short cropped hair, young, minimal make-up, very trendy.

'At this time, we are withholding that information in the interests of the ongoing investigation.' More arms were waving at me wildly. 'By doing so, the public are not at more risk.' A couple of arms dropped.

Ethan was sitting in the middle of the room, his look serious, arm in the air with the other reporters. I pointed him out. 'Ethan Gale?'

He paused a moment before speaking. I rubbed one of my damp palms down my trouser leg and kept it there, conscious of fidgeting.

'Detective Inspector, do you think the death of Finlay McDonnell could have been prevented had you acted more swiftly with Lianne Beers?'

It's his job. His job, just his job.

My mouth was dry. I swallowed.

'No.' I swallowed again, trying to get saliva to my mouth to help it function. This was not a good time for it to fail. 'I don't think anything we could have done would have prevented Finlay's death. The timeframe was too tight. As you can see, we are holding this press conference at the earliest opportunity now we know there is a problem, letting the press and the public know there is an ongoing investigation and we need their help and support.'

His job. That was all. Just his job.

32

He was sat in the witness interview room, a square box with a table and four chairs, looking calm and relaxed. An arm draped over the back of the chair. One leg crossed over the other. Not a care in the world.

'What the hell, Ethan?' I couldn't believe he'd had the balls to ask for me.

'I wanted a quick word.'

'So you thought asking to see the DI in charge of the investigation after the press conference was the best way to do that?'

'Han, all they will think is that I'm here trying to get more info from you.'

I sat down in the chair across from him, the thrum of the busy station permeating the door. 'And what is it you are here for?'

He smiled. 'I wanted to talk to you properly. I can't just see you like that, across a room,' he waved his arm to indicate the distance, 'and not be able to have a conversation.'

'But you have to. It's how it works. It's our jobs. We're not in a relationship anymore, Ethan, or did you forget that?' I certainly hadn't. I wish I could, this would go so much easier for me if I could.

He sighed. 'I didn't forget, but it doesn't mean I don't think about you.'

I looked down at the bare wooden desk. Scratch marks scoured into it. Names. Insults. Lasting memories of others seated here before me. 'Okay.'

'I know how you tick.'

'How's that?' The thrum quietened.

'My question. You'll take it personally.' I looked at him. Dared him. 'It wasn't.'

'You asked if we were to blame for further deaths. How else am I to take it?'

'Like a question from a journalist, but then what you're supposed to do is realise who I am, realise you know me and know how I feel about you and know there's a difference.'

I missed this man so much. 'But do I?'

'Do you what?'

'Know you?'

He stood. 'Han, stop thinking with your head, feel that question and let me know the answer if you ever figure it out.' He picked up his bag. 'Tell them I was pushing it, looking for an exclusive and you blew me off.'

And with that, he opened the door and walked out.

33

She was a woman. The report stated a woman was investigating the deaths. DI Hannah Robbins. It was the first time he noticed the name of the investigating officer. But it was the first time the police had stepped out from behind their desks and confronted what was happening. This wasn't their fight. He had no quarrel with them. His fight, the one he was taking right to their doorstep, was with the pharmaceutical companies.

It was interesting to know her name, though.

To know who was chasing him.

That was a horrible thought. It made him feel bad. Like a criminal. He wasn't a criminal. He was only after what was right. He was after the giants. For the little man.

For a little girl.

He didn't need to be chased by the police. By DI Hannah Robbins.

Isaac didn't like that he had access to the other names. To Lianne and Finlay. He had never wanted to know those names. He had never wanted to know anything about them. They weren't to enter into this. This was to be about sending a message to pharmaceutical companies through the use of their own failed products. He could distance himself from it all. Buy the goods, contaminate them, place them back in the shops and walk away. Far away. He wasn't there when anyone was hurt. He didn't see them, he didn't know them. He didn't want to know. He was at home with his grieving wife.

Their own bubble of hopelessness.

He dropped the paper into the large garden bin so Connie wouldn't read it. Not that she was reading anything any more, but he'd do his best to protect her. He'd failed his daughter so the least he could do was protect Connie from having to think about the real fat cats behind Em's death. She needed to heal in her own way and she wouldn't have the energy to fight back. But he was the husband, father, and the protector. He'd do it now.

There was a problem though. The reporter had failed. Ethan Gale.

He hadn't named the poison used.

Reading the articles was hard, but this would have to continue. Isaac had to get his message out there.

34

She was about forty feet away from her front door on Petworth Avenue, Toton. Detached houses in a small cul-de-sac. Black Lycra clinging to her body, cerise pink flashes down the sides accentuating toned muscles and a fitness level I wished I possessed. An elasticated iPod armband was wrapped around the top of her left arm and narrow white earphones sneaked out and looped into her ears. Around her waist was a plastic bottle hooked into a belt. I could still hear the beat of whatever music had been driving her as she ran towards what she thought was comfort and safety. Instead, she was face up on the sun-warmed grey concrete pavement, on display. Arms splayed. Head tilted back, rubber shock pads still stuck to her chest and blue gloves on the floor around her where the paramedics had left everything as it was. They'd heard the news reports, as had everyone else, and knew that they needed to leave the scene as intact as they could after they had attempted to save life. I stood over her, horrified at another senseless death. We didn't know this was a murder yet, but we'd been called out by the uniformed inspector anyway. She was young. Only thirty-six years of age. Not an age you'd expect to die on the way home from a run. One of her neighbours had looked out of their window and had seen that she'd gone down. He'd called the ambulance that had responded quickly, but too late to do anything for her.

My thoughts tumbled through my head as I waited for Jack to attend. Martin and Aaron were talking to neighbours and obtaining details to come back later for longer statements.

What was driving our killer? Because we did have a killer. This was no accident. Not with three suspicious deaths. How could three apparently unconnected people die from digoxin toxicity? Which is a presumption I was making, even though Jack wouldn't confirm it for me until we had the lab results in, but I knew deep down that this was our killer; this was the job we were already chasing our tails over. How was he targeting his victims?

A deep-voiced screaming followed by further shouting came from the cordon at the end of the road. I turned and saw a man of similar age to the woman on the ground, fighting with two uniformed officers. A car abandoned on the road behind him. He was screaming and yelling, arms flailing, trying to get past the officers and the cordon. I walked towards them and saw Martin and Aaron leave the neighbours they were talking to and walk in the same direction.

He wore a smart shirt and trousers, but you could still see he was a fit man and though his arms were not connecting with the officers, his physique was strong enough to be pushing them further and further into the thin plastic strip of barrier that had been stretched across the road. His emotions were disconnecting his arm functions from his brain and they were just waving about rather than actually doing any good or getting him anywhere. Once broken, I knew he would make a run for it and we couldn't have this scene compromised any further than the paramedics had done. Which of course they always had to. Saving life came before anything else, but this was different. He was in pain, but we had to stop him, no matter how strong his grief. His eyes were streaming. Tracks littered his face.

'Angela! Ange! Oh my God. Oh Ange.'

Aaron and I reached the battling threesome simultaneously. I knew his name from the neighbours.

'Mr Evans?'

'Angela!' boots scuffed the road as the two officers tried to keep traction to hold him back. 'Angela! Oh God. Oh God. No.'

'Mr Evans. Please. I'm so sorry. You'll be able to hold her soon enough but first we need to know what has happened to her and there are procedures.'

'Oh God. Oh Ange.' The arms had stopped flailing.

'I'm am genuinely so sorry for your loss.'

He looked at me. Looked at me in my all white protective garb. The garb that says something really bad has happened. Deep, pools for eyes. He stopped pushing the officers and sank down onto his knees.

35

Lance Evans shook intensely as he perched on the edge of his neighbour's pale blue floral sofa. The neighbour, Chloe Anderson, was in the kitchen making several cups of tea because that is what we do when grief strikes us in the heart of our community and homes, we make tea. It is the go-to soother of choice. It keeps hands and minds busy for those few minutes it takes to make it and once made it keeps the hands still of those grieving and those attending to them. It's not about the hot steaming fluid itself. It's the action and inaction it causes. So now, Chloe was creating her own distraction as a neighbour brought his life-altering, severe and hard-edged grief into her lounge as we attempted to talk to him. Cupboard doors banged and crockery clattered. And still Lance Evans shook. Tears spilling from his eyes, down his face and onto knees that jumped up and down from the balls of his feet.

'It's just you two at home is it?' asked Aaron.

'Yes. Yes. Yes it is. I mean ...' He scrubbed his head with his hands. 'It was. Oh God, no. What happened? To Ange? What happened to her?'

'That's what we're trying to find out, Mr Evans.' I kept my voice calm. Even.

'And why are we here? Why can't I go home?' His voice was rising slightly. I willed Chloe and her tea to come through, imagining her actually hiding out in the kitchen to avoid this.

'We don't know what killed her.' I'd had opportunity to speak with Jack as he examined the body, before I came into the house to speak with Lance. 'Our pathologist is concerned it may be something she has ingested so we will need to search your home to see if the contaminant is there.' *Ingested*. We were now looking at something a whole lot more serious. Products were being contaminated. Our residents were being poisoned from who knew where. Our victims were scattered around.

I looked back at the broken man in front of me.

'Our own home? But I'm fine.'

'I know. So we're going to go through some questions with you about diet and contents in the house a little later. Not right now.'

Lance Evans dropped his head into his hands and started to cry heavily. Chloe walked in with a tray in her hands. A teapot, three cups and a plate of biscuits, though I doubted anyone was in the mood for biscuits and Aaron wouldn't have a drink. I smiled at her and she gave me a tight smile in return as she placed the tray on a side table before hastily retreating back into the kitchen. She had been hospitable offering up her home to us, but from what I could see, she didn't really know the Evanses and was uncomfortable with the situation. I would make sure she was told we were grateful.

I poured out two cups of tea as Mr Evans let out his grief. Aaron sat quietly. Waiting until we could continue to speak with him.

'Is there anyone we can call for you, Mr Evans?' I asked.

He looked up. His face now red and bloated. 'No, no one. Not here anyway. We only moved here recently because of my job. Ange was still looking for work, which is why she was out running at this hour. We didn't need for her to work, but she said she needed to, she couldn't stay at home all day and do nothing but keep house. She left a job to follow me here. We left everything for my career. She put me first. This should have been me. Not her. She didn't deserve this. She was kind and generous and the brightest light in my life.' His sobs started again.

Aaron looked at me, getting pretty uncomfortable now. So Angela Evans had no family around her to be in conflict with and she had already given up her career for her husband, so he wasn't gaining anything by her death that we could immediately see. It seemed we had another brutal death and no strong leads.

36

Jack's voice was tense as I answered the phone in my office. I could tell we had a problem.

'It's the same thing isn't it?' We were cutting out the small talk, the usual friendly chitchat today. This was bad news.

'It is, Hannah,' the pathologist replied. 'The results are in from Angela Evans' blood work, I had them put it through immediately. It's positive for digoxin toxicity.'

'Crap.'

'I'm sorry to be the bearer of such bad news. The good news, if it can be called that, is it looks as though it killed her quickly with a myocardial infarction. She was obviously more sensitive.'

'Any indications of how it entered her system, Jack?'

'Well, as you saw at the PM a few days ago, there were no puncture marks, so that rules out injection. You've searched her home and asked her husband and neither of them was taking heart medication so she didn't accidentally take too much. The most likely scenario is ingestion because, as with the previous two victims, there were no puncture wounds.'

'I was wondering if we were looking at a product contamination case and you're backing that up.'

'Have your CSIs identified any item from the searches as a possible mode of transport into their systems yet?

'No, they're still working on it. With three addresses and a multitude of items to test, without knowing which ones to look at first, it's taking longer than we'd like. There aren't any items that match up across the addresses either so that's not helping the situation.'

'I can imagine. I'm sorry, Hannah. These cases are difficult to work. Have you heard from the offender, any demands?'

'Nothing.' I picked up my pen and started doodling on the pad in front of me. 'So, as of yet, we can rule out blackmail. I can't see any political gain from the victims or the areas, sabotage could well be our motive or just plain old excitement.'

'That's a scary thought.'

'Isn't it just?'

'And on top of that, we've had no luck with any of the witness interviews from the bus that Finlay McDonnell died on.'

'Whatever the cause of this, they're making it far from easy.' I nodded into the phone. 'I'll email you a copy of the report and post the hard copy. Let me know if and when you need me for any briefings at all.'

'Will do, Jack. Thank you.'

Funny how we give thanks, even for the bad things in life.

37

He was optimistic. It had to be working now. There was no way they couldn't be paying attention. He'd done too much.

He gently opened the door to Em's room and checked on Connie who was curled up with her arms wrapped around Em's pillow, her face pushed into it, her shoulders quietly shaking.

He closed the door. She never wanted to be disturbed at these times. This was her time with her daughter. A time when she felt connected to her. Through the space they were both sharing at different points, Connie believed she could feel Em with her. Anywhere else was just a desolate wasteland.

His hand squeezed hard at the injustice and the paper he was holding crackled, breaking the quiet on the landing. He loosened his grip and walked away, leaving his wife to her grief.

Downstairs, he put the *Nottingham Today* down on the kitchen table again. He didn't need to open it up today, there was the story of the deaths right there on the front page. He was excited by what he would read. That his plan was working. That people were sitting up and taking notice.

The headline didn't give much away as to the content of the article:

Nottingham Police Unable to Find The 'Poison Killer'

It indicated there were deaths by poison but the police hadn't yet caught him. That much he was already aware. He was excited to know what the rest of the article said. To read that the poison had been identified as digoxin. To see if the reporter had asked for quotes from the pharma companies and to hear their thoughts. He wanted to hear they were going to address issues with the drug, that because it was obviously a dangerous drug to the public, they needed to look at it in more detail and make sure it was doing the job it was intended for, as the risks with it were so high.

Isaac grabbed the coffee he'd made and pulled up the chair to read what the reporter had written.

He gripped the newspaper as he read, the crisp grey paper rustling in protest. There was no mention of what the poison was. Why hadn't they mentioned the poison? Without that, his plan fell down. How would the pharmaceutical companies know, and the medical professionals? There was no mention of it being a heart medication. A heart medication that killed people. Why were they not looking at the big companies, pointing the finger at them?

His head pounded. His grip growing ever tighter on the back pages. The *Today* was only interested in targeting the police but the police weren't the issue. He knew the police had a difficult job. He wasn't going to make it easy for them. He'd watched a few crime shows. Not that he needed to worry about fingerprints or anything; it was all random and he wore thin gloves bought from the chemist. He was far away from the victims when he injected the poison into the items. He was going to keep going as long as he could, as long as it took for those who needed to notice, to notice and to actually care. That was the difficult thing. The pharmaceutical companies might notice. They might make the right sounds to the press but getting them to genuinely care was another issue. He had to keep going, keep pushing until they had no choice, until the public demanded they put all their billions into actually saving people, instead of lining their pockets.

The article ended. It was worthless.

With both hands he grabbed the paper up and screwed it into a ball, throwing it into the corner of the room.

He still had work to do.

38

Evie Small looked at me with a deep sadness in her eyes.

'What is it?' There was no smile. No laptop in her arms, no biscuits, just a newspaper in her hand. A newspaper. The *Nottingham Today*. My stomach lurched. What now?

'Have you spoken to Ethan lately?'

Evie was the only person I'd trusted with the information about Ethan. I'd needed someone to talk to and she was the best friend I had. She didn't judge. She listened and she cared. As EMSOU's analyst we worked together often and in turn, drank together often, and we had become firm friends.

'Not since the press conference. Why, Evie?'

She pushed the paper towards me and then wrapped her arms around herself as she stood on the spot. Not moving, her top lip pulled in as she bit at it. I sensed trouble. I opened up the paper and there it was. On the front page. He would be proud. *I* should be proud. I willed him on to do well but for it to be at the expense of me, of a job I was working?

Nottingham Police Unable to Find The 'Poison Killer'

A 34-year-old woman has been found collapsed on her street in Toton, Nottingham, after going out for a jog. Paramedics tried to revive her but she died at the scene.

Angela Evans leaves behind a husband, Lance.

The couple had not long moved to Nottinghamshire following a promotion that Mr Evans had recently accepted. The couple did not yet know anyone in the area.

Angela Evans will be the third victim of the so-called 'poison killer'. His previous two victims are; Lianne Beers, 29, of Bramcote and Finlay McDonnell, 16, of Beeston.

When asked for comment Lance Evans said, 'Angela was the sweetest, gentlest and most giving person.' He pleaded for the killer to turn him or herself in and not to harm anyone else saying, 'it's not just the dead who are hurt, but also the living that are left behind.'

Nottinghamshire police has asked anyone with information, however small they think it might be, to come forward. Information can even be provided anonymously via the tip-line, number below.

Detectives are baffled as to the motive of the killer, as no demands have been received and no one particular product, item or source has been identified as being the target.

Police have stated they are working all the angles and will update the public as soon as they know anything further. They ask that everyone is vigilant and self-aware.

No one can say if the killer will strike again and if so, where that will be.

The Police and Crime Commissioner's Office informed the Today that they are fully behind the investigation as they want to provide the grieving families with answers as to why their loved ones died and they need to provide the public with real assurances about their safety.

With this being the third victim of the killer we are now in the realm of a serial killer. Two words that the police will not want the public to worry about.

If you saw Angela Evans as she was out running or you are friends with her, please get in touch with police so they can build a picture of her last movements.

If you are a friend of Angela's get in touch with the paper, let us know what she was like as a person. We'd love to hear from you.

How could he write this? How could he write this and not tell me? Yes, we were giving them quotes, but the rest of it …

Was he angry with me? Did he have a right to be?

I dropped the paper onto the mess that was already covering my desk.

'Thanks, Evie.'

'I'm sorry.' Her arms were still wrapped tightly around her body, accentuating her waif-like figure.

'What for? You didn't write this. I'd look stupid if I saw him without having seen this first. So, again, thank you.' I smiled. Or I tried to. What was I supposed to do about Ethan now?

'I also need to worry about if Grey and Walker have seen it. He's right, they won't be happy with the words serial killer being thrown about. And how did he get a quote from Lance Evans? They've obviously waited for the Family Liaison Officer to leave before they've gone knocking on his door. Leeches. Lance Evans won't have the ability to deal with it. He won't know how to tell them to get lost. All he'll want is his wife back, his life back. This violation of his space will be an unknown for him. Of course he's going to say he loves his wife and wants the killer to stop.' I was furious. Imagining the crumbling man I'd met on the street, having journalists banging on his door when he was alone and distressed. 'I'll speak to the FLO involved and make sure he tells Lance that he doesn't have to speak to them and he doesn't have to answer the door to them. Though, now he's given them a quote I hope they leave him alone.'

'And, how are you?'

'If I don't have to worry about you chewing half your face away,' she let go of her lip, 'then I'll be fine. I'm not sure I can say the same for Grey though.'

'How is he?' She relaxed a little as we moved away from the subject of Ethan and his coverage of the investigation.

'Stressed, as you can imagine. What with the PM results coming back from Angela Evans as digoxin toxicity, he's feeling the strain. He's getting pressure from Catherine. You know how she hates bad publicity and slow clear-up rates, anything that can reflect badly on her department. Then he's going to see this from the *Today*. I'm sure

I'll get more of a feel for how he is when I see him at this morning's briefing. Will you come in for it today, please? You might be able to help us out. Get details where everything has occurred, map it out and see what ideas you can come up with? Any help we can get we will be gratefully received.'

'Of course, Catherine emailed early this morning about the case. Though I'm going to be at the opposite end of the room to Grey. Just in case he spontaneously combusts.'

39

The briefing room was heaving, even though it was only eight a.m. The airwave radio set, was on Aaron's desk and tuned in to the local area. It was quiet. From experience I knew it would scream into life later and Aaron would hand it off to someone else to manage because he couldn't stand the constant noise on his desk. It distracted him, made him grumpy and bad-tempered.

I was pleased to see Catherine had drafted in extra staff, though this much chatter in the room was going to stress Aaron out. He was already sitting at his desk with his earplugs in.

There were many familiar faces that I had seen in my years working over the force area, but there were also some unfamiliar ones. We had the full HOLMES 2 team setup, which included manager, receiver, reader, indexer and inputter, as well as our own intelligence unit and Evie as our analyst on a permanent basis for the length of the investigation. I imagined the new death had given Catherine cause to rise early and organise it all.

I thanked everyone for coming in early and at short notice. Aaron took out his earplugs as the noise died down. 'As you may know, we've had several deaths that have been caused by digoxin toxicity.'

'Lady Westholme, Ma'am?'

Catherine, who was standing at the side making sure her organisational skills had gone to plan, gave the interrupter at the back a glare. Whether she understood the Agatha Christie reference or not, she obviously didn't care, though I imagined she didn't get it. I saw her more as a literary fiction kind of reader.

I nodded my understanding and continued talking about Angela Evans and how this had exploded without warning.

'We are working this under the operation name Veridical. We have no links between the victims so far, so I want a large part of the investigation team to work on that, to do the victim work. Find out if any of them link back to each other in any way. If they have mutual acquaintances between them. Check bank and credit card bills, locations of such, schools, jobs, subscriptions to clubs, magazines, online spaces. Speak to everyone they know and liaise with their FLOs so that you always have the support of the families as you do this. I don't want it to look as though we are being intrusive on the victim when all we are doing is trying to hunt down a common denominator and find a killer before he finds himself any more victims to house FLOs with. If you've come over from another force area EMSOU, thank you. If you're here from another division on temporary secondment, see DS Aaron Stone who will partner you up with someone and point you in the direction of Theresa, the HOLMES inputter, for actions.'

Aaron nodded as I pointed him out and a bunch of eager faces looked towards him. Ah, the uniform secondments. Usually a good bunch to have because they were always thrilled to be seconded to a homicide investigation and got on with their work really quickly and for some reason they loved to be wearing a suit to work. I think it was the novelty. Personally, I liked the days when I wore a uniform.

You never had to think about what you were going to wear in a morning and never had to worry if your arse looked big in anything because it was known that it was going to look big in the awful uniform work trousers, but they were practical and robust for running about, throwing yourself about in and cleaning up in the washing machine.

'As well as tying the victims to each other we need to progress the separate digoxin investigation. It looks as though we have a killer using digoxin as their weapon of choice and the most likely way of administering it is by product contamination. So far the victims have been spread out so we have a list of patients within Nottingham who are being prescribed digoxin and we need staff to research the names, see if any of the patients are known for violent offences, for making threats against people for any reason, and we also need staff to knock on doors, see how the patients are doing, make sure they are still taking their medication in as much as a police officer can make that kind of assessment.'

The room was silent. We had our work cut out for us.

40

1 month ago

The medicine was in the cupboard. Isaac thought he would move it before Connie saw it was gone. And also before she noticed them lined up and started crying again. For what they represented. The bottles of medicines that were to keep Em alive. The sole purpose of it being there in the cupboard. Chemicals in tablet format, created to keep her alive.

Failed.

Em would never take another again.

Isaac shook as he collected the bottles. Picking each bottle up delicately so as not to wake Connie, he wrapped his fingers around to dull the rattle of the residual tablets in their cool plastic casing. He pushed each bottle deep into his coat pocket and looked at the void in the cupboard where Em's lifeline used to be.

The deep ache inside him threatened to erupt like an all-consuming monster, its claws ready to tear him apart from the inside out, his heart, emotion and tears, his lungs, the very breath torn savagely from him, the eruption leaving just the monster with no heart, no breath, nothing to care for.

The monster erupting would be angry beyond anything Isaac could imagine and vicious with it and that, he didn't want Connie to see. He took what breath he could pull in and breathed as hard as he could and as deep as he could, into his lungs that hurt so much. He reached from his pocket, where his hand still rested, closed the door of the cupboard and took one last deep breath. The anger needed a release valve, but not at Connie's expense. He knew what he had to do. He knew where the blame lay for this.

With another breath, much calmer and quieter now, Isaac walked out of the kitchen, picked up his car keys and headed out towards his allotment on Bessell Lane. His sanctuary.

A place he was safe and a place Connie was safe from.

41

The building that housed Curvet was large and bold, with clean lines and lots of glass. You could have been forgiven for thinking you were walking into a futuristic hotel, if it weren't for the high level of security we'd had to pass through just to get through the front door. And that was as far as we'd made it so far.

This place was more secure than the police station, but with billions of pounds worth of secrets inside, it didn't really surprise me. Up until this point I'd only ever really heard about pharmaceutical companies, yet here we were, Aaron and me, standing inside the pristine glass jar that was Curvet Pharmaceutical. The nearest company to us that produced digoxin, they were based on the outskirts of Derby. Away from other factories and workers, to keep themselves safe. There were a hell of a lot of drugs here that people would want to get their hands on. I wanted to talk to someone about their security protocols and also about any disgruntled employees they might have.

Above the reception desk hung a giant curved television screen preaching the gospel that was Curvet. What it could do for you. How it could heal you. How it supported the community it worked beside. How it was campaigning to shape the younger generation and how it was helping Third World countries with the medicines they produced. Watching their message, I could easily believe all the world's problems could be helped by Curvet.

But, if this were true, then why were we not seeing more evidence of it? Aaron was patiently waiting for our meeting to start, not even watching the show that was being shown above the head of the well turned-out receptionist.

'Can I get either of you a drink?' he asked, as if reading my thoughts.

'Thank you. I'd love a tea, green if you have it.'

'Of course. And you, officer?' he asked of Aaron.

'No, thank you. Can you tell us how long we'll be waiting?'

'A few minutes, I'm afraid. Mr Treadway took a call before you arrived, so you might want to have a seat.'

I ushered Aaron to the leather seating and dropped into the sofa that was more comfortable than the one I had at home.

Fifteen minutes later, we were five flights up and in the largest office I have ever been in. Treadway was a slim man who took his own health seriously from the look of him. I didn't imagine it looked good if you ran a place like this and were the unhealthiest person here. The office space took up a good quarter of the side of the building. All the glass made it feel like we were sat outside. We were in the middle of an unusual run of hot sunny days and the air conditioning felt blissful against my face as I kept my suit jacket on.

'How can I help?' he asked.

I let him know about the digoxin deaths and asked if there was anything in his accident at work book that would cover something like this, to which he showed suitable horror. Treadway stated he had read about people dying but hadn't realised it could be linked to his factory.

'We can't say for sure that it is; we're only making enquiries at this point. You're the closest pharmaceutical company to Notts that manufactures digoxin so it's only wise that we come to speak to you.'

'Of course.'

'Can you show us your accident at work book?' Aaron asked. 'To see if there are any individuals who may have a grievance against the company.' He clarified.

'Yes. Yes.' He walked over to his desk and spoke into his intercom asking the person at the other end to bring it in to us. Then he came and sat back down.

'Thank you,' I said.

'Anything I can do. This is horrific. As well as the deaths being utterly appalling, you can imagine what this will do to us if it gets out that we are linked to it, so on a purely business level, we have to clear this up as fast as we can.'

Aaron grunted. I looked at him and willed him to stop. Craig Treadway smiled at him. 'I know, it sounds callous, but we have that reputation anyway, so we may as well admit to it, embrace it and get on with it. That way we deal with it and resolve the issue.'

'We appreciate it.' I glared at Aaron and hoped he could contain his thoughts today. 'What about other potential disgruntled employees, have you had to fire anyone within the timeframe we are working with?'

'I can check, but hiring and firing isn't something I have anything to do with, unless of course the firing is to do with a major breach that needs to be brought to my attention, and we haven't had one of those. The same goes for accidents at work. I'm not saying we haven't had any. We haven't had any of the level I would get to know about, but whether there are any in the book that I wouldn't need to be informed of, is another matter.'

Treadway made eye contact with me.

'It's only the serious stuff that makes it to my office I'm afraid. Which is the stuff you'd want to know anyway, I suppose?'

'Exactly. And talking about stuff you would know about, are there any instances of drugs mistakenly being labelled incorrectly and going out as something else? Could that be something we could be looking at?'

The door opened and a young woman walked in with a large black book in her hands. Aaron reached out to take it from her. She froze and looked to Treadway.

'It's okay, Amy.'

She handed the book to Aaron, who started flicking through the pages. Treadway studied me a moment, considering his answer to my last question. Aaron flicking, eyes moving, but his head side on, alert to where the conversation was going.

After a moment that had yawned in front of us, the silence thundering in my ears, Treadway had compiled his answer and spoke. 'The word mistakenly would indicate that we wouldn't know about it if it had happened, because there would have been a mistake and not a work in progress, so, no, at this point, I'd say not.' His gaze was steady. 'What I will say though, because I want to help, is that we will do an inventory of all our stock and make sure all our numbers are as they should be.'

I nodded.

'Does that sound satisfactory to you, DI Robbins?'

'Thank you, that would be really helpful.' Aaron carried on flicking pages. 'So, you don't think anyone has been fired but we can check up on it.' I confirmed what he'd told me earlier. 'How happy do you think your employees are, Mr Treadway? Are they likely to be disgruntled and still be at work?'

'Ha, that's the big question. How many places of employment can we ask that question of?'

That was a scary thought, many people hated their jobs, and passionately, which meant, inside this building, right here, right now, could be our killer.

42

Treadway was correct in that there had been no job losses in the time frame we were interested in. He had a very efficient HR department. There had been a retirement within the last month but the man in question had worked at the company for his entire working life. Forty-five years. It wasn't often you found that any more. Gareth Rice had been a model employee and had retired to a cottage in Devon with his husband, Bernard. He'd worked in the offices, not on the factory floor. They'd had a good send off, from Curvet and from his family and friends as they made the move, we were told. They were a well-liked couple that spent their spare time walking. They loved the outdoors, hence their move to the coast.

We'd make a request to Devon and Cornwall to check on the couple to cover our bases, but I couldn't see Gareth Rice as a lead we needed to spend time looking into. If Curvet had any place in this investigation, it was either with a disgruntled employee still in their employ or someone else with a grievance against them.

'Do you get any hate mail?' I asked of Chris, the HR woman we were now talking to, again sitting in an immaculately clean office. They must use an army of cleaners to keep this place glistening to this level.

'Oh yes. Animal rights groups have a particular soft spot tucked away for us in the hatred box of their heart.'

'How often do you receive mail?'

'A couple of times a month, and it's pretty graphic. You wouldn't believe how graphic it is and how sordid their minds are.' She shuddered. 'It's not as though we test on animals here. All we are is a production and distribution centre, but that's still enough for some to hold us in contempt. I can't sleep at night after reading some of the stuff they send, so I don't know how they manage to create it.'

'Do you still have it?'

'Yes. We keep it all. The groups are also why this place is the fortress it is. Otherwise you wouldn't get staff working here. They wouldn't feel safe. Cars get attacked. It gets really scary when the groups go on a spree.'

'And these sprees, do they happen often?'

'Not so much now, they used to a lot more often, but it has tailed off in recent years. They like to target the places where they know the animals are, we're more for those who can't be bothered to travel.'

'Anything recently?'

'Not in the last couple of months, no.'

'But,' Aaron joined in, 'as Mr Treadway already mentioned, this wouldn't be good publicity for the company if it got out that Curvet was linked in any way to the spate of poisonings, would it?'

Chris shook her head, ponytail swishing behind her. 'No, it wouldn't look good for the company at all. The stocks would take a real dive.'

43

Ross stood in the wood-panelled dock to the left-hand side of the judge who sat under the Royal Coat of Arms. *Dieu et mon droit* (God and my right) *Honi soit qui mal y pense* (shame upon Him who thinks Evil of it) emblazoned underneath it, a representation of the Garter behind the shield. The judge's face was pale and jowly. He was leaning forward on his elbows, listening intently, wig firmly in place. Ross couldn't remember when he had last seen a female judge but he knew they did the circuit here.

Ross glanced over at the twelve jurors in the heavily wood panelled court room, who all peered back at him, a look of undisguised interest on their faces. The room smelled clean and polished as always.

His shirt collar felt somehow tighter today. It wasn't a new shirt; he'd worn it plenty of times before. Maybe he'd shrunk it in the wash last time he'd washed it. It felt close, stifling. The collar was choking.

His hands clasped in front of him. Palms sweating. Sliding. Unable to grip the other hand. He intertwined his fingers as the defence barrister reminded him that he was still under oath and asked him if he was aware of that fact. Ross nodded.

'For the stenographer, DC Leavy.' The barrister's black gown looking a comfortable two sizes too big as they all did, sliding over one shoulder in a relaxed fashion that Ross certainly wasn't feeling.

'Yes. Yes, I'm aware.' He raised himself up. Pulled back his shoulders. Tightened his fingers together. It hadn't felt like this when the prosecution barrister had taken him through his statement yesterday. Yesterday was a breeze. A walk in the park. His collar fit perfectly and his palms were cool and relaxed. Fuck, this guy they had on trial was guilty as hell. Why was he the one sweating and why was he being treated like the criminal here?

'So, I'll ask you again then. Were you aware of the fact that my client who is currently here on a charge of murder, had previously been assaulted by his wife on no less than twelve occasions – and that on one of those occasions, a knife had been used?'

44

She looked as though she was about to explode. I hadn't ever seen her lose her usual controlled poise. Her hair had the look of fingers having ravaged their way through it and her face was colouring up at a rate I was getting concerned about. If she was going to lose control any further I wasn't only concerned about her, I was concerned about myself. Who knew what rash decisions were going to come out of this? Grey sat beside me, fingers twiddling rapidly in his lap. The faster Superintendent Catherine Walker paced, the faster Grey's fingers moved. Again, I didn't think that was possible. I'd seen him stressed before. I took a deep breath in, ready to interject in the tirade. Like preparing to hold your breath underwater for an undisclosed period of time.

'Ma'am, if I can?' The pacing behind her desk stopped. I exhaled. Grey's fingers stopped, just for a moment, as though he was now holding his breath.

'Hannah?' It was like an icy blast from the Arctic had directed its force at me.

'How has the judge left it today? What do we need to do?' Grey's fingers moved like whippets out the gate.

'How do you think he left it, DI Robbins? The prosecution barrister had to approach the bench and admit he was not aware of the facts of the case that had been admitted in open court. The judge went on to tear strips off him and Nottinghamshire police for their incompetence which, I'm reliably informed, was in front of the public viewing gallery. Amongst the gallery was a member of the press. After immediately dismissing the jury for the day, the judge told the prosecution that they had until tomorrow to decide if they wanted to continue with the prosecution of Pine for the murder of his wife. I then, as you can imagine, received a very irate phone call from the head of the East Midlands CPS, asking what the hell was going on. Does that clarify it enough for you?' She was still standing behind her desk; her hands had run through her hair at least once as she related this to us.

I ran my own hands through my hair. Something Grey was unable to do, which I suppose explained the finger twiddling. 'Where is Ross now? Has anyone spoken with him?'

She sighed and finally sat down. 'No, I think he's still on his way back or hiding somewhere. I got you and Anthony in as soon as I heard. What is going on, Hannah? How has it got this bad? I thought it was a straight up and down domestic murder and your team could handle it. It's why you were getting the Cat C murders – because they were the ones where there were supposed to be no issues and I know you needed a break after ...'

I nodded. I understood.

'He's royally screwed up, Hannah. We can't take this. Not right now. Not on top of the inquest. We don't know how the cards are going to fall there. Another mistake, well, it's just … You can't afford it.

'He has to go, Hannah.'

45

The stuff in the hate mail to Curvet was shocking. The venom people spewed and actually put down onto paper amazed me.

There were threats to burn down the building. To trash people's cars and homes. To do to the people what was being done to the animals. To lock the people in cages and stick needles in them. Whatever they could think of, they had written it down. I fully understood why Chris had said she couldn't sleep after reading some of it. I thought I was going to have some problems. A glass or two of wine might be needed to help things along.

Of course there were never any return addresses. I'd have to get the letters ninhydrin tested for fingerprints, but there were going to be multiple prints on the letters now. Postmen, sorting office staff, postmen again and Curvet staff. We could get lucky though. It was a line of enquiry we needed to take.

Martin finished talking me through his visit to Finlay's school and how there had been no issues noticed by them. Finlay had been a quietly popular boy. Not one of the cool kids, but neither was he ostracised because he looked different. He'd been confident in himself, and in school that held a lot of weight and stood him in good stead. I was getting frustrated with everything, the lack of movement on the investigation, when Ross walked into the major incident room. His shoulders were slumped, head down, hands in pockets, looking for the entire world as if it had indeed ended. He didn't know the half of it yet. I needed to talk to him, to know what was going on with him and to know how something as big as this had been missed. I'd trusted that he could run with a CAT C murder. I had to shoulder some of the blame myself. I was his supervisor. I had also missed it. Or I had missed the fact that he had missed it.

I watched every person look up from what they were doing as he walked in. News travelled pretty damn fast. Tight smiles were offered. None were passed back. I stood. 'Ross,' I nodded him towards my office. He threw his jacket over his chair. Took a deep breath and walked back out.

'How are you?' I asked once we were both behind my closed door. He still hadn't lifted his head since entering the office. I wasn't going to make the same mistake this time. Sally had needed me to push her, to make her talk so I could listen and make supervisory decisions and I had failed. I would not do that again. Though bolting the stable door sprung to mind.

'I'm sorry, boss,' he mumbled.

'Sit down.' I took a chair on the same side of my desk as Ross was standing. I didn't want the desk between us as a barrier. I wanted him to talk.

He slumped into the chair next to me. Heavy, leaden. Though he was doing his best to hide his face from me, I could see how pale he was. Washed out. I worried about how this was going to run. It didn't matter what Catherine had said, I was his supervisor and I would deal with him, but I needed him to open up and at the minute his body language was telling me he was doing the exact opposite.

Maybe he was going to tell me he wanted out of the job. Had I allowed it to get this far? How had I missed the signs? We were all so screwed up, but now I needed to step up and pull us back up to the mark and that included Ross.

'What happened, Ross? You have to tell me. I can't do anything about it if you don't talk to me.'

46

Ross finally looked up. He saw his DI, Hannah Robbins, sitting beside him, elbows on knees, leaning forward. The typical positioning of anyone wanting to show they were actively listening. He knew her. He knew she tried hard and that she meant well. He had to try and talk to her. To tell her what had happened. How he had screwed up. How he had failed her. The team.

Her dark fringe had grown slightly over recent months and it hung down now, just about covering her eyes. If she dipped her head they'd be gone and he wouldn't feel the weight of her soul as it searched him, because he knew that's what she was doing. She was looking and she was analysing. What did she see in him? A failure already? Or did he have a chance?

Daria Pine. It had all started there. Or rather, as Ross well knew, it had started long before that. It had started with Sally – but he wasn't going to use her as an excuse for his poor behaviour, his poor investigative skills.

Daria Pine. The woman stabbed to death in her kitchen. A woman who had lived and breathed in that house, torn down to a corpse with procedures to be carried out around it as she lay splayed on her own kitchen floor, still bloodied and shredded.

Daria Pine. For all intents and purposes, a straightforward job. Her husband there with the knife in his hand and a confession in the interview room. With the physical evidence seized by CSIs and the post-mortem evidence and the admission, it was straightforward getting a charging decision from the CPS.

Now he was here, but it looked as though the whole case was going to be lost.

47

6 weeks ago

The sun shone like an evil blast of hell, bright in the sky, reminding those around Isaac and Connie that things would still go on as normal. They'd attend this funeral, give their condolences, look saddened for one taken so young, while inside feel relieved their own nearest and dearest were still with them. And then they would, as the sun shone above them, and it probably would again tomorrow, live their lives uninterrupted by loss or grief. Real grief, pain, and that barren, barren loss.

Connie stared at her wardrobe. Half her clothes already on the bed or scattered at her feet. Trousers and blouses. Dresses. Greys, blacks, navies and greens. All selected, held up for scrutiny and discarded like trash.

She stood erect in her pants and bra, staring into the space that held the remainder of her clothes. Her arms hanging lifeless by her sides as though being pulled by an unknown force through the very floorboards she stood on. Her shoulders slumped under the invisible tension.

All colour had been drained from her this past two weeks, and her skin now looked loose on her tiny frame. Soft and malleable. Isaac couldn't bear to watch her torture herself over what she should wear today. Who cared what she looked like for her only child's funeral? What was the significance of the dress code? Em wasn't here to appreciate it and even if she was, her life signified doing what you loved best, not doing what pleased others. Isaac didn't see that it was really down to their style of dress on how much they were judged to be grieving. He stalked from the room. Already dressed in a pair of black trousers with a white shirt, paired with his polished black-laced shoes, but only because he hadn't put any thought into it. He'd picked them out because it was the norm. It was his funeral outfit. The clothes he wore for other people's funerals. He never ever expected to have to wear these clothes to his daughter's burial.

Connie sighed, she sighed from the bottom of her very soul. Her pale drawn face awash with silent tears.

48

Ross walked out of the office with a bigger slump to his shoulders than he had come in with, though I wasn't surprised considering the full set of circumstances on the Pine case I had provided him. He was overburdened with guilt. I could see that. I didn't feel good. I had to do something to protect him, to help him through this. I was determined this wouldn't be the thing that beat him and ground him out. Catherine might want him out of the unit, but there was no way I was going to let that happen.

He'd led me through the job as he'd seen it. Simple in his eyes. But he'd skipped so many crucial steps. He'd taken everything at face value and with a confession in custody I could kind of understand why, but he wasn't trained to work that way. He was trained to do a full investigation, to check everything out. I could see that when he spoke of Daria Pine he was really talking about Sally. Her prone body on the floor. The stab wounds and the blood seeping out covering her clothing and the floor. He couldn't separate the two, he was seeing his friend instead of seeing the victim and he wanted to feel the victory of the charge and conviction and I hadn't picked up on it. I had failed as badly as he had failed. I wouldn't let him take the flack for this alone.

Daria Pine had been a domestic violence abuser. Robert Pine had been injured by her on multiple occasions. He'd phoned it in on at least four occasions and another time the hospital reported it as he attended with a knife injury. The other occasions had been reported by well-intentioned neighbours who had heard the screaming of the couple and had seen Robert punched in the face at barbecues and other events, but he had never agreed to go to court and support a prosecution. He informed the OIC each time that he had been afraid of how it would look. A slight woman like Daria, abusing a solid man like himself. No one would believe him. Regardless of his injuries. They would want to know why he hadn't just protected himself from her. He couldn't. He loved her. She was diminutive. He was a physically imposing man. If he defended himself he would hurt her. What she did, he could cope with. It would stop anyway. He was sure of it. The reports had included photographs of bruises on Robert's torso and back. On his arms and legs. Reports Ross hadn't searched for and hadn't found. It was these very reasons that Robert had kept quiet about the abuse during his interview. In his eyes, he had committed the crime. He had used a knife and stabbed Daria. He wasn't going to talk about what had happened leading up to that moment, just as he refused to support prosecutions against the woman when she had beaten him. A man of his size had stabbed his wife to death and those were the facts as he saw them. He took the blame. It didn't matter to him that she had been the one threatening him with the knife first and could possibly have killed him this time.

Of course Ross had submitted the knife to forensics and it had come back with sets of prints for both the couple, but that was to be expected, as it was the family home. He hadn't asked the question of when she had last used the knife. That one question alone could have opened Robert up and led the investigation down a different path.

And we had failed to do a simple background search that would have led to further interviews and questions and maybe a different outcome when presenting the case to the CPS charging decision maker. Robert Pine was now on trial for straightforward murder.

I could see why Superintendent Walker would say she wanted Ross gone, even if his record was previously unblemished. This looked bad for her. I went to see Anthony.

We'd worked together for several years now and though I knew he hated the stress of the job I also knew he was great at making sure we were all covered the best way we could be. That the jobs were done the way they were supposed to. He was afraid of comeback, so he did investigations exactly by the book and he expected his teams to do the same. And even though he wasn't running the investigations he monitored them and expected updates, and if you stepped out of line he wanted to know why. In this way, he was also fair.

DCI Anthony Grey was a good man. But a worrier.

I respected him.

'We're short staffed,' I continued.

'I know, it's not a great situation to be in. With governmental cuts and our recent losses,' he looked me in the eye and I maintained the contact.

'Only the other day, I spoke to a divisional sergeant who was complaining about having staff taken from her. I think the stolen bicycles can wait for a while, don't you?' he continued.

'Absolutely. I'd have thought the sergeant would have understood that, with the fact that we have no idea where the poison killer is going to strike next. We have no geographical profile. No boundary line. Nothing. Why the moaning?'

'Oh, it's not that she doesn't understand the scale of the job we're undertaking. It's that she is still being assessed on her figures. Her clear-up rates. She's still expected to perform with less, and bear in mind she already had less before we came along and took what we needed.'

'What? So the powers that be are still monitoring the divisions that we are taking staff from and expecting them to perform the same as before?'

'Not the same, Hannah, better and it's not the powers that be, it's coming from the government. The ones making the big cuts also want us to do better and this sergeant is stressed. She's only been in the role a year. I went to see her with a bee in my bonnet and left feeling sorry for her.'

'You soon forget how hard they have it in uniform on division once you leave, don't you?'

'You sure do. Anyway, what brings you here to my door – and not Catherine's?' He grimaced at me, which I knew meant he wasn't really kidding.

'As I said, we're short staffed, so we need to keep Ross on.'

He sighed.

'We can't work as we are, it's impossible. We're understaffed, you've acknowledged as much. Taking Ross off now as we run a full multiple murder investigation just doesn't make sense. I need him and I won't let him go.' There, I'd said it.

Grey tapped the edge of his desk as the cogs turned in his head. I could practically hear them squealing. He'd have to take this up to Walker.

'You haven't told Ross yet?'

'No, with everything that we have going on, doing the paperwork to move him to another department isn't at the top of my to-do list. Besides, I want to keep him.'

'Walker told you to get rid of him. How do you want me to explain this to her, Hannah?'

'Yes, he's screwed up but we're as much to blame for that as he is. We're his supervisors and we failed to supervise.

'He's a bloody good cop, Anthony. I could really do with him working this. Once he puts his head down, there's no stopping him. He has no qualms about the hours he does; he goes above and beyond, checking and cross checking facts before passing them on. Last year, he picked up several pieces of key information on the Manders' case by keeping his head down and working it from his desk.

'Tell me, are you planning on reallocating this investigation or leaving it with us to follow through? Because if you're leaving it with us then I'm going to need all hands on deck – and that includes Ross.'

He rubbed the lines that were creasing his forehead.

'The other units are running a nightclub stabbing and a gang shooting. There's nowhere else to send this. You're going to have to keep going with it.' He drank his coffee. I waited. Watched the traffic moving outside on St Ann's Wells Road. The sun glinting from the washed and polished cars travelling about their business. He put his mug down.

'I'll take the issue of Ross up with Walker and see what her stance on it is. You're putting me in a very difficult position.'

I stood. I knew we were about done. 'I know, and I'm sorry. We've had a shit six months and we need to try and pull together not apart. I'll keep him in line.'

'Make sure you do. I can't cover you forever.'

49

The nerves danced in Isaac's stomach as the newspaper lay folded on the kitchen table. This daily routine was something akin to sticking needles in his skin. Each word became a piercing of pain driving home the loss of Em and the impotence of him as her father to protect and failing that, to avenge, to make right.

His fingers hovered over it as his mind raced through the possibilities of what lay in store. Would they get it right today or would they still be running on the wrong track? His aim was simple enough, for this void that lived inside him and Connie, to be noticed by the companies who could do something different, something to help, the newspaper had to report the use of digoxin in the deaths of local people. Fear clouded his brain and his fingers refused to move. All he needed was the ball to start moving, for the idiots in their ivory towers, those who had never seen real loss or pain, who only reported on it, to see this for what it really was. A message. And to distribute that message to those who had the power to make a real change.

The floorboards creaked over his head. Connie was moving about. He couldn't sit here like this; she would ask what he was doing. He had to make himself move. Turn the pages. Look like he was reading the paper, not looking for a specific article. His heart hammered in his chest. The floorboards stopped creaking and her gentle footfalls started to descend the stairs. He had to open the paper.

His hands shook as he unfolded it. Hands that had loved. Had protected. Had shielded. Had failed. Hands that had fought, worked, battled and now were being used to hurt … but he had no choice. He wouldn't allow Emma to have died for nothing. If the drugs failed her then the world needed to know, so that others wouldn't be failed in the same way.

He read the headline and as he did so, Isaac felt every muscle within his body tense. He needed to scan the full article, to see if the drug was mentioned while trying to avoid the personal details that might be listed in there, but he could already hear Connie at the bottom of the stairs and he didn't want to let on how fraught he was. Isaac took a deep breath in, then slowly exhaled. As he did so, the kitchen door opened and she walked through.

'Morning, love, I popped to the shop for the paper, I didn't think you wanted anything, I'm sorry I forgot to ask, I hope there wasn't anything you wanted, it was just a paper I wanted, just a paper.' The words came out in a rush, tumbling, tripping over themselves.

'No, you're fine.' Connie walked over to the kettle, lifted it, shook it, testing for water, then took it to the sink and filled it from the tap. Isaac looked down at the article and started reading. 'Coffee?'

'Mmm?'

'Coffee? Do you want one?' Connie put the kettle back on the base and flicked the switch.

'Oh, yes please. Just reading the paper. The one I bought from the shop.'

'Yes, I can see.'

He stood up, scraping the chair on the tiles as he did so. 'Let me give you a hand with those drinks. I'll get the cups out.' His movements were rushed and jerky. Connie yelped as his elbow swung into her arm, causing the mug she was holding to fall from her hand and hit the worktop.

'Isaac!' he stumbled back, bumping into the chair he'd just vacated, a screeching sound rearing up from the floor as its legs ground against the tiles. His eyes were wild with panic. He quickly grabbed hold of the chair, steadying himself, took a deep breath and stood still.

'What on earth are you doing?' she picked up the cracked mug and rubbed it with her thumb, a gentle, weary caress. *World's Greatest Dad.*

'I'm sorry, I don't know, I wanted to help, I was reading the paper, but wanted to help.'

'Well, for heaven's sake, Isaac, sit back down with your paper and let me make the coffee before you do any more damage.'

Isaac looked at his big thick hands and rubbed his face with them.

'Isaac.'

He slowly dragged his hands downwards from his face and looked at his wife.

'Sit down. Let me get on and make the drink.'

He sighed, moved the chair and shuffled into the seat, the newspaper still on the table in front of him, his hands now shaking. He heard the kettle whistle to boiling point behind him. He couldn't sit here and do nothing he had to read the paper. He had to do what he'd told Connie he was doing. There was enough lying going on as it was. If he delayed opening the newspaper much longer Connie would wonder what was wrong with him and ask him why he was acting so strangely. He couldn't face those questions. Not from her. He didn't know if he had it in him to lie to her about this. He didn't know how she would feel about it; if she would be angry with him, or if she would be in agreement, her anger driving her forward as much as his. Isaac couldn't face that conversation; he couldn't bear the idea of her looking at him with disgust on her face. There was little conversation between them nowadays but she was still his wife, and more importantly, she was still Emma's mum.

He heard the fridge door open as she continued the task at hand. He rubbed his face again and took a deep breath as he tried to steady his nerves, uncertain as to what he would find inside the *Nottingham Today* and what his reaction to that would be. He didn't want to be reacting badly to any article inside the paper in front of his wife. He had to get a grip of himself.

The milk sloshed into the cups and he unfolded the paper.

There was nothing in there about digoxin. He raged inside. Feeling as though he was holding a wild animal within, clawing and fighting to get out, but he had to sit here and be calm and civilised, because that's what they were, him and Connie.

Civilised.

If he was so civilised he wouldn't be doing this, he understood that, somewhere in the dark recesses of his mind. But that comprehension was so far embedded in the depth of his despair that there was no carving it out and dragging it into the light. The pain and anger driving him forward pained him, nearly as much as the reason for it.

But, he couldn't stop now.

50

The evidence we had now seized from Angela Evans', Finlay McDonnell's and Lianne Beers' respective addresses made a mountainous sight. During briefing, I'd tasked Ross with being the exhibits officer for the case which meant every single exhibit that came through on this job had to then go to him to be logged on the main case log. I could see in his eyes that he hated such a paper intensive role but like a scolded puppy he had put his head down and got on with it. It was an important role but it was also station based, so I would be able to keep a close eye on him. As well as the visit to Curvet we were looking at who in the county was currently prescribed digoxin. This hadn't been an easy action to initiate as patient confidentiality had previously prevented all this information being collated together in one place, but once the Health and Social Care Information Centre had started compiling all medical information anonymously with patients listed only as numbers, several police forces had put in requests for a database with names to be added, for instances such as this. We now had a database running where we could search the drug in our county and see who was prescribed it. The new database known as HEAD (Health Explained and Accepted Data) was being trialed in Nottinghamshire, Lincolnshire, Essex and the West Midlands. We were lucky that we were one of the forces in the trial, otherwise we would not have been able to access the details of people being prescribed digoxin, just their patient number. What the hell use was that when people were dying in the streets, I didn't know.

There were a lot of ongoing enquiries. As I mused this over, I stood and watched Ross record all the new items that had been brought in.

Finlay's parents had sat there helplessly as we worked our way through their house and removed everything from foodstuff to personal hygiene products and cleaning items. Their shock at his death was no doubt compounded by the emptying of their home and of Finlay's personal items. It wasn't easy doing this, but not only did we need to find out what had happened to him, we didn't know if his parents or siblings were at risk. If that risk was still in the home. Their silence filled the house like a heavy weight. When we left, they thanked us. Now we had the task of working through all of this stuff with the CSU to identify the culprit and from there, find out where the item had been bought.

Ross had his shirtsleeves rolled up and his hair flopping down over his face as he worked. He used to take such pride in his looks. Sally would tease him that he was a pretty boy. His hair immaculately groomed with wax holding every strand in place, his face smooth and young. Fresh. Eager. Now his face no longer had that fresh-faced youthful appearance, though I knew we had all changed over this past six month period.

The surgery had repaired the wound in my arm. Fixed me up externally. But there was the ongoing physio to strengthen the arm and muscle back up, as well as the insidious pain I lived with. A permanent reminder I hadn't been able to save Sally, no matter how hard I had tried. That was a wound, which for me would take some time to heal. And Martin had taken to living his life more energetically when he wasn't at work. Every opportunity he had, he was away with his wife and two dogs, or with his mates, taking on the country roads on their motorbikes.

Aaron. Aaron, I couldn't fathom. His surface was dark and his depths unseen. I just hoped he was talking to someone.

51

It had been warm all day but there was a chill to the apartment. It was always colder inside than it was outside, the hardwood flooring and painted walls keeping it cool. I dropped my keys on the table and went straight for the kitchen, where I had a bottle of Merlot open on the side. Putting my bag on the worktop, I pulled a glass out of the cupboard then rummaged through my bag for the painkillers. They went down easily with the wine. The throbbing was unbearable. The pain deep. Intense. Close. Personal.

I put the cool wine glass to my forehead and breathed.

What a day.

What a week.

What on earth was happening to my life?

Grabbing my bag, which contained the *Nottingham Today* I'd brought home, I walked over to the sofa and made myself comfortable. We were front-page headlines. Ethan's dream to move on to a national paper might come true. But at what cost?

I read the article again, wine glass propped against my forehead.

Detectives are baffled as to the motive of the killer as no demands have been received and no one particular product, item or source has been identified as being the target.

Police have stated that they are working all the angles and will update the public as soon as they know anything further. They ask that everyone is vigilant and self-aware.

No one can say if the killer will strike again and if so, where that will be.

It felt strange reading the article he'd had written, especially with being the SIO of the investigation. The pressure at work was immense and this outside element, the press watching so keenly and Ethan most of all, really didn't help.

I picked up my phone, took a slug of Merlot and dialled. The *Today* in my lap, headline face up, Ethan's name mocking me.

'Hannah.' A note of surprise in his voice.

'Hi, Ethan.' *What now?*

'It's good to hear from you. How are you?'

'How do you think?'

'I don't know, that's why I'm asking. And it's not like you to make first contact. I'm glad you phoned.'

'Are you?' I took another drink. Why was I being so antagonistic? Things had been okay between us when we'd been out for the meal. Admittedly I wasn't expecting the ending. And at the station it was, I don't know, but I had no real reason to have a go at him for being him.

'Yes. Of course I am, Han. I've told you I'm there for you. I'm just not sure where your head's at, what you want. It's why I give you the space you need.'

'I know. I'm sorry.'

'I try to talk to you but you won't listen, you won't take my calls. *You* pushed me away after ...'

Ah, blame. 'Is that why you're going after me now, Ethan? Because I wouldn't take your calls?'

'Going after you?'

'In the *Today*. The headlines.'

'God, no. That's work. And you know that's not even heavy, Han. It's reporting of facts, what I do. The job's interesting as well. We've never had anything like this in Notts. Come on, I'm not doing this *to* you. I know you'll be doing everything for this case.' I wanted to have his arms around me and for him to make everything all right like he used to, but nothing would be right again. I'd failed and I deserved what I was getting.

'I'm sorry I phoned.'

'Don't go Hannah, we can talk. Let's talk. I can—'

'I'm sorry, Ethan.' I was, I felt so frustrated. I didn't know how to sort this mess out. I wanted him, but how could I be with him when we were both working the same case again? We'd worked the same case before and look how well that had gone.

I ended the call, Ethan's voice echoing in my head. The softness with which he said he wanted to talk. The callousness with which I'd hung up the call. What had got into me that was making me such a bitch? I missed him; but I didn't know how we could make this right. Too much water had gone under the bridge. That had been made obvious when we went out that last time.

We'd been together at a period in time that had caused a crack in a relationship that was too new to be able to survive it. Our jobs had caused that crack to open up into a crevasse too big to cross.

52

Zamaan Khaleel stood behind the counter of the corner shop, his corner shop, reading the paper. He skimmed through the paragraphs, looking for people he knew, areas and items of interest that might affect him and his local community. He did it every day. Living and working here in Stapleford for all of his adult life meant that he knew everyone and he knew their business. The downside to that was that they also knew his. He used his forefinger and thumb to separate two stuck pages as a couple of youths he knew walked in. He knew them to be about twenty years of age. Bouncing on the balls of their feet, jeans hanging from somewhere mid arse. He split the pages and turned one over.

His daughter was only two and as she slept upstairs in the comfort of her surroundings with the protection of her mother, Zamaan worried about her. About the life she would have. They had a profitable business here. Their shop was the only one nearby when local residents needed their fags or a chocolate fix in the evening and the big supermarkets that were closing a lot of businesses down were too far away, so they had a stable income. He wasn't worried about that. But he worried that the teachings he would provide for his daughter would not be enough to save her from the trappings of westernised ways and behaviours.

An article caught his eye. Three deaths in the city, police were appealing for witnesses and the media were sensationalising it. The article elaborated on the differences between the victims. The ages. The locations of death. One of the victims died publicly on a bus. A third on the street. The reporter knew one thing for certain, that the police had no current suspects for the three deaths, and no idea if there were going to be any further or how to stop them. He postulated that the poison could have got into the victims by any means, but at this stage, with such variety of people, it was likely to have been through food or drink. Of which sort, they couldn't say. In fact the article couldn't say an awful lot, if you looked at it properly.

Zamaan wondered about the source and hoped it would be sorted soon, then turned the page again. The only other crime articles in this one were to do with too much car crime and a robbery in the city centre where the offender had used a flick knife to obtain a wallet and mobile phone from a man in a suit, no doubt already walking about with his phone in his hand, looking face down towards the pavement. Not that he should need to look around him, but times had changed.

As he turned the page Khaleel heard a wet thud come from the back of the shop. He could no longer see the two lads who had not long ago entered. The shop was filled with shelving and cardboard display units, which held items like chocolate or cheap wines and beers. It was crammed with as much as he could get into it and this was at the expense of having clear sight of everywhere.

A deep-throated laugh went up and another joined it, both turning into higher-pitched excited laughter. Khaleel closed his paper and hoped Farzaana stayed upstairs with their daughter, Salimah. An uncomfortable feeling was running through him.

He rested both hands, palms open and down, on top of the paper and sighed. He looked under the counter, the little red light assured him the CCTV was in working condition and recording. He kept his stance open and non-threatening, his mobile sitting to the side where it had been pushed as he'd opened up the newspaper.

A third male walked into the shop. Khaleel recognised him as another regular. Slightly older than the two already at the rear. He was short for a male and wore his blond hair slicked back. A black leather jacket and brown pointed shoes were his trademark items of clothing. He appeared to carry a lot of weight with the younger group. Khaleel pulled his phone nearer to him. A cackle went up at the rear of the shop and as the older male went out of sight towards the others, silence descended.

He dialled Farzaana. She picked up on the first ring. 'You know you'll wake the baby. What are you doing?' she barbed at him straight away.

'Hush. Listen to me.'

'What is it?'

'Whatever you hear downstairs. Do not come down. Are you listening to me?' His voice was low. Rushed.

'Why? What is this about, Zamaan? What about Salimah?'

'Just stay upstairs. You'll be safe. I don't know. It's a feeling.' He was ready to put the phone down. Something else was thrown now. The sound of low thudding and growing excitement. His nerves were fraying. No longer were his palms face down. His free hand was tapping out a beat on the edge of the counter top and it wasn't a melody.

'Zamaan, you're scaring me.' She looked to him for support, protection. Everything a husband should do and he took his role seriously. They were his family; he was going to protect them. These people just wanted to blow off steam. He knew others like them, had stood up to them and they backed away, but he didn't want his wife or daughter down here just in case.

His voice cracked under the strain. 'Do as I say. Do not come downstairs. Whatever you hear. Phone for the police if you become frightened and I don't come up. You have your family. They are a good family. They will take good care of you. Of both of you.' He was being overly cautious now. All it would take was for him to stand up to them. But there was a weird vibe in the air. He was uncomfortable. He couldn't phone the police now simply because he was uncomfortable. What kind of man would that make him anyway?

He didn't hear her cries in response. Zamaan put the phone down and came from behind the counter.

53

Zamaan Khaleel tried to live a good life. He'd done as his parents asked and married Farzaana. They'd had their first child and planned to have a second very soon. The business was booming. People around here wasted money easily, on the things in life that were not important, so his family both here and back in India prospered. Today these things worried him as he stepped from behind the relative safety of the shop counter. A barrier to all those who entered his shop, his livelihood. His stomach twisted in on itself causing pain and a feeling that he really needed to go to the toilet as he heard more things being thrown. Thudding, laughter, the noise of items falling from shelves onto cold, hard floor tiles. There was something in the laughter though, it wasn't all fun, there was a heightened sense of pack mentality, of – fear. He knew what it was because he was feeling it so acutely now, but why? Why were they in his shop feeling and acting this way?

Khaleel turned the corner where the nappies, cotton wool, cotton buds, and powdered milk were shelved and saw the three men. Their lips stretched tight across their teeth as they howled with laughter. On the floor at their feet and around the wider area were fresh fruit and vegetables. Cartons of fruit juice spilled their contents from cracks in their sides, like leaking rivers breaking their banks.

'Can I help you?' It was the only thing he could think of to say. Benign and helpless, but what else could he offer? These were customers. People he knew and saw on a regular basis. They were his community.

The older male looked at him. Straight in the eyes. No menace or malice.

'You know what they're saying don't you, Zamaan?'

A pain twitched in his head above his eye. He didn't move.

'What who are saying?'

'The papers?'

He brought his thumb up and massaged the spot that throbbed.

'What are they saying and what does it have to do with me?' Zamaan voice was intentionally low. Conversational.

'We're being poisoned. All of us. Any of us.' He had an apple in his hand and he threw it at the floor. It landed with another thud and juice sprayed up to the group of men who stood around it. No one moved from its path.

Khaleel now dug his thumb into his head and drove it towards the pain as though he could push it out the other side.

'And my fruit and vegetables, my stock? How do they come into this? I've served you a long time. Haven't I always been good to you?'

'Use your head, Zamaan. You could be a target as much as we could. We could be targeted through you. We're doing you a service now. You don't want these goods in your shop. Anything not sealed you want rid of. We're helping.'

The younger two bounced on the souls of their feet. The sense of good, of empowerment, flowing into them, driving them. 'Yeah, we're helping, look.' One picked up two oranges and threw them at the shelves, knocking even more bottles from their places.

'No! Stop.' He couldn't help himself. This destruction was unnecessary. He'd read no such thing. 'Just stop. Leave my shop alone. Out. Out. You have to get out!' His hands waved them away. Towards the door. It was too much. They had lost their minds. This wasn't the way to behave.

Another apple went past his head and skittled boxes of fruit bars down to the floor. There was so much mess and the laughter had started up again. The older male looked at Khaleel as though he was to blame, that he hadn't listened; a look of annoyance mixed with pity. Zamaan couldn't take it. This was his life. He was building a future here. For his family. He stepped forward, the ground wet and slick under his feet, his hands waving towards the door. 'You must go now. You must go now.'

'No, we don't go; we have to destroy the poison in here. They're poisoning us. Weren't you listening? Are you deaf?' Laughter again. Like hyenas. He needed them out. His head throbbed. His shop was a mess. 'Here, see if this helps with the deafness.' An orange came hurtling towards him. It hit his head, catching him off balance. He threw his arms out even wider, his shoes trying for purchase on the floor but it was slick with fruit juices of every description. His hand caught the edge of the cold metallic shelving unit but he was already going down, his feet had started to let him down. A pain shot through his arm as it scraped and banged against the units. When finally he could hold on no more, he collapsed in a heap on the floor with the rest of the smashed-up fruit and veg, in front of the watching men. His head slammed down hard onto the metal shelving, his temple forcibly hitting the corner of the stand and the world went black. There was no more mess for Zamaan Khaleel to see.

54
7 weeks ago

There was a post-mortem. They desecrated his baby. Opened her up like a piece of meat. He'd watched enough television to know exactly what they'd done to her. They'd crowded around her. Maybe told a joke or two. After all, this was just a day job for them. Then they'd looked at her medical history, seen what was wrong before she came in, assessed her externally and make sure there was nothing amiss. She'd have been there on that steel table, naked and cold. No dignity afforded in death. In birth, you're wrapped immediately, warmed and cooed over. In death, you're stripped down, laid out and examined, no longer seen as a person.

His hands gripped the arms of the chair.

Then the pathologist would have taken his scalpel and dug it into her beautiful clean skin and sliced it down her body. She wouldn't have moved. Not a flinch.

He threw himself forward, his head into his knees, his hands coming from the chair to grasp at his head.

'Isaac?' Connie walked in.

'I'm fine.' His voice muffled from his lap.

'I'm getting something to eat, do you want anything?'

'No. No food.'

He heard her leave again.

They violated his baby girl. As clear as the day outside, they violated her when they didn't need to.

They were trying to cover their own tracks, but they couldn't fool him. They were all in it together. Health and pharmaceuticals.

They were incompetent. Em should never have died. Not at her age. Not in this day and age. She should have lived. She should have been able to live through this, survive it, fight it and win. He knew that. He wasn't going to let them get away with this. They provided the medication that was supposed to keep her alive and now she was dead.

55

The briefing was due to start any minute now but I scanned the *Today*'s article in front of me, wanting to finish it before I went in. The byline was Ethan's again. The headline more shocking than the last. Murders alone were bad enough but murders caused by panic were on another level and the press were playing that up. *Ethan* was playing that up.

The owner of the local community store on the B5010 in Stapleford, Zamaan Khaleel, 29, has been killed in the store he had made his home. A post-mortem is scheduled with a Home Office pathologist. Nottinghamshire police are investigating and are appealing for witnesses and ask anyone with information to come forward. Any and all information can be provided in confidence.

Zamaan Khaleel is survived by his wife, Farzaana, 27, and 2-year-old daughter, who were above the store in their home, just metres away, at the time of the attack.

Mr Khaleel was found by his wife after he phoned to tell her of trouble, warning her to stay upstairs. After hearing everything go quiet she went down and found his body at the back of the store.

The Today *has learned that a group of men were seen*

entering the shop just before Mr Khaleel was murdered. Detectives have refused to speculate as to the motive of the attack but confirm that nothing was stolen and the contents of the till were intact. They want to speak to the three men seen entering the shop in relation to the incident, as soon as possible.

The timing of the attack on Mr Khaleel coincides with the press conference given by police asking the public to be vigilant of goods they purchased.

A neighbouring shop owner said, 'Police need to be doing more than issuing words of warning, they need to arresting the "poison killer" and keeping our streets and shops safe. Panic is rising and more people are dying.'

Thanks Ethan. Thanks very much. As if the public weren't panicking enough, you decided to give them a big heave-ho push by quoting frightened members of the public.

We really were up against it now.

56

There was no need to raise my voice. The incident room was quiet. Everyone was waiting to see what I would say. Events were taking place at a pace beyond which we were ready or prepared for and we needed to stop being on the back foot. No one here was comfortable with being so far behind an investigation. I'd even managed to talk Catherine into allowing me to keep Ross on the team because we needed all hands on deck. I'd noticed he had made more of an effort with his overall appearance today. He still looked like he had been caught in the headlights of an oncoming articulated lorry, but he was a cleaner-looking roadkill.

As usual, Martin was the complete opposite of how Ross had been presenting himself recently and I loved that about him. He was always the yang for the yin and now was sitting using an old letter opener to pick bits out of his front teeth. I had no idea where he'd got the opener from, I didn't realise people still used them. He never became flustered, was always calm and could always be relied upon. Aaron was poised over his notepad with his pen, ready to take notes as we progressed through the morning's briefing.

Not only did I have the investigation team here, but I had Claire Betts the press officer. Between her and Evie, they kept me sane at work. Jack Kidner was here as well as the county divisional commander, Chief Superintendent Trevor Youens. Youens was a buttoned up kind of guy; not just that his appearance was immaculate, but he was obsessed about going by the book.

Youens wasn't happy. This latest development of the shopkeeper killed on his area appeared to be linked to our investigation. The CCTV seemed to show that it was part of a group type hysteria attack and the blow to Khaleel's head that killed him, though not directly struck by the men in the shop, was a direct result of the incident that evening making it a murder investigation.

This was going to make Youens' life hell now. He'd be responsible for reassuring the public in his division that he could keep them safe, he would have to make plans to actually keep them safe, so for that, he needed to know what we had. He had made it clear on entering the briefing that he wanted everything. There was no brook given with that statement either. It wasn't a request or a pleasantry before we started. He had to come up with localised community plans for the safety of residents.

We also had the briefing video linked up to his intelligence unit, so they could be in the briefing without leaving their office and be able to take what they needed and research it for their own safeguarding needs. We had our own intel officer, Dave Morgan, present.

And finally we had the four family liaison officers who were placed with each of the bereaved families.

It was a busy incident room with a lot of active minds at work. Only I wasn't sure we all had the same goal in mind. I needed to catch the person who was randomly killing residents of our county and Youens was responsible for the safety of those residents, but in a different capacity. He had to make sure no one else was killed because of the public outcry caused by the killer we were hunting. Two goals caused by the same person.

I thanked everyone for coming and let them know we were in for the long haul and that leave passes would be authorised once we had resolved this investigation, but for now, none would be signed through.

I began the briefing on what we had so far, starting with the death of Lianne Beers and ending with the public order offences and murder of Zamaan Khaleel on the B5010 in Stapleford. Then I let Jack go through the post-mortem results of the first three murders where we knew that Lianne, Finlay and Angela were all killed with digoxin and yet none of them were taking it for medical conditions. Then Doug, from the Crime Scene Unit, talked about the lack of forensic results. There was so much evidence gathered for testing from the home addresses of the victims that they were still going through it, so we had no real idea the mode of transport into the victims but the press was leaping onto the mode as being food related after speaking to a so-called 'professional'. I saw Youens roll his eyes at this comment and it took all my strength not to mirror the action. It was frustrating when you had people making guesses at what was happening within an investigation and even worse outside the investigation from the point of view of the offender. He knew the difficulties with investigations but at this point in time he was only concerned about his own back and how to police such a high profile issue.

'We have a difficult one here. I know you will give it your all. We're a good team. We can pull together and work this.' I had Ross's attention. Martin relaxed further back into his chair. Arms in their usual position, clasped behind his head. Letter opener back on his desk. 'It's not easy. I think I can safely say we've ruled out suicide.' Grey shook his head. I carried on, ignoring him, 'It's unlikely we have an industrial accident of any sort. Curvet has been helpful and open as much as we can tell; they are the largest producer of digoxin around here and they're not reporting an accident of any description. Admittedly, they do have a lot to lose if this was their fault, so we can't rule out a cover up, so we'd need to find out how that cover up would happen. The pharmaceutical companies do have oversight in the form of the Medicines and Healthcare Products Regulatory Agency, which is a government agency, so we can follow that line of enquiry.

'The other link to Curvet is that they could be being targeted by means of product contamination, so their name is muddied. If an animal liberation group is involved they usually go for harmless items such as salt in the health section products that the pharmaceutical companies make, though there has been one instance where high levels of laxative was placed in probiotic yoghurt cartons, so it's not out of the realms of possibility that this is what is happening. They don't seem to have lost any employees recently, so the only disgruntled employees we would find would be ones that are still working there and it's one huge place. For their part, Curvet is doing an inventory of their products to see if any of it is missing.

'No matter how hard we work on them, their friends and family, it appears the victims are random, which firms up the idea that Curvet is likely to be the target. I'm waiting for the results of ninhydrin testing on the hate mail to come back. We do need to keep working on the victimology though. We can't relax and miss something. Look at each person as though they were a murder in their own right and forget they are part of a series, that way we look at family, friends and possible conflicts with people. This could be one targeted murder, with two others committed to throw us off the scent. We can't cut any corners. We look at each one on its own merit and we look at them as a whole.

'It's a lot of work, I know. Overtime is authorised. You're going to be earning it. I know we already have enquiries ongoing with the digoxin users from the list from HEAD. We still need to work through that because each name needs to have checks made against it and a visit made.'

We really did have our hands full. We needed all the analysts and detectives we could get to work the actions and make the visits. Grey was propped against a desk now, picking at his fingernails. He'd be taking all this in and would go back to his office, write it all up and stress about the situation. The level of morale in the job had changed over recent years.

'There is one problem we've come up against though, boss, in relation to digoxin users.'

'What's that, Martin?' We didn't need more problems, we needed answers.

Martin leaned forward in his chair. 'You can actually buy digoxin over the Internet, so even though we are checking out the registered users, there is a capability to go online and buy it without a prescription.'

Shit, was anything going to go our way in this investigation?

'Okay. Work with the actions we have so far and see what comes of it but bear that in mind. It might be that we end up with a suspect and we need to seize their computer to check the Internet history to see where they got the product from.'

My head and my arm throbbed as we worked our way through the meeting. Youens was tough and unforgiving of anyone who didn't have the information he needed at their fingertips. He had trouble on his area and not only did he not want it but he didn't want it escalating further.

I gave him all we had, which at this time wasn't a great deal and his face set hard like stone as he looked at me. I could play that game. I could stare him out, but it wasn't what I wanted. I wanted to do this in a way where we both worked together. Knocking heads with another supervisor in another area wouldn't be conducive to our investigation and I knew knocking heads with me wouldn't help him with his community work either. In this matter we needed to work together.

His plan was to put a larger uniform presence out to reassure people. To have them around local smaller produce sellers. To have them popping in and buying anything they needed from those shops. If they had time to eat, then to do it publicly where they could be seen by the general population. How his staff felt about this when we had no idea where the poison was coming in from, I had no idea, but then again, we all had to buy our food items from somewhere. We all had to eat. His PCSOs would buoy up his small team of uniform officers as his numbers had dwindled considerably during government cuts this past five years. We discussed bringing down some extra uniforms from north of the county to help cover the task at hand and agreed it was something our unit needed to request.

The pace of this investigation was rapid and was wearing me out so I knew it would probably be doing the same to my team. It was also moving in ways we couldn't predict. This new turn of events with the death of the shopkeeper was shocking. Shocking in his death and shocking that it was fear in ordinary members of the public that had caused it, producing a mob mentality. Because of the timing of the incident we firmly believed it wasn't racially aggravated but that our initial killer was turning ordinary members of the public into killers. Chief Superintendent Trevor Youens was correct in that we needed to get on top of this before it spiralled out of control, only I wasn't sure we could. I needed to know what was driving our offender. Usually in cases of product contamination, we had communication, a letter of threat or blackmail, but we'd had neither yet. We were sitting on our hands, not knowing what they wanted or why they were doing it and it was this fear of the unknown that was also gnawing away at my insides.

Where was the poison being administered and were the victims carefully chosen or were they random victims of chance? Questions I needed answers to before we had another one on the slab.

I jotted it down on my list of things to do from this meeting. Staff was a major problem when jobs went the wrong way, ever since our budget had been cut by several million pounds per year. Superintendents fought like hell to keep every single one of their staff and I couldn't say I blamed them because they were working down to the wire themselves. With each member of staff taken off them, the risk grew for the remaining people in their divisions. Though the officers were dedicated people and worked like hell, but with the paperwork and the immediate low-level call volumes going up, they were drowning. I felt sorry for us all as we sat there. I rubbed my head again and tuned back in as the guy on the internal briefing screen from Youens' intel unit reported that there was no further chatter that any shops were going to be targeted. We agreed that though this was the case as it stood now, we needed to be vigilant and keep to our community safety plan – and hope to hell we got a good lead on our killer before the city really started to panic.

57

It was dark. Quiet. Warm. The quilt, heavy on top of me, nearly covered the top of my head and my face almost smothered itself into the pillow. The scent of vanilla with something else mixed in wafted through my half-waking, half-sleeping state. The feeling was one of comfort and relaxation. My body was a heavy weight on the mattress, as though it had decided it had given in from the grind I had been putting it through. I relaxed further into it, my arms star-fishing out from under the pillow my head was pushing down on. A breath escaped and muscles I didn't realise I had been tensing let go. I felt myself gliding further towards a blissful slumber. I let out another breath and…

What? Where? What? Hell. Shit. What? The ringing broke through. My thoughts scrambled to collect themselves back together as my head felt like a fuzzy morning from a night before.

'Hello.'

'DI Robbins?' the voice was tentative.

'Yes. What is it?' Damn. Not tonight.

'There's another one.' Not tonight.

'Okay. Where?' Dammit.

'Well,'

'Spit it out.' I shunted myself into a seated position. I couldn't have this conversation lying down.

'She's at the QMC.' The Queen's Medical Centre hospital?

'She's been moved from the scene already?'

'That's just it. The victim is still alive, Ma'am.'

'I'll be right there.' I took details and ended the call.

I needed to get to the hospital.

Damn. This had been such a bad idea, but I'd needed it. A couple of glasses of red wine and the need for some comfort, not just comfort, but the need for him. I missed him. It had been easier to cut him out of my life at first, but now he seemed to be everywhere I looked. His name in every situation, drilling into my mind ... and this is where it had landed me.

I turned to my left, breathed in the warm scent of his aftershave, before ending what should never have started – even though I wanted nothing more than to curl up around him and stay there for the rest of the night and play hooky with him the next day. To pretend neither of us had jobs to go to. Jobs that would decimate this and stop all chances of anything happening. Jobs that had already come between us, or was I making excuses? Was I the one to blame for how it had failed to work?

Ethan stirred, turning over and pushing the quilt away from him. I watched as it slid over his hip, exposing skin I had not long ago caressed and kissed. With a couple of painkillers and a couple of glasses of red wine inside me the previous night, I'd sent an irritated text to his phone, which had brought him to my door, his body shaking with frustration and anger at my constant inability to see things his way. We'd yelled at each other for ten minutes. I wanted him to stop reporting on the poisonings to which he'd replied I was an idiot, it was a job. He wanted me to listen to him and stop taking everything as a personal slight. I'd told him *he* was an idiot, I had a career and people's lives were at risk. We yelled in circles until he stalked into the kitchen and helped himself to a glass of red wine and seated himself on the sofa. He told me he was tired of fighting with me.

Now, I shook his shoulder to wake him. 'Ethan, you have to go.'

58

She filled the narrow hospital bed. Her bulky frame nearly spilled over the sides but the raised bars of the bed appeared to be acting as a restraint. Her skin was pallid. Her bleached hair yellow on the starched white pillow with a slight green tinge from the overhead bulb that was on in the dark ward.

There was coughing and shuffling as patients attempted to get comfortable and to sleep in uncomfortable and unknown beds. Nurses chattered at the night desk, their laughter reaching us. A normal working shift for them meant normal working engagement with their colleagues, despite the late hour.

Aaron nearly looked as distressed as Dawn Barry, the woman squeezed into the bed in front of us. His hands flicked up to his tie and he straightened it again, for the fourth time that I had seen. Not that it had moved in that period of time. I know it wasn't great being woken up in the middle of the night, but he knew it was a part of the job.

'Can you tell us what you were doing before you started feeling ill, Dawn?' I asked as she pawed at her face, wiping away strands of hair that were sticking to it. Her blue eyes glued themselves to me.

'I'd been out for a meal with me mates and when I got home I grabbed meself a tub of ice cream before I went to bed to cool me stomach down. We'd eaten a Mexican meal, you see. It wasn't agreeing with me.'

'Then what?'

'That's when it happened.'

'I need you to tell me exactly *what* happened, Dawn. It's the only way we can help you, if you tell us in your own words what happened.'

'Well, I ate half the tub,' she stopped and looked at us. 'The Mexican food was really spicy. I don't eat spicy food and I hadn't eaten it before. I didn't realise.'

'It's okay, carry on.'

'So, I ate the ice cream and I started to feel worse – and not over-eaten worse, just worse. Really bad. Like I knew something was wrong, bad. Then it was like something out of *The Exorcist*, I was spewing out to the other end of the room and it was coming and coming and coming. And it was bloody as well. I felt like I was going to die. I was on me knees I was. My phone was in me pocket so I dialled 999 and left the line open cos I couldn't actually speak. Then I don't know what happened, I woke up here and they said they'd pumped me stomach and they've took a load of blood from me and then you turned up and here we are. And by the way, I feel like shit. What the hell happened and why are you here?'

'Have you read any papers recently, Dawn?'

'Can't say I have. They're full of crap aren't they? You can't believe half of what they tell you, there's always an agenda, so no I haven't.' I couldn't argue with half of what she was saying, there certainly appeared to be an agenda at play when reporting on police activity. 'Again, why?' She was trying to prop herself up but her body was weak, her elbows buckled under her and her body slumped back down onto the mountain of pillows that was raising her up. 'Shit.'

A howling sound started up further down the ward. Aaron went straight for his tie. The laughter at the nurses' station stopped and the howling became louder, punctuated with swearing and then finally sobbing. It was a minute before I realised the three of us had not moved and had stayed silent as the horrific sound had pierced the ward. I looked back at Dawn, who wasn't looking too happy.

'Is there anyone we can call for you? Who can come and sit with you for a while after we've gone?'

'No. It's fine. I'm gunna try and get some sleep if this racket dies down. I've texted a couple of mates and they'll see me in the morning. They pumped my stomach, though I don't know the hell why. I'm knackered. You telling me what's happening, then?'

I looked at Aaron. How to tell someone they could be a part of a bigger picture, one that was being reported on in the news was never easy, as we didn't know what reaction to expect. 'We've had some deaths, Dawn. Deaths that are suspicious, highly suspicious and they've been caused by poison. We were called out tonight because your symptoms have been pretty severe and possibly caused by the poison that has killed our previous victims. You may have saved your own life by having your phone on you and being so quick thinking.'

'Fuck me. Wait till I tell the girls.' Well, she wasn't overly fazed by it. Dawn's pale face shone out at us in the yellowing light of the night-time ward. For all her joviality she was still heavy against the bed, no energy lifting her. 'And that's why you asked about the papers; it's been in the papers, has it?'

'Yes, there have been a small spate of victims so far and we were really glad you didn't make it another, I can tell you.'

'You and me both.' Her hand grasped out to her left for something on the personal cart to the side, but she wasn't looking at what she was doing. Her hand tapped with an increased urgency and her face changed colour to a pale and mottled green.

'What is it, Dawn?'

'The sick bowl. I need the bowl.'

I passed her the bowl and she heaved over it but nothing came out. Tiny droplets of sweat gathered across her brow and she shrank into the pillows. As if waiting for this moment, a nurse appeared.

'Officers, I'm afraid you'll have to leave. Dawn needs her rest. We'll let you know if there are any sudden changes.'

'Okay, thank you.' We both stood. I opened my folder and grabbed the medical consent form. 'Dawn, I need you to sign this so we can access your medical records from the hospital in relation to tonight's incident.' I pushed pen and paper under her hands and she gave a half-hearted scribble before we were politely but most assuredly shown out of the ward for the night.

59

'The initial test results have come back from Dawn Barry.' Aaron grabbed the chair in front of my desk and made himself comfortable. I don't know how he did it, looking so bright and alert on so little sleep. I was exhausted and knew I looked it. After leaving the hospital last night I'd returned home for the few remaining hours I had before the start of the new working day. But because I was so hyped up with the case running through my head, with having a live victim in the hospital, making mental check-lists of all the enquiries we could work through because we actually had her to talk to, my brain wouldn't switch off. Plus, nosing its way into all the work related noise in my head was the evening before with Ethan, and how he'd ended up in my apartment and in my bed, unsure how I felt about it, meaning I only ended up with a couple of hours' broken and disturbed sleep. A sleep that didn't feel like sleep. That felt like the sleep of the undead. Where the mind is still working but the body is trying to rest and recover, heavy on the mattress, unable to move. This morning my head was a blurry mess with not a coherent thought in it. Yet here Aaron sat, looking for the entire world as if he'd had a full and heavenly night's sleep, yet I knew differently.

I needed his body clock.

'It seems she wasn't poisoned by digoxin,' he said.

'So what does this mean? We spent the evening with her and all it was was a girl who had drunk too much? Who the hell had called us in for it? Who decided it was poison? Who can't tell the bloody difference between a pissed-up girl and life-threatening poisoning?' I shot off multiple questions at him. I was already exhausted from this job without it getting me out of bed for a drunk girl.

'They made the right call, Hannah. Dawn *was* poisoned. Well, she had a poisonous substance in her system.' He crossed his legs. 'Just not by digoxin. It was a different poison.'

I rubbed my arm. 'What was it?'

'I've just finished a call with the hospital and they've run the tox screen and she doesn't have digoxin in her system, so now they're testing for other substances that specifically match her symptoms. She's still quite ill so they're treating her symptoms aggressively.'

'Crap. So do we have a killer who is changing MO ... or do we have a copycat on our hands?'

60

A walk to the local shop on Pasture Road would blow some wind into his head, clear it out a little. He was feeling tense. Cluttered inside. The continued reading of the newspaper reports was hurting his head. Providing too much information. When all he wanted to know was that the drug was being listed, he was getting personal details of those involved. No matter how much he tried to skim read he couldn't help but pick up specifics he didn't want.

Isaac bent down and laced up his shoes, and decided the day was warm enough to go without a jacket.

'Connie, I'm popping to the shop, do you want anything?' he shouted through to the living room.

'No, thanks.'

The air was clear. The sky blue and cloud free. It was one of those mornings people loved to wake up to, where they felt happier and more alive. For him it served only as a reprieve from the black thoughts that shrouded his mind. It made a little room for him to be able to think again because the darkness made thinking an impossible task. Everything had become sluggish and stagnant. The sun that shone now would carve a little room out in that gloom and allow him to keep on going.

The walk was short. A couple of streets. Houses that pretty much looked like theirs. Streets he'd walked up and down the majority of his life. They'd lived together as a family on Kennedy Drive for as long as he could remember and for all of Em's too short life. He could walk this route blindfolded.

This morning there were kids in uniform slouching in small groups, trying to make the walk to school drag out as long as possible. Rucksacks on backs, bags slung over shoulders with work nearly falling out and ties pulled down away from necks. The young rebelling against the regime that the adults tried to inflict on them daily. Cars pulled away from driveways in a hurry to get to work after seeing these children off. All sights he was used to seeing, yet sights he was now tired of seeing. Isaac was tired of it all. Tired of the normality, the banality. All he wanted was the *Nottingham Today*. He needed to see what they were reporting today and if they were getting it right. So far they had been useless, but they had to pick up on the truth of the matter now. All the poison was the same. How could they ignore that fact?

It was still early and though the day was bright, the sun was not hot. Despite himself, Isaac found it pleasant and he hated that feeling. He picked up his step and quickly made it to the shop.

There were a couple of people in his local paper shop. Isaac selected the *Today* from the pile on the floor and paid for it, giving no attention to those coming in for their daily bits and pieces before their day really began.

He kept the paper folded and slid it under his arm for the walk home. Reading the article was to be done in the privacy of his kitchen. Especially when he had no idea what he was going to read.

Naturally, Isaac's steps homeward were quicker. He kept his head down so he didn't make eye contact with anyone and within minutes the door was closed behind him and he was safely locked back in the cocoon of his home.

He slid off his shoes without unlacing them and rushed into the kitchen, his socked feet quiet on the floor.

'It's me,' he called out to Connie.

'Okay.'

With the paper on the kitchen table Isaac sat himself down with a strong hope of what he would read coursing through him. It was front-page news again.

Fourth Person Poisoned

Another person has been poisoned and is currently in hospital after ingesting food bought while shopping.

Staff at the Queen's Medical Centre has stated that the woman from Radford, is poorly but in a stable condition.

She is the first person to survive the poisoner who has, so far, killed three people in the past couple of weeks.

DI Hannah Robbins, leading the hunt for the killer, has confirmed that Nottinghamshire police are managing this poisoning as part of the ongoing murder investigation, stating, 'We are awaiting full forensic testing on this woman's blood work, but we are treating this incident extremely seriously. She has been very lucky to survive and it's important that we talk to her.'

Police state they are making enquiries with the woman, who at this time does not wish to be named, to try to ascertain where she had been and what she had consumed.

But, for now, how do we know what is safe to eat?

The thoughts wouldn't slide through his mind. They felt jumpy and kept stalling. He read the article again to see if he had read it correctly the first time but the text was there in black and white, completely blocking all function for him. What was happening? He hadn't placed any products where this woman lived. How had this happened? What had happened? The police were now making a terrible mistake. This wasn't him.

This wasn't supposed to happen. This wasn't his message. This person was ruining everything!

What about Emma? What about the pharmaceutical companies? What about the medical authority? They had to answer for what had happened and the question was getting lost in this mess now. This ... This person was ruining everything. This shouldn't be happening. It couldn't.

The paper was pushed off the table and his anger rose like a tidal wave gathering momentum but he had nowhere to send the energy it was creating. Isaac looked around in panic as he felt it grow from the pit of his stomach and rise into his chest, his head pulsating. There were cups and bowls on the drainer that had been washed. He grabbed a cup and threw it as hard as he could against the far wall near the door. It smashed and dropped. Crashing down in a quick movement. It wasn't enough. It was all getting ruined. His Emma wasn't getting noticed.

Ruined.

He picked up another cup and threw again. It crashed and dropped. He let out a breath of air but there was still swirling fog in his head. He looked at the drainer again and picked up a bowl. That went to the wall and smashed to the floor.

His chest relaxed. He reached for the last bowl and threw it. The momentum; less now. It broke up and lay with the rest of broken crockery. Isaac's head felt heavy, his body heavy. He was tired. He slumped down the cupboard doors and sat on the floor, spent.

When he looked up, Connie was standing in the doorway, quietly watching him.

61

Dawn was lying in her hospital bed, looking no better now that daylight streamed through the windows rather than the awful dim lighting of the night-time ward. Her eyes were closed and she was curled in the foetal position, facing us as we entered. Her eyelids flickered, then opened.

'Hi, how you doing?' I asked.

'Oh, hi. Dreadful. They said I've definitely been poisoned. The treatment for it is awful. I don't know which is worse – the poison or the treatment.' She pushed herself up on the pillows but stayed curled up, arms wrapped around her stomach.

'They put a tube down my throat and washed my stomach out.' She grimaced. 'What the hell did I do to deserve that?'

'Not pleasant.' I didn't have the words. She was lucky to be alive, but it wasn't what she wanted to hear right now. 'I'm sorry you have to go through this,' I answered her, pulling up a chair to seat myself at the side of her. Aaron remained standing. Stiff and unyielding.

'Then I had to drink this awful black stuff. They're torturing me.'

'I'm sorry, Dawn.'

'Thanks, it's not your fault. Do you know who's doing this, then?'

'No, that's why we want to talk to you. We had to be quick last night but today we have a bit more time. The staff have allowed us to come in before visiting hours so we can speak to you without disturbing the time you have with family and friends.'

'Oh, thanks. I don't really know what else to add.'

'Well, we need to know where you ate last night, who you were with,' I took out my major incident notebook so that I could take notes as she spoke. 'What you did before you went out, and then between the restaurant and home and finally at home. It would also help if you could tell us if you have had any specific run-ins with people or upset anyone or if anyone could perceive themselves to have been hurt or upset by you, even if you don't think they should have been.'

'Wow, that's a lot of information.' Her eyes closed and we waited.

'I know, I'm sorry, Dawn. I know you're tired, but it's the only way we can work our way through this and try to get to the bottom of what is happening.'

'It's okay. At least I'll have one hell of a great story to keep telling me mates over and over on our nights out, won't I?' Dawn tried to smile but the joy just wasn't in it.

62

3 weeks ago

His hands shook. Like huge rugged mountain ranges being shaken from the core of the ground beneath. But that's what was happening. His core was shaken. His very belief system. The system he trusted had failed and they needed to know that. Isaac had been a hard-working man all his life, but he couldn't figure any other way to get their attention. Em would have done. Em had the smarts, the brains, but Em wasn't here and that was the point.

The stone pestle and mortar from Connie's kitchen worked in those mountainous hands, grinding up tablets until they were powder. He was careful, delicate almost, that he didn't spill any. There wasn't much to waste and he had a message he needed to deliver; it could take time. He had to get their attention and when he had their attention, he had to be sure it was maintained. He wanted them to be worried, to look at the drugs and assess how they worked. If it wasn't an ideal drug, then they needed to change it for another. Isaac wondered again if it was a cheaper option. Had Em died to keep costs down?

How much would the pharmaceutical companies put the cost of his message once he'd finished delivering it? Would it even be enough for them or would it be another drop in the ocean, like Emma? He hoped that it would be the negative press that would swing it for him, because the message itself probably wouldn't faze the companies. He had to make a splash. He had to make this showy.

63

The newspaper was thrown across my desk.

Fourth Person Poisoned

Another person has been poisoned and is currently in hospital after ingesting food bought while shopping in the local area.

I read the article in the *Today* with Catherine Walker stood over me, scowling.

'This continuing press coverage is killing us, Hannah.'

'It's not good, Ma'am.' I had to confess, though I had of course contributed to the article and she wasn't mentioning that. We needed to be seen to be speaking to the public, reassuring them and the best way of doing that was through the media and our own website, but more people read the local news than the social media of the police. Catherine was upset that there was constant coverage though, but as long as the killer continued to poison then the paper would continue to print.

'Not good?! They're actually going to be blaming us next. We need real results. I know you've had a rough six months.' She paused, I waited.

'You were stabbed,' she continued. 'I know it takes time to recover from an injury and at the same time your past investigation is being looked at by the IPCC. You haven't been in charge of a major investigation since ...'

Where the hell was she going with this? 'Ma'am, what is it you need?' My patience with her was running out.

'Your team is screwing up.'

Really? I crossed my arms.

'Just look at Ross. He completely screwed that job up. And it was on your watch, Hannah. I'd hate to see it happen, but the reality is, you could lose your position at the end of the IPCC investigation. The pressure is going to be piled on as this investigation drags on unresolved and people continue to die. I'm wondering if you're still capable of leading a team, with everything you're dealing with.'

I straightened my back. 'Ma'am; yes, Sally kept a huge secret last year and she paid for it dearly. We all paid for it. But the organisation has a responsibility to Ross. We need to make sure he is attending his mandatory counselling. But,' I gave her a pointed look, 'I think the best place for him, the place where he can be properly monitored by people who know the situation, is here with me as his supervisor and yes, I am his supervisor. I am more than capable of leading the team through this. This is no ordinary homicide investigation. We're dealing with product contamination. It's not something that comes through any force's door on a regular basis. I believe we can deal with this just fine.

'We have a lead on this one they have written about. Ross and Martin are talking to Dawn Barry now to obtain the details we need to progress it. Everyone is waiting for those details to act on them.'

Her face went a shade darker.

'Ross?'

'Yes, Ross.'

'Why has he been tasked with such a serious and clearly, potentially evidential task? After what I've just said? Have you lost your mind? You have your choice of detectives and officers with great records out there in the incident room and you send Ross.' Catherine's voice raised an octave.

'Ross is perfectly capable of taking this statement, of getting this information from Dawn. In fact, his statements are of an excellent evidential standard. And I've sent Martin with him anyway. Ross needs to get out of the incident room and get some air.'

'He can get some air in the car park, Hannah. He does not need to get air with a witness who is our only surviving victim of the county's first major product contamination case.' Her hands clenched and I took a breath in and pulled my shoulders back.

'He made us look like imbeciles. Do I need to remind you of that?'

I exhaled. 'No Ma'am, you don't. But I believe that Ross has learnt from that experience and he is in need of the support of the service, not hostility and anger,' I lifted myself higher, 'he has been grieving for his colleague and has been struggling and we need to be seen to be supporting him, not hounding him out and bullying him because he was affected by what happened. How would that look? At a grievance procedure, say?'

Her mouth parted and her hands splayed.

'I hope you know what you're doing, Hannah.'

She walked out. I looked down at the newspaper on my desk.

So did I.

64

I brewed myself a green tea, made a black coffee, then picked up the half eaten pack of chocolate digestives I kept in my desk drawer and walked down the corridor to Evie's office. I pushed my way in with my bum as my hands were full and as I turned round Evie was already looking at me, a smile on her face, lifting her glasses up onto her head and leaving them nesting in her curls.

'I see you take advice well and have brought biscuits with you as well as drinks,' she said.

'You are definitely the one person I listen to, Evie.' I handed her the coffee, put the biscuits on the desk and sat on the spare chair inhaling the green tea vapours winding their way up out of my mug.

'Ah, so on that point, who is it you are not listening to?'

'You're so wise.'

'That's why you come here.' She grinned at me and leaned towards the biscuit packet, pulling one out and stuffing half in her mouth. I have seen her eat a whole biscuit in one before but she obviously wanted to be able to speak today. I picked the next digestive out of the packet.

'I've had a run in with Catherine and needed a tea break. Where better to do that than with my best friend?'

'Ah, um,' Evie mumbled through the biscuit, waving a finger at me.

'My thoughts exactly,' I replied, smiling at her before taking a bite of my own biscuit. This was why I came in here. I knew she would make me smile.

She swallowed hard. 'Sweetening me up with biscuits and sweet talk, it must have been bad.'

'It was. The article in the *Today* started her off, then we got into the Ross situation and how I'm managing the investigation.'

'She didn't send the bad news through Grey?'

'Nope, I was lucky enough to get it all from the horse's mouth today. Grey is probably getting his own version right now.'

'Oh dear. Poor Grey. I'm not sure he can cope with Catherine on the rampage.' The rest of the biscuit went in her mouth.

'Neither do I. Though I think part of the reason she is rampaging is because she is stressing over the pending result of Sally's inquest. Grey is even more fretful than usual for exactly the same reason.' I washed down the biscuit with my tea.

Evie swallowed again. 'And you?'

'Me?'

'Yes, you. How are you with the inquest still hanging over your head, what's the effect on you?'

I paused. Put my cup down. It was a good question.

'I don't know.'

Evie looked at me.

'Really Evie, I don't. This job has had my full attention. It isn't giving me time to think too much. Having to deal with the stress of Catherine and Grey is enough of a knock-on effect for me without me adding my own stuff to the mix.' I picked my cup back up and drank.

'Don't hide behind those excuses too long, Hannah. More harm will come of it than good and I don't want to see the outcome of that.'

65

I looked at the faces of the team on this manhunt. A dedicated team and I was proud of them. Even Ross who was trying hard to do what was needed without moaning about the shit job he'd been given. Martin continued to be his shoulder to lean on, or tried to. He was there for him. Always chatting, talking about the job, about life, how it continued for him, his wife, and his dogs. I often overheard them as they sat doing something mundane where they could talk and work at the same time. I could see what Martin was doing. He was a great guy, a great detective, not easily spooked or excited and I didn't ever want to lose him from my team. I knew there were plenty of other departments out there he could apply for but I hoped he was settled enough to stay here for some time at least.

Things were happening quickly and we all needed to be up to speed on it all. I'd taken three painkillers as my arm was killing me and I didn't think two would even take the edge off. I needed my thoughts to be focused on the job at hand, not on the deep throbbing ache that pulled my mind away from whatever it was dealing with.

'We have a lot of information to get through, so listen up. You might want to get your incident books out and take some notes.' The room rustled in one seamless movement as green incident books were pulled onto the tops of desks and onto knees where room wouldn't allow for desk space.

'Several things have happened and have come to light as we've been working,' I continued, 'so it's going to be a long night as we tackle what we've got. When we've finished in here you need to make the calls home that are necessary. OT is already authorised. I hope it's not going to be a problem for anyone.' It wasn't a question. On an investigation like this people expected to work long hours and rarely was I asked for time off before a job was finished. Sick children or spouses were the usual exceptions to a working rule.

'We've had another public order incident. More shoppers trashing foodstuffs because they couldn't figure out if it had been tampered with or not and the staff member there at the time was unable to calm them down sufficiently. Luckily no one was seriously hurt but there were arrests for public order offences. This time in Beeston, so following this briefing I have to head straight into another briefing to deal with that side of it. We need to be supporting divisions that are dealing with the fallout of this; after all, we're the ones who have not yet got a handle on who this is or what their motive is. Going into meetings like that is not something I enjoy doing, so we need to get a grasp on this and now, please.' I was actually giving them the toned-down version of how I felt about going into the next briefing. Not enjoying doing it was a massive understatement. I think if someone gave me a spoon and asked me to gouge my eyes out with it I would probably consider it, if it would get me out of what was coming next.

'Why Beeston in particular? Finlay seems like an age ago now?' a voice from the back of the room asked.

'I don't know. I imagine they're worried this problem will come back to them as it is moving about and has no discernible pattern. It's not helped by the hysterics from the *Today*. That's something else we need to deal with.'

'As far as we're concerned,' I continued, 'and I'll update you after this next briefing, we are doing everything we can to keep the public safe. The hospital staff are keeping in touch with the CRCE, the Centre for Radiation, Chemicals and Environmental Hazards for anyone not conversant with the acronym, to keep on top of the public safety issue. There is nothing to be done to protect them that we aren't already doing. We could consider a public televised piece on what to check for – tampered food etc., but I'll discuss that at the next meeting with Claire, Catherine and Grey, and feed it back down.'

Pens scribbled away in notepads as heads bent over in concentration.

'Regarding the property seized from Dawn Barry's address. The CSU have found the item that contained the poison that made her sick and identified the poison as an off-the-shelf rat poison, which matches up with what the hospital identified from the tox screen.'

Heads flipped upwards. All mutterings stopped and phones that were being texted from were quickly slid into pockets.

I tucked my hair behind my ear. 'It was in the carton of ice cream she ate. There was a small puncture mark in the tub, which is how the offender got it inside without notice. It was pushed up as close to the lid and under as he or she could get it. Dawn is recovering slowly. Her body was badly affected by the poison. She went into convulsions and was also jaundiced, which indicates a problem with her liver. She's in good hands and should make a full recovery. Rat poison, however, isn't what we've been dealing with up to now. I made a phone call to the National Crime Agency and spoke to one of their profilers and from what she was saying, this is likely to be a copycat and not the original poisoner.' There was a collective groan from the room. 'But we still need to identify and arrest them before they continue their spree.' I paused and looked around. This was going to be a long explanation. I looked behind me, gauged the distance, walked backwards to a desk, and perched myself on it.

'Karen, the profiler, says that this offender is likely to have committed the offence because of the high level of publicity that has surrounded the murders. Copycats desire the media attention that is being directed at the original crime. It's usually a male and though this is probably publicity driven, it does not mean he would not have offended in some way without the trigger of the press frenzy. Look at the world we live in, everyone is obsessed with how many people are looking at them, how many followers and friends they have. Locally this is the biggest thing to happen in a while, especially as we've lowered the rate of gun crime in the county.'

'So, are we looking at someone who hates their mummy?'

'Is that a serious question?'

'Erm.' A scratch of a balding head, one of the seconded staff. 'Yeah, I suppose it is; this psychology stuff isn't much of my thing.'

'No, then. They'd be targeting women specifically and doing it from the get go rather than copying someone else.'

'But, he's craving attention?'

'Yes. The attention that's building daily because of these murders has built up in his mind and he wants a piece of it for himself.'

There was a mixture of nodding and shaking of heads as the strangeness of this statement sank in.

'Martin, tell us what Dawn said when you saw her please.'

'Well, she's been lucky to survive. There was a pretty high dose of rat poison in the ice cream and in her system. It's causing all sorts of problems for her. She didn't taste it because she was drunk when she ate it. According to the experts, this guy really wanted to kill.'

More head shaking.

'Dawn said she only bought the ice cream the day before she ate it as she loves her ice cream and tends to get through a lot of it, which is why she can be so specific. She bought it from the shop round the corner from her home address.'

His look told me he'd finished.

'Good, thanks.' I looked at the rest of the room again. 'Ross, I'd like you to go to the shop to pick up the CCTV for as far back as it goes, speak to the store owner and any and all of the store workers to see if they saw anyone suspicious around the ice cream freezer.'

I turned to Martin, who was working on looking at finding links between the victims.

'What have you got?' I asked.

'Unfortunately, I still can't find a link between any of the victims. I looked through all the relatives' statements and there was nothing there. I then looked through the victims' bank accounts and I couldn't find anything there either. They didn't go to the same takeaways, restaurants, gym clubs, or hairdressers. There is nothing to link two of them, never mind all of them. It's harder with Finlay McDonnell but I did take a lot of information from his parents' statements and the extra information that has come in slowly from their FLO. Nothing. It's so frustrating.'

'Okay, keep looking, there has to be a crossover somewhere. Also, I heard back from Curvet after they did an inventory check and they don't have any missing stock, so the digoxin is not coming from them.' Another dead end.

'Aaron has the rest of the actions for everyone else, so let's get going, we have a hell of a lot to do. This isn't even the original enquiry work!'

66

By the time I got back from my meeting with Youens I was stressed and wanted to run to the kitchen to find that spoon for my eyes. The amount of times I'd had to admit I didn't know something to him made me feel like I didn't have a handle on the case and it annoyed me as much as it had very obviously annoyed him. He'd said the investigation was toxic to his area and infecting his residents and turning them into monsters. Because of course they were never predisposed to this behaviour before our offender started his business of randomly poisoning people.

We needed to get a grip on this and get a grip now before more bodies dropped on either of us.

Ross was already back with the CCTV collection and was sitting in the CCTV viewing room going through it. I spoke to Martin who was stretching his legs around the incident room.

'So, the owner of the shop is a woman in her late fifties. Doesn't understand how any of her products could have been tampered with. She hasn't seen anything but she was more than happy to hand over all her CCTV discs as she doesn't want to get a reputation for being one of the stores where there is dodgy food. She asked Ross if she should be closing the store or anything. He didn't know and called me, and to be honest, boss, I don't really know. Has our offender put this stuff in more than one tub, or even in more than one product?'

he asked, looking a little more pensive than I was used to seeing him, his hands in his pockets as he stood in front of me, shoulders slumped forward.

'As we've identified her store as a source of one of the outbreaks I think we need to inform CRCE and let them take the lead with those questions don't you? It's not our area of expertise. She needs to keep the shop closed until they contact her and go from there, but they're very good and will be in touch with her soon,' I answered.

'I did tell Ross to keep it closed until I'd spoken with you to be on the safe side.'

'Great. Thanks, Martin. And how's it going with checking the CCTV? What about any other staff?'

'She has two other part-time staff members. Ross took statements from them. They both say the same thing. Nothing suspicious seen and this is out of the blue to them. After getting back in, Ross volunteered to start viewing straight away, so I've left him to it.'

'And we're running background checks on the owner and the staff as well?'

'Yes, I've started it but still have a lot to do.'

'Great. HOLMES will be able to identify if any of the nominals are known to each other, which will help us to see if there is a link anywhere.'

'I fed all the names to Diane to index on HOLMES before I continued with my stuff.'

'Thanks, Martin. I'm glad I have you on the team right now.' I made a move towards my office. 'How's Ross doing?'

Martin walked with me. 'He's doing okay, I think. He's subdued. But you'd expect that, with what has been happening. He desperately wants to stay here, that much is obvious, so he's doing all the jobs, even the tedious ones that will hopefully show him in a positive light. I know it's not my place to ask, but they're not going to boot him, are they?'

'Not if I can help it they're not. Not if I can help it.'

67

It was late, the sun had set and the heat of the day had finally given way to a cooler easier evening. A light was on in the upstairs window. He'd be sat in bed, glasses perched on the end of his nose, book in hands, drooping into his lap as his head nodded downwards.

I had a key but I didn't like to use it. Not now, not when he was in bed. I knocked softly on the glass pane and waited. Then knocked again because in his fitful sleep pretence of reading he wouldn't have heard me the first time. I checked my phone for texts or missed calls as I waited for him to rise and answer the door. Nothing had come through. I didn't want to use the Q word, even to myself, but a silent phone was good news.

A light went on.

'Who is it?' the voice behind the glass asked. Did I hear fear? I forget he ages as I age. But mostly, I think he's lost on his own.

'It's me, Dad.' It had been a couple of weeks since I had spoken with him. It always caused me to feel guilty but with the pressures of the job and the difficulties in the relationship, I didn't seem to be able to call him or visit any more often than I did, but this was different.

'Hello?'

'Dad, it's Hannah.'

'Hannah!' the joy in his voice nearly broke my heart. The door swung open and his face shone. 'Come in, come in. How are you?'

I picked up the four carrier bags at my feet, my arm twinging, and walked over the threshold. 'I'm good. You?'

He looked at the bags, stepping back out of my way, confusion crossing his face. 'Good. Good, yes,' he paused, 'how's the arm?'

'Still sore, but you know ... still healing.'

'Yes. These things take time. Don't push it, Hannah. Take care of yourself.' He grabbed at the bags, taking them from me.

'I am, Dad, I am ...' I gritted my teeth. We walked into the kitchen. 'Look, I called for a specific reason this evening.'

'Okay.' He dumped the bags on the kitchen worktop.

'I've brought your weekly shopping round so you don't need to go out to the supermarket and buy it yourself.' He looked at me in silence. 'If there's anything I've missed, text me.' He frowned. 'Or call. And I'll bring that round as well.'

'What on earth for? I'm quite capable of doing my own shopping. You know that, why would you do this?'

'You've read the papers, Dad. Please do this for me. I'm not asking you to stay indoors or anything, just to stay out of food stores. I don't want you to get caught up in anything and get hurt. You can still go about your daily business as usual. Please, Dad?'

He sighed. 'Okay. But only because you actually asked, Hannah, and not because you told me to.'

'Thank you, Dad.' I rubbed my arm. 'It's because I care.'

'I know. And when I ask you for something, it's always because I care as well.'

'I know. I'll order your shopping online for next week, as I'm not sure if I'll get time to do it again. But, I don't want you doing it until this is resolved. I hope that's good with you?'

He looked at where I was rubbing. 'Hannah?'

'What is it?'

'She was worried as hell, you know.'

'Yeah, well she lost all rights to be worried when she lost her rights to freedom, didn't she?'

He sighed. 'She's paying for her crimes in prison but she's still your sister. You were stabbed. She couldn't get to you, see you. It hurt her.'

'I have to go. I need to get some sleep before I get back into work early tomorrow. Night, Dad.'

Another sigh. 'Night, Hannah. And thank you.'

I wrapped my arms around him and he squeezed me tight. 'Night, Dad.' I had to leave; we were about to go round in circles again. He couldn't grasp where I was coming from. We were all he had since Mum died, I knew that, but I couldn't forgive Zoe. She was my sister, but my anger towards her was still too raw to speak to her, it was still too raw to speak about her.

The position she had put me in before she'd been arrested was unbearable. She'd nearly cost me my job, my career – or she would have done if the people I knew had taken things at face value.

68

2 weeks ago

People forget. It's easy for them to move on with their lives. To not pick up the phone. To not visit. *Life is busy* they say when they bump into you, their eyes wary. Like rabbits caught in the headlights. What should they do? What should they say? They'd forgotten, but they can see it's not been that easy here for you. They look about them for a reason to leave quickly, their mouths moving rapidly with platitudes, trying to fill the void with anything but the truth – that it all became too difficult, so they forgot and they moved on. They don't know the loss, the pain, the heartache, loneliness, and the deep soul-wrenching agony of something torn away. They forget the promises of help, support and of being there for them that they uttered at the start. Those promises had expiry dates on them, yet they were unspoken. Presumed known. But what were they supposed to do? They had lives.

Lucky them.

Now, as they stand here, Connie looks shrunken to Isaac. Like a rag doll that has been put in the wash on hot, and high spin, and left on the side to dry in the sun. Shoulders curled over, as though she wants to hide herself away as much as she can. He knows she doesn't like to go out of the house but the necessities need doing and he hates to see her wither inside so he pulls her out with him once a week but when this happens it hurts.

How are they supposed to move on from this so quickly, or at all? It's not a pet dog they've lost. There isn't a time frame for when the pain will start to lessen. Here they were in that awkward position of being the people no one wanted to bump into. Connie didn't have the strength to pretend she was any better than she was, and stammered at the inane babbling of their so-called friend. The odd hand that reached out and touched her arm for a split second made her jump. Human touch, aside from Isaac's, wasn't something she had experienced in a while. It was alien and forced. He could see she wanted to cry out. To howl out at the world. But she held it in. They both held it in. But the agony of holding it in was tearing them apart shred by tiny shred.

Eventually, the empty chatter stopped. An excuse was found and the used-to-be friend moved on. Connie sighed. Isaac felt the knot of anger in his gut grow ever tighter.

69

The morning papers were nearly as much our nemesis as the killer. I could see this etched on Catherine's face as I sat in her office with Grey, the morning briefing only fifteen minutes away. She was calm. It was as though she had worked out there was no point in raising her blood pressure because it was all misdirected anger. I wasn't going to defend the *Today* because of Ethan, but there would be no story to write if there were no killings of this kind to write about.

'**Police Failure Puts Residents At Further Risk.** Really? They're going with that today?'

I didn't answer her. It pretty much explained itself as a rhetorical question as she turned her back to us and looked out the window at the secure police car park below. Last night had seen another public order incident over food stuffs and this in a supermarket. The *Today* was obviously running with it. The pressure to bring in the killer was mounting with the people of the city getting nervous.

'I want Claire in here as soon as she gets in this morning. We need to be responding to this.' She turned back to face us. 'We can't sit back and let them take pot shots at us and watch the whole of Notts crumble before our eyes. We need to get in front of it. Or at least catch up with it.' She was obviously calming down as she now sat in her chair, smoothing her trousers down at the knees. 'We've been on the back foot this whole time. I have to admit that. I never in a lifetime expected something of this magnitude to ever come across my desk and have to be dealt with while I sat here.' She eyed us up as though looking into our souls for evidence we might repeat her confession of not being prepared or acting correctly to a job. I didn't move. I had Grey at the side of me and that's what supervisors were for. If anyone was going to be eaten alive today, it certainly wasn't going to be me.

Grey was statue still, which was unusual for him. The man who always fidgeted with his fingers was rigid. With fear? Someone needed to speak next, not just allow Catherine to speak to herself, which was likely to get her more annoyed than she already was as she spiralled around in anger at the situation.

'I'll speak to Claire, Ma'am. Make sure she's apprised of your request to see her. We still have a lot of enquiries to continue with today so we could make some headway that will knock the *Today* off their perch. But I agree, it's not good for the community. Chief Superintendent Youens will not like waking up to this today, either.'

She groaned. 'Don't remind me. Another call I'm going to have to be smoothing over. It seems that recently I am spending all my time making promises we can't keep or apologising for things we do.' She looked at Grey. 'And the hammer is not just going to fall on my head.'

His fingers twitched. 'I'll go back to see Youens while Hannah gets on with the investigation. It'll keep the coast clear for her to work.' His throat scrambled to get the words out, his Adam's apple bobbing up and down hard in his scrawny neck.

She leaned back, seeming more appeased. 'Okay. Let's make today matter.'

Ross was already in the viewing room continuing to go through the CCTV from the shop. He must have got in early. This was a throwback to his good days.

'How's it going?' I handed him a coffee and kept the mug of green tea for myself.

'Boss,' he acknowledged. 'Slow going. Lots of activity. This woman has a good business on her hands. It's really busy. Customers coming and going at all hours, but at least I know what area I need to be focusing on.'

I nodded.

'I've made a note of the date, time and description when someone goes into the freezer and takes out ice cream, even if it isn't Dawn,' he continued. 'So far I haven't seen anyone stand and meddle with one and place it back in but I'll keep watching.'

Ross seemed more like himself. His eyes were brighter, more alert. There was less of a roundness to his shoulders.

'How far back does the CCTV go?'

'She keeps it for twenty-eight days before recording back over it. It was due to be done again in a week so we have three weeks to look through. It's lucky with things like this when we don't call on the day they've just erased everything.'

'True. Though Dawn was even luckier she was on the ball that night and called an ambulance and also that it wasn't the digoxin that was in her system.'

'We've a great camera angle here, boss; we stand a good chance of ID-ing the copycat at least.'

'Good work. Keep at it, Ross.'

'Yes, boss.'

'And Ross.'

'Boss?'

'Get a haircut, will you.'

My phone was ringing as I walked into my office.

'DI Robbins.'

'Ma'am, it's Penny from CSU.'

'Hi, Penny,' I replied.

'We have some results for you which I've emailed to you, but I wanted to phone to make sure you got it and the email doesn't sink in your inbox.'

'That's great. Phoning was probably a good idea because the way my inbox works, it's like a game of chance some weeks.'

I opened up my computer with my spare hand as I spoke. 'What do you have, Penny?'

'We finally found the source of the digoxin in Lianne Beers' address. It was in a microwave ready meal, one of those breakfast oat things and it was enough to take effect fairly quickly; well, to make her feel ill and then kill her.'

'And how did it get in there?'

'The packaging was already damaged. It had a discounted sticker on it from the local shop so she wouldn't have been surprised with the damage or have been worried by any tampering because she wouldn't have seen it as tampering. The actual digoxin was injected into the paper-card case of the meal under the lip, so the box was open and injection site wasn't visible unless you were looking.'

'Oh Christ. Seriously? This is one smart offender to target already damaged items.'

'I know. It has now narrowed down our testing range for the other jobs that are in. We can look for any food products that have a discounted sticker on first and put that to the top of the queue if you're happy with that?'

'Absolutely. Thanks, Penny. I've found your email and will read it fully for details including markings on the sticker etc.'

'No worries. We'll get working on the next job. Thanks, Ma'am.'

Discounted goods. Damaged packaging. No wonder this poison was getting into people. We were up against someone who really wanted to hurt people.

70

Lianne Beers' address was still closed off as a crime scene. I hadn't wanted anything disturbed in case we needed to go in again, and we did. I'd informed Sean Beers that unfortunately it was still an active crime scene and access wouldn't be granted until we'd finished with it. We needed to find out where she bought the ready meal so that meant going in and searching bins and desks, drawers, bags and purses for receipts so we could then isolate the shop and close it down while we checked all goods within it. We also needed to check with the other families to see if they also shopped there. It wouldn't go down well with the store if we closed it but we had to stop further deaths. I hoped it was just that one shop that had been contaminated and not a variety of shops, but we wouldn't know that until the search team completed their task. I paced my office. Martin and Aaron were heading up the search team. I knew it was in good hands but I couldn't shake the itchy feeling that was creeping its way up my body. All I could do was keep walking. We had to get this guy. My arms itched. I wanted to shake them and shake them viciously. My scar throbbed.

I looked at the phone, then walked back around the desk and started pacing again.

At 5.45 p.m. Aaron called me to say they had the receipt for the microwave breakfast meal and the name of the shop where the goods were bought. They were heading over there next and the search team was coming back in to collect more evidence bags. I rubbed my arm hard and sighed.

'Thanks, Aaron. Finally, something seems to be going our way. Let's hope the shop is the same shop they all shopped at. I'll call the FLOs and get them to ask the families if they do and we can go from there.'

'We're going to need extra staff here for the search, Hannah – or do you want us to just collect the items on the discounted shelves?'

'Good question.' Shit. We couldn't seize the entire shop but we couldn't risk leaving any items out there that had been compromised. 'Take the discounted goods and all the microwave meals that are not discounted then hand the information over to the CRCE, as with the Dawn Barry case.'

'Okay. Send me those extra bodies and I'll update you shortly.'

'Great. Thanks, Aaron.'

Was this the break we needed? I hoped so.

I walked into the incident room and identified some staff, asking them to leave what they were doing and to meet Aaron at the shop close to Lianne's address.

Next I made the calls to the three FLOs. One to update the Beers family and the other two to ask the families about their shopping habits. Though we had already had this discussion with them about their shopping routines, in grief, things could easily be missed. If we asked a direct question we could know for certain, though in all probability it was unlikely they all shopped at the same place because of how spread out the victims were. They all had their own closer supermarkets and their own closer corner shops, they had no need to go further afield unless they were maybe visiting someone and had stopped off or were working in the area etc. I knew, again, we were one step forward and yet, no further forward.

71

Yesterday had proved to be a long day and night. Quick drinks with Evie in the Pitcher and Piano, on High Pavement, Nottingham, for an hour allowed me to wind down as my brain was twisting in knots and functioning at warp speed, or at least it was attempting to.

The Pitcher and Piano was an old converted church with bare stonework, high ceilings and beautiful arches.

Evie was great for my health, making me laugh at her tales of dating escapades. Like the man who had spent an evening with food stuck between his two front teeth and try as she might she'd been unable to tell him and the entire length of time he'd sat with it, it had put her off him, even though she'd been fully capable of doing something about it. There were the men who still lived with their parents. In this day and age, with the cost of housing, that wasn't unusual in itself, but as Evie put it, when they still looked as though they'd been dressed by their mother, she drew the line. By the time I'd pulled myself into bed I was feeling ready for sleep and more ready to take on another day.

And, now we were here. As I'd imagined, none of the shops that the victims bought their foodstuffs from matched up. We were no further forward, other than knowing one shop our killer had used and accessed and being able to deal with it forensically and the obvious one of potentially preventing further deaths from that location.

CSU were working at full pelt and we were getting complaints from other divisions and departments because their submissions were being put on the back burner. Catherine, Grey and I were fielding those calls when absolutely necessary, though the head of CSU was a fairly formidable woman and you wouldn't want to cross her.

Having two killers out there was not making our job any easier and we'd made a decision not to disclose this to the press as of yet because we didn't want to invoke panic or nudge another person into joining in the mayhem because they figured it would be fun and something to do for the week.

It was later that day when I went in to see Ross that the copy-cat part of the investigation lifted off. Ross was sat staring at the screen, his head tilted heavily to the side as though he had a weight hanging from his right ear, tugging it down.

'Ross?' I asked.

He jumped. Head straightening.

'Ma'am.'

'What is it?'

'This guy, Ma'am. I've been looking at the image, rewound it a couple of times, I think he picked it up.' He looked at me. 'The ice cream,' he clarified. 'Then put it back down in the freezer again. I can't quite make out what he's doing with his hands though. It's what I'm replaying it for. He's doing something. I'm not happy with it.'

I grabbed a chair, my heart lifting in my chest. A breakthrough? We were due one. Dragging the chair over to Ross I sat with him and noticed I was pulling the same bizarre stance, as though twisting my head meant I could see around people and corners. Moving my head moved them out of the way.

Eventually I decided it was enough. I wasn't happy with what he was doing, we were going to ID him, search his premises and interview him.

'Take this to intelligence; see if the guy is in the system already and if so, we'll act on this today.'

He was like a cat on hot coals, jumping up the minute I opened my mouth. 'You think it's him?'

'I think you've done a good job going through all this, Ross.'

72

He'd taken to getting the *Nottingham Today* delivered. The walk to the newsagents had started to feel like a walk of shame. He didn't want to endure that, so he'd asked them to start delivering it. Connie had been surprised even though she hadn't said anything, but they'd been together long enough for him to be able to read her face when she was surprised or annoyed, happy or sad. Sad, that was something he had no need to practise any more. Sad was the default setting. Surprise was a glimmer, a shimmer, and a passing glimpse of someone else inhabiting his wife's body. To be honest, it had caught him off guard to see a different emotion cross her face but he removed the look of astonishment from his face because all he felt was guilt. He didn't want to cause her any more distress than she had already been through, and was living with, on a day by day, hour by hour, second by second basis, and the fear of losing him would be too much for her to bear on top of having already lost Em, so he wouldn't do that to her. He wouldn't give her that fear to live with. He would hide what he was doing, so that Connie could get through her days in the best way that she knew how.

He'd continue this alone.

73

He was sitting at the same kitchen table where Em had told them her news. Back then it had been devastating, but back then there had been some hope. He remembered the talk of treatment plans, of doctors and drug treatments.

Isaac thought his child would survive this. She was strong and today's medicine was advanced. But it hadn't happened that way, so now his hand had been forced. He hadn't wanted this, but what else could he do? There was no way they would listen to him if he wrote a neat little letter and wrapped it tidily in a neat little envelope and posted it off to them to be opened by a neat little receptionist. This was the only way they would sit up and take notice.

Connie was upstairs, lying in Emma's room. The room hadn't been changed, touched or emptied of anything. She often walked into the room and came out several hours later, face flushed, streaked and her eyes somewhere else. Lost to him.

He straightened himself in the chair, pushed his shoulders back and felt a calm settle over him. They had to be getting anxious about things now.

He unfolded the *Nottingham Today* and looked at the front page.

Police Charge Man With One Count of GBH

Police have charged 24-year-old Lewis Armitage of Lenton with one count of GBH after he admitted to adding rat poison to ice cream in a store.

The 22-year-old woman has been seriously ill after buying the ice cream and ingesting the rat poison and was kept in hospital for a week.

Armitage is still being held by police and will appear at Nottingham magistrates' court today for a remand application hearing.

A neighbour of Armitage said, 'I'm surprised by this news, Lewis is a quiet neighbour. We rarely see him. He spends so much time in his flat.'

Nottingham has recently suffered with a spate of poisonings, which has resulted in the deaths of three Nottinghamshire residents, including a sixteen-year-old boy. As of this date the murders are undetected.

Progress of the multiple murder case appears slow and police are not offering much. Two businesses have been closed down, creating a further two victims. The authorities have refused to disclose what poison is being used, for investigative reasons, but are warning the public to be cautious when buying food goods and to check all seals and packaging carefully. They advise shoppers to only buy goods that are properly packaged and not damaged in any way.

Isaac put the paper onto the table at the side of him and clenched his teeth until his jaw hurt. Why were the police refusing to name the digoxin? How could he get his message out there if they wouldn't work with him? This was stupidity. What 'investigative reason' was there that prevented the basics of the case from being disclosed? Someone somewhere was not doing their job and they were now going to end up killing more people because he now had to up the stakes. He couldn't have done all this for nothing. People had lost their lives. That was an awful thought. He wouldn't allow them to have lost them for nothing, in vain. Isaac couldn't just give in, so he had to push harder. It was the only way.

He'd done his homework; he knew that if the medicine were given to someone who didn't need it and in too high a dose, they would die from it. He wasn't doing it for any other reason than for those in power to sit up and take notice, so that someone listened to how Em could have and should have been saved. He needed them to realise that the drug wasn't working properly, that they had work to do before more people died. At their hand, not at his. He was doing it for a purpose, to stop any more victims like his daughter. The pharmaceutical companies were doing it out of sheer negligence and the need for higher profit margins rather than wanting to help anyone. They had to notice.

Whoever was responsible for the decision to not name or report the digoxin was now going to regret it – because they had just sealed the fate of several more people.

74

Damerae Rabasca loved noise. The sound of people talking. Shouting. Bad-tempered people. Happy people. Traffic. Car horns.

He loved the exhaust fumes that made the city streets all the more grey. Flat-fronted buildings. Local markets, spilling out onto the street with their wares. The oppressive heat that seared them all together. This was his home. And it was his. All of it. No one sneezed without his say so.

It had been his ever since the house fire that had killed Odane last year. Not so much a house fire, as a firebombing. O hadn't seen it coming. His closest friend. But Damerae took what he deserved. It wasn't going to be given to him on a silver platter and no matter how close they were, O was a selfish cunt. Treated him like one of the guys on the street. And Damerae deserved better than that. So he took it.

They'd just finished breaking Dean's right leg that night and Damerae had driven Odane home, as usual. O was laughing about how, when they'd taken Dean to the rear of The Happy Tyre Man, he'd pissed himself, because he'd known what was coming. After all, you didn't get Odane Hajric and Damerae Rabasca dealing with you themselves – unless you've royally fucked up. And you couldn't fuck up more than by stealing from them. Did Dean think they wouldn't notice he'd been skimming off the top of the coke and taking their profits? O had laughed. And he'd laughed. And he'd laughed. It was his crazy high-pitched, I-want-to-break-some-bones laugh. And Damerae had sat at the side of him and forced himself to laugh along.

The snively little cokehead, he'd managed to gasp while shrieking with laughter. *His face was a picture. And did you hear that crack, man?* Oh Damerae had heard the bone crack all right. He had no problems with the breaking of bones. Dean deserved every painful second of it, and more. If he Damerae had his way, both his legs would have been gone. No, what Damerae was silently seething about was how O asked the question about it being 'their' profits. O was the man – everyone below him was below him and he made sure they knew it. Damerae didn't see a share of the profits. He was paid the same way as everyone else, by selling and enforcing for Odane. Long-time friendship and loyalty didn't count for anything and Damerae had had enough. So he watched O walk into the house and pulled away as usual. Not half an hour later, the house had been razed to the ground and a new chain of command was already in place.

Now Damerae stood here, feeling it and loving it. He watched as his baby-mama came waddling towards him, skinny white arms swinging wildly at her sides as she huffed her way up Ilkeston Road, flip-flops slapping at the soles of her feet. She was hot, her face was red, but it wasn't surprising, she was huge. Due any day now.

'Damerae, what'd I say to you?' she bellowed as she walked.

Damerae didn't hear what was said next as a weight pushed down on his chest, crushing and squeezing, forcing him down to the floor.

The sun-warmed pavement rushing up to meet him was the last thing he saw.

75

This was a man whose dead body I had fully expected to be standing over one day – but with blood slipping from bullet or stab wounds, a violent end to a violent man. Not this, not him face down in the middle of the pavement with not an injury on him.

The rustle of the paper Tyvek suit told me Aaron was now standing at the side of me as I looked down at Damerae Rabasca. Doug Howell, the CSI, was taking photographs of the body. I was aware of eyes watching us from above as residents in the flats peered out. We'd kept a wide crime scene cordoned off but those people in their homes could look out as much as they wanted.

I clenched my fist in my pocket.

I'd already shouted at someone who had opened their window to lean out and over the scene, asking if they wanted to be arrested for murder because they were currently contaminating the scene with their DNA by leaning right over it. They had rapidly closed the window and now had their nose pressed to the glass.

'So, Damerae Rabasca?'

'Yes, I wasn't expecting this one,' I answered.

'What are you thinking?'

'I'm suspicious. As head of The Niners I'd expected him to be killed in a gang-related incident, not to keel over in the street. We need the PM doing quickly and the tox screen results as fast as we can.'

'Ah, young Hannah and my favourite detective sergeant.' Jack's voice came from behind me. 'You enjoying keeping me busy?'

'Hi Jack. Well, I do like to keep you out of trouble.' I grinned at him. I thought, as a pathologist, his job was grim, but he was always so upbeat. So open to the good in life. I wasn't sure how he did it, but his attitude was infectious.

'So, what do we have?' Jack asked as he snapped on his gloves, pulling them over the elasticated wrists of his own paper suit.

'Well, here we have Damerae Rabasca, twenty-four years of age. Head of the gang known as The Niners; so called because of their penchant for 9mm automatics, though, out of interest, more recently they've been using the Glock semi and the odd Mac-10.'

'Lovely, lovely.'

'The gang marker is a tattoo of a 9mm bullet on the back of the neck – you can see his is clearly visible from this position – but to identify each other easily and quickly,' I pointed down to his right hand, open as though waiting for someone to hand him monies owed.

'The bandana on his wrist?' asked Jack.

'Exactly. Red, because no matter how bloody it gets, it's not going to upset the gang colours.'

'Well, he had no need of it today, did he?' Jack hitched up his trousers, and crouched down to the body, taking Rabasca's core body temperature.

Doug continued with his photographs.

'Any witnesses, Hannah?'

I looked down the street to where Martin and Ross had been. 'Yes, his heavily pregnant girlfriend, Gemma Spicer. She said she was walking towards him and he just went over. No sound, he just went down.'

Jack pushed himself back up. 'You know what I'm going to say.'

I nodded.

'I can't tell you anything from this. I need to do the PM and I'll do it as soon as we move him from the scene. I'll supervise the removal and I'll get the tox screen off straight away. He's a young, fit man. Find out from Ms Spicer all the illicit drugs he was taking so we can ascertain if they played any part, but looking at him, it doesn't look like a typical drug overdose, what with the surroundings and him looking well. Once I've done the PM I'll let you know the results, but we won't know what we've really got until we get the tox screen back if it's what we're all thinking.'

I huffed, I couldn't help it.

'I know it's a slow and frustrating process, but that's science for you. I've sped up the process as best I can. Everything that comes through that looks as though it's to do with this case is marked as high priority and is moved to the top of the list and dealt with first.'

'It'll come, Hannah.' Aaron backed him up.

'Good man, Aaron.' Jack slapped him on the shoulder and Aaron tried not to flinch.

I glared up at the flats again then turned to Aaron. 'What if Rabasca was the intended target all along? All the previous victims may have been a smoke screen. Rabasca had more enemies than any one of our victims, though I'm not sure if any of them have the wherewithal to be able to pull something of this scale off. Not just the scale, but using such a poison and being able to administer it in such a way … but we can't rule it out. It could also be that the previous deaths were just fortuitous to Rabasca's killer and they decided to make it look like it was a part of the same job so we don't look anywhere else. With someone like this guy, we need to think very carefully.'

'I don't know, Hannah, you're right about the level of thought that needs to go into something like this. These guys are just point and shoot.'

'We need to speak to Gemma Spicer,' I said.

76

There were no tears.

She stood in the clean, sparse kitchen, stomach touching the worktop, arms stretched out in front of her, making a cup of tea. I'd offered to do it for her but she'd looked insulted. As though I'd insinuated she was incapable of doing something quite so domesticated. When she finished she spread her knees wide and pushed her bum down to the floor so she could reach the tabby cat that had been circling her feet. She rubbed the top of his head.

'Stop fussing now, Norman, I've to talk to these here plods.' She reached a skinny arm up, grabbed the worktop and pulled herself back upright before walking past me, back into the living room, carrying her tea with her.

'I'm sorry for your loss, Gemma.' I sat opposite her on the worn but clean sofa.

'Why you sorry? You lot aren't gunna miss him, is you?'

'If someone has done this to Damerae, we have every intention of investigating it fully, but first, we need to wait for the post-mortem to find cause of death.'

'Of course you are.' She tried to take a drink but it was too hot, so she settled the cup on top of her expansive stomach instead, folding the material of her top over to shield her from the heat.

'He's your partner and to lose someone is always hard, but I can only imagine the difficulties in your situation, with a baby on the way.' I tried to connect with her. Aaron, I noticed, was leaving me to it, probably recognising that dealing with heavily pregnant women was not one of his strengths.

She grunted at me. 'What do you know? I'm no worse off with him dead that I would have been had he lived. He wouldn't have been a dad to this kid. All he were interested in was running that fucking gang of his and ruling with his iron dick. I were there to just hang off his arm whenever he needed me. It's no loss, let me tell you.'

Gemma was honest. I liked that. And I could work with that.

'Okay, what can you tell me then about his enemies, his recent life? Has there been anything you've noticed out of the ordinary?'

'You're not listening to me, are you?' She tried her tea again, this time managing to drink some.

I waited.

'I were only there when he wanted me. It's not like I were his confidante. I'm a mere woman, meaningless to him, a trinket on his arm and about to be his baby mama. I'm not stupid. I accepted him for who he was.'

I nodded my understanding at this comment.

'His life were about making sure the Niners were the top gang. He was always looking for trouble. But I ain't heard any threats against him, if that's what you're asking. I don't think anyone dare. Not after what he did to O.'

'So, that was him?' asked Aaron.

'Yeah, that were him all right. Came round that night all hyped up. Pumped, he was. Told me if I told anyone, he'd kill me. I believed him. Kept me mouth shut.'

She looked from Aaron to me. 'But he can't kill me now can he?'

77

Grey's fingers twitched on the desk in front of me. His once-blue eyes, now sliding into a murky pond colour, froze me in my seat. He had to have known this was coming but the feeling in the pit of my stomach was telling me something else. It had been four days since Rabasca's post-mortem. Four days where we'd talked to Gemma Spicer at length, worked with source handling to see if they could task their informants with obtaining intelligence on whether this was to do with Rabasca and the gang world, though I was told it was sensitive work and we'd hear back when they were ready. And so far, we hadn't. When we'd moved his body from the street we'd recovered a Glock, which was a change of weapon for him; it also tied him to a shooting that had occurred a couple of weeks ago, so I passed the weapon and the information onto DI Amanda Lawrence who was the SIO for the case. It appeared the death of this man cleared up many cases – apart from our own.

I focused on Grey's fingers, which always fascinated me. They were his giveaway, his *tell*, the thing that told me if he was anxious about what was happening. At this moment in time, his fingers were doing a merry dance on the desk top. He couldn't keep still. He moved his pen from one side of his laptop to the other, without looking away from me.

'And he's sure?'

'Sir, it's science, of course he's sure. Jack would never guess and he'd only ever phone and tell me when the results are in, never before.'

'Did they double check?'

'Sir?'

'Did they double-check the results? The sample? It could have been from one of the other victims.' The pen moved back to its original place. His stare was getting harder, a steely glint, a warning.

My stomach twisted in on itself. Grey was clutching at straws. I knew he hated that this case could get any bigger.

'Sir, they tested the correct sample. Jack and his team are scrupulous.' I ran my fingers through my fringe, buying a little time, mere seconds. 'There is no mistake. Damerae Rabasca had digoxin in his system and no other cause of death was evident. We made enquiries with his girlfriend Gemma Spicer on the day he died and she had nothing obvious to offer. It could be a rival gang – or one of his own, bearing in mind what he did himself. There had been no suggestion that anyone would make a play for Hajric's hold on the gang so when it happened it took everyone by surprise, including the Niner's themselves, according to the intelligence that came in following the incident. Spicer's disclosure last week tied up a long-running investigation.

'But, my feeling in relation to this, is that it's simply a part of our bigger picture. This has come unexpectedly for everyone who knew him. Spicer stated she doesn't know anyone who is ill or taking any medication. Of a legal variety, anyway. I lean towards believing her.

I'm not sure any of the gang members from either side are smart enough to pull this off. We've brought her in and got her interview on camera to cover our bases. She's not the most helpful of witnesses but she went along with us.'

Grey closed his eyes.

'On the positive side,' I tried to help him process what was happening, 'We no longer have a problem with the copy-cat. Armitage was kept in on remand and won't be going anywhere for a while. That's one file for court that is currently being put together and wrapped up.'

'Okay, Hannah. I get that, but we still have a huge problem. No one sleeps. No one leaves. No one has a life until we get to the bottom of this. Am I understood?'

He'd stopped moving. I wasn't sure which was more unnerving. 'Yes, Sir. I'll let the team know where we're up to now.'

I left his office wondering if my boss wasn't in need of some heart medication himself.

78

If they'd had a dog, he would have had some warning that the paper had been delivered but they couldn't have a dog because Connie was allergic to most pet hair. So instead, the first he knew was when he saw Connie walking down the hallway from the kitchen. He was standing in the doorway of the living room about to get himself a coffee when he saw her. Sauntering. Towards the *Nottingham Today*. Which lay like a bright hot burning beacon of his guilt on the mat. Screaming out the horror he was inflicting in the name of justice for their daughter. Justice she would never understand. It was this guilt and this knowledge that she wouldn't understand and that she would be put through so much more pain that made him rush past her.

Isaac was panicked. Blinded by fear, his vision tunnelled and dark. The brightness of the *Today* searing into his brain and leaving no room for conscious thought, nothing but getting hold of it and saving her from its cruelty. Because the *Today* was cruel. Its portrayal so far had been cruel and unfair. It had been incorrect and it had been nonfactual.

Connie was the love of his life. He had chosen to spend his living breathing life with her and they had produced a miracle together. How could anyone ever think he could hurt her? And yet here she was, on the floor, leaning against the hallway wall with her hand on her head, asking him what an earth he was doing. There was blood on her hand when she pulled it away from her head. She looked at it before she spoke to him again.

'I was fetching you the paper with your coffee, Isaac.'

79

His head screamed like a flock of angry birds in the air, fighting over the smallest of food scraps. How could this have happened? He looked down at his fragile and shaken wife, now pale with shock. He crouched down to her, trying to hold back the noise in his head and held out his hand to her.

'Connie, let me help you.'

A look of confusion crossed her face. She dropped her hand from her head then looked away from him and put her hand back up to the small wound that was bleeding like a bloody great gash had opened up across her skull.

Isaac didn't know what was happening. How had he got to the place where he had injured his wife, when all he had been doing was trying to protect her?

Eventually she was settled with a strong stewed tea on the sofa in the living room. She insisted she didn't need to see a doctor, that she knew what signs to look out for if she had a head injury but that he was overreacting and there was nothing wrong with her. She wasn't feeling sick, or dizzy, she only a slight headache and would keep an eye on it. It was, Connie explained to him in a tone she reserved for talking to a young child, a small bump, and nothing serious. Bumps and bruises happen as part of life. It was the look on her face that made him ache though. She was scolding him for his fussing when she should really have been yelling at him for his behaviour in making her fall to the floor in the way she did. If it wasn't for him rushing at her that way she wouldn't be on the floor and she wouldn't be looking out for the signs of a head injury or scolding him for fretting over her. He would never stop fretting over her.

She was all he had left of Em.

She shooed him away and he was torn between wanting to stay and worry over her more and get back to what he had been rushing towards, the *Nottingham Today*. Isaac turned back and had one last look at her before he left the room and was stung by the look she was giving him. Her eyes were narrowed in on him while her fingers gently tapped on the cup of tea she was holding. He kept walking.

He picked up the *Nottingham Today* from where it still lay on the doormat and took it into the kitchen, sneaking a look at Connie who was drinking her tea and staring out of the window.

Again, it had made the front page. Little else made front-page coverage lately. It was dominating the local news. It was also starting to gain national coverage but all he was interested in was what was happening on a local level. This was the place that had let them down and this was the place that would carry on paying … until those who played fast and loose with the lives of those who trusted in them made their drugs safer, and the community more aware.

Killer Strikes Again

A 24-year-old man was found collapsed in the street and pronounced dead at the scene, with no obvious signs of injury. An incident that mirrors that of jogger, Angela Evans of Toton.

Damerae Rabasca was with his girlfriend at the time of his death. She is eight months pregnant with his child and does not want to be named. She describes his death as violent and sudden.

Mr Rabasca is the fourth victim of the killer who is using poison to murder his victims.

In a recent development, Nottinghamshire Police have released a new media appeal asking for any witnesses who may know who the offender is and are offering a reward for

any information that leads to his arrest.

Detective Inspector Hannah Robbins from East Midland's Special Operations Unit – Major Crime, based in Nottingham said, 'At the moment, we don't have much detail on where Mr Rabasca could have obtained the products he ingested, or where he has been the last few days, it is possible that someone could help us with those enquiries and help us build a larger picture of his last moments and in the process, narrow down where the poison could be filtered into the public domain.

'If anybody has any information that they believe could help our enquiries then please contact police.'

They are also advising caution when buying, using, cooking and eating foodstuffs, telling the public to check all seals and labels, lids and tops to make sure they are secure, but warning against panic. You can contact the tip-line number printed below.

He slammed the newspaper down on the table and looked up at the door. The space there was empty. He was glad Connie wasn't standing there. How could he explain his anger? His fury. His utter contempt for multiple organisations that were letting people down and letting people die. How could they stand by and watch this unfold and simply do nothing when they all had it in their power to do more? To stop it. All it needed was an admission of guilt and their culpability would come to an end.

Right now, however, he was failing. He was obviously not working on his plan hard enough. He was failing Em and it could be argued that he was now failing her more than they ever did. Unless he could get things back on track, he had been nothing but a failure for his daughter.

80

Bridgette York loved her new sandals. They had wide pink flowers on the bar that ran across her foot and in the centre of them were the cutest white buttons with smiley faces on. As she walked, she watched her feet. She watched the flowers. To make sure they were still smiling. She'd only got them yesterday so they had that lovely smell about them as well, but without bending down close to them she couldn't smell it and she had hold of her mum's hand right now. It did mean she could walk and keep looking at her flowers without bumping into things. Well, not too many things anyway. Occasionally she heard her mum tut as she hit her side on a shelf as they rounded the corner in the shop. Her mum was trying to do some shopping but she was also trying to stop Bridgette from walking into anything and Bridgette knew that the tuts she heard were not aimed at her, how could they be, she was protected by smiley-faced sandals. Her mum was tutting at herself because she had been unable to stop Bridgette from bumping herself again. Never mind. Bridgette grinned down at her beautiful, sunny, smiley sandals.

She felt her arm twitch as she was manoeuvred around the end of another line of shelves but she didn't look up, she knew her mum was keeping her on the right track. And then Bridgette bumped right into her mum. Right into the back of her legs. With no warning. When she'd stopped to choose shopping from the shelves Bridgette had been guided to a stop in front of the shelf but this time her mum stopped abruptly in the centre of the aisle and Bridgette had walked into her.

'Stay behind me, Bridgette.'

She looked up from her sandals.

She couldn't see anything because her mum's legs were in the way so she shifted a little to the side and looked in the same direction as her mum.

'Bridgette, I said stay behind me.' She was pushed back behind her mum's legs. Mum had never been that rough before. Bridgette twisted her neck so she could look around instead.

In front of them was a group of people. She could only count to ten and Bridgette thought there were less than that but the people were moving about, shouting, so she didn't know if she was counting right or not. They were angry and there was a woman in the shop uniform who was trying to talk but they weren't letting her, they were shouting at her so loudly.

Her mum stepped backwards one step and nearly stood on her sandals. Her hand went tighter around hers and Bridgette started to feel a bit strange. She didn't know what was happening or why her mum was acting weird. She looked down at the smiley flowers again.

There was a crashing sound and the voices grew louder. Suddenly her mum let go of the shopping trolley and Bridgette was snatched up from the floor and they were running back the way they had just come. Past the fridges and freezers which made Bridgette cold. Little bumps grew on her arms and they grew on her legs because she had a dress on. She was cold even though it was warm outside. The sun was shining and her flower sandals could look up to the sun and smile.

She watched over her mum's shoulder as the shop whizzed past, cold and blurry, her mum's handbag bouncing against her bare legs as her mum ran towards the doors. She could still hear the shouting, she could see people running towards the voices as her mum was running away from them.

'We'll be in the car in a few seconds, sweetheart.'

It was the last thing Bridgette York heard her mum say.

She never saw the car barrelling through the store's sheer glass window and barely had time to register the sound of shattering glass and screaming, panicking people – before her world went silent and there were no more flowers smiling for Bridgette York.

81

It was carnage. There was no other word suitable for what was in front of us. The car had been moved from where it had mown down mother and child, because the fire service had needed to get to the mother to save her. She hadn't died. Her young child wasn't as capable of taking the impact.

The mother's injuries were severe and life threatening. Her status, as defined by the hospital, was currently critical, but her daughter hadn't made it that far. She was pronounced dead at the scene. Her mother had been rushed away, unaware of what she was leaving behind in her unconscious state. The doctors and nursing staff had a difficult job ahead of them, not just with Trisha York's physical needs but with the emotional needs that she would present when she woke from her surgeries.

The Honda Civic had been pulled out of the store window and now stood quietly in a disabled space near the doors.

Shattered glass lay in fragments along the shop floor. Sharp and bloody. A tiny pink sandal sparkling with shards caught up in the leather straps, discarded during the havoc. The early evening sun innocently reflecting rainbows.

The child, four-year-old Bridgette York, still lay in situ amongst the twinkling pieces of glass.

Damaged.

Rebecca Bradley

Not pretty or sparkling.

Her face; smashed and bloody.

Her legs bent out of shape.

Bone protruded from her arm, splintered and torn.

Blood congealed in her hair. Matted to her head.

We worked quietly and we worked quickly. To get Bridgette York out of here as soon as we could.

This was the work of our poison killer. This time, he hadn't used poison, but his reach was even more deadly than before – because this time he had managed to put the fear of God into others to now do his bidding.

82

Nottingham Today – online article

Four-Year-Old Girl Killed By Car In Supermarket

A four-year-old child was killed and her mother was seriously injured when a Honda Civic ploughed through the window of Tesco supermarket on Carlton Hill.

Trisha York and her daughter Bridgette were in the store when a disturbance flared up in one of the aisles. One witness states that on seeing the fracas, Trisha picked up her daughter, dropped her shopping and headed for the exit. As the argument in the store became more violent, Trisha was seen by several people to start running with Bridgette in her arms.

One witness said, 'She looked horrified at what she saw, she grabbed that little girl off the ground so quick. I could see what she wanted to do, she wanted to get out of there. Protect that little one.'

Staff at the local Tesco store in Carlton Hill say people were running in all directions, both away from and towards the main area of the chaos.

Shelf stacker Glen Moore said, 'It was scary. It started with one woman asking how she would know which items were safe to eat and soon everyone was getting involved and people got frightened and then angry and it blew up.'

It is reported that as Trisha and Bridgette York were about to reach the exit of the Tesco store, a car was driven into the large shop window, hitting the mother and child head on.

Shop assistant Liz Butler said, 'This guy ran out of the store, he was furious, I'd seen him in the middle of the row over which items were safe to eat, then the next time I saw him he was stumbling out of the car that had smashed through the window. He looked shocked when he saw that little girl and her mum. I don't think he was aiming to

hurt anyone. He was angry at the food situation.'

Bridgette was announced dead at the scene and Trisha is in a critical but stable condition after fire crews cut her out from under the wreckage of the car. We have been informed that she is currently unaware of the death of her daughter but family are at the hospital with her.

Trisha York is married to husband Ian and they have a son, Edward. Extended family are supporting them at this time.

The supermarket has issued a brief statement saying they are extremely saddened and sorry for the loss of Bridgette's life and the injury to Trisha York yesterday and regret that it occurred at their store, offering their deepest *condolences to the York family.*

In relation to the fact that customers are concerned about products available in stores, the supermarket state that their products are all safe but to take precautions they *are no longer selling off discounted goods, to prevent any tampering.*

The driver fled from the scene on foot and was later arrested at his home address by police. David Burnett is still in police custody.

83

The heat of the day slid away, leaving the night with a sharp chill. Outside, the car park was close to empty, with only a single marked police car and four staff vehicles standing in the car park. The car that had come through the window had been taken away on the back of a low-loader by the police.

In the far right corner, over the meat counter, a bulb flickered continually. No one cared enough to notice, let alone change it.

Liam Scott was the store manager and he had never known a day like it.

He was considering resigning. His mum had always wanted more for him. She wanted him to attend college or university but he had insisted on leaving school as soon as he could and had taken the first job that he'd been offered. In his defence, he had been able to progress through the company and work up to the position of manager, but he would never have imagined that managing a store would leave him in a store at night, virtually alone, after a child had been murdered while he had been on duty.

He used to think the idea of being so close to a real life crime scene was thrilling but he now knew otherwise. There was nothing thrilling about seeing a young child dead in your store.

Bridgette's mum had wailed like a broken animal when the car hit. Unable to move her legs, pinned beneath one of the wheels, her screams pierced the air around her, with the only word escaping being the name of her daughter. But Bridgette was silent. Bridgette couldn't hear her mum's screams and eventually the screams had slipped away as unconsciousness took her.

All those customers that had taken their phones out, minutes after they had apparently got over their shock, sickened Liam. There was no social value in death. In murder. In this whole craziness that was overtaking the city. His mum was right. He should have applied himself more. Dreamed higher. Now was the time to do that. This was the push he needed. When he finished up here he was going to do something about his situation.

He handed steaming mugs of coffee to the two cops guarding the scene at the front of the store, then stepped away. He was anxious around the uniforms but there was only him and three other staff left in store, and it was creepy being here when it was so quiet, so he stayed close to them.

He could apply for jobs in the city, in offices where nothing happened. He could study online and progress things from there. He had the brains. This wasn't what he wanted.

Tim from the bakery walked towards him. A huge grin on his face.

'So, what're the odds our store would be affected by all this then, Liam?'

He sighed. Everyone loved a drama. 'I don't know, Tim. Extreme, I imagine.' He straightened the boxes of cereals on the shelves in front of him.

'Oh you bet they were, but look at us now.' Liam didn't think it possible but Tim's face split into a wider grin.

'Right in the thick of it aren't we?' Tim's hands were firmly in his pockets, no inclination to do any work.

'I suppose we are.'

'Something to go home and talk about tomorrow, eh?'

'I'll be sleeping tomorrow, Tim.'

'Oh, yeah, course. But, after that.'

Liam had stopped listening. He could see a group of about half a dozen youths approaching the two police officers at the front of the store. They were dressed in dark nondescript clothing; jeans and dark hoodies, and it looked as though they were all carrying things in their hands. Their shoulders were bunched up, their elbows bent, and they looked ready for trouble. Liam felt a prickle of fear run down his spine.

'So, what do you think?' Tim was still talking.

'What?'

'About the girls? Are you not listening? They'll be interested in what we have to say. I might get myself a decent date out of this.' He rubbed his hands together.

Liam's stomach rolled over.

Voices were raised and easily heard through the broken pane at the front of the store. The group were angry with the police. The police called for back-up using their radios.

There was a smash as one of the group threw what looked like a brick through another of the store's windows.

Tim stopped blathering and looked to where the sound had come from.

The group were shouting, he could hear words about murderers, arms were being waved for added emphasis and the crowd in front of the officers grew.

Things were getting frantic.

Both officers turned, threw their mugs on the ground. One looked Liam in the eye and shouted at him to get further back inside.

He didn't need telling twice. He grabbed Tim by his sleeve and pulled him towards the back of the store. Tim was rooted to the spot.

'Tim!' he shouted in his face without letting go of his sleeve. He didn't like the sound of the group that were outside. They were angry and it was obviously targeted at the supermarket. As far as Liam could see, he was affiliated with the supermarket and he didn't want to hang around to see how this group would deal with that fact. He pulled on the sleeve again. This time, Tim finally moved.

Liam heard the dulled whirl of the double doors sliding open and another smash. Glass shattering. Then another. There was a wine display at the front of the store; this was obviously being hit by something.

Liam paused for the briefest of moments as it struck him what was happening. He was about to be caught in the middle of a riot where the people outnumbered the police. The store was being entered. Emotion driving actions couldn't be contained. They weren't safe. As that moment froze in his mind it dulled and slowed, dragging his dark thoughts in like a black hole. The smashing and shouting and screaming were filling his head. If he and the other members of staff were caught by this group, they'd be trashed like the produce in the rest of the supermarket.

Tim no longer needed to be persuaded to run. He was the hundred-metre sprint champion three years running at school. Though the hundred-metre sprint was only a short distance and nowhere near as long as the length of the store. The back of the store was where the stock came in and the loading bay doors were. He'd forgotten Liam had been tugging at him to move. His instinct took over. But he could hear him panting behind him. Ragged and strong.

Tim was channelling that feeling of having competitors at his heels, waiting for him to let up, slow down, fall, and it pushed him on and forward. And instead of fellow runners at his heels, he had attackers. People who wanted to do him harm.

He wasn't going to look back to see how close they were. He'd seen them when they threw the brick through the window and he wasn't going to hang around to see how quick they moved. He'd heard stories about out of control mobs. Panic-driven flash mobs who lost all identity of the person they usually were and became part of a pack.

Hunted in a pack.

Tim's heart hammered in his chest, so hard that he thought it might break right through his rib cage. It slammed hard. His vision was shrinking. His breath ragged.

He kept running.

Down the aisle.

Through the door, down the corridor.

Into the huge, cool storeroom.

He was nearly out and free.

The loading bay doors were closed.

Tim looked around him. Panic sucked the air right out of him. His breath was coming fast and uneven. He felt as though he had run twelve one-hundred-metre sprints, one after the other. How the hell did you open the bay doors? He was hot and his brain was slowing. He couldn't think.

Liam caught up with him and bent double, panting.

'Kirsty and Don are behind me. I saw them running across the back of the store from the clothing area.'

Yeah, but that didn't solve the problem in front of them.

'How do we open the doors, Liam?'

'There's a large red button at the side of the door. You open them; I'll go and see what's happened to Kirsty and Don.' Liam ran off in the direction he had come from. Into the store. Towards the oncoming mob.

Great. As soon as the doors opened he would be out of there, not waiting around to be someone's football.

He felt a little safer in here and walked down the concrete ramp towards the huge steel doors, trying to get his breath back. It was harder than he imagined. Sucking in air seemed to be a struggle and his chest hurt. But he was safe now. As long as he could get the doors open, he was out of there.

84

The room was silent. I seated myself on the corner of Aaron's desk. Martin had wheeled his chair over to us, Ross stayed at his own desk with his head down and a couple of the other staff obviously listening in. It was shocking that it had come to this. We were losing control of the situation – not just this incident, but also the situation as a whole. The bigger picture. The digoxin killer. This was his doing. He may not have started this incident at the supermarket, or this may or may not have been his intention, but he bloody well was behind it, and sitting here, listening in on the airwave, hearing colleagues relaying information from the ground back to the control room was frustrating and a little bit frightening. I didn't doubt any one of the people in this room would say they were frightened by what was happening, by what had happened so far. They'd be on the wrong side of the blue line not to be. This was something we hadn't seen before and it was natural to have a fear of the unknown.

The air crackled and fizzed with the sound of breathless cops trying to relay messages of activity on the ground to the control room. It made trying to keep up a difficult affair. I had to tune myself into the sounds, something I hadn't used to such an extent for a while now. There was a time I could be wearing my radio and tune it out into the background as I talked to witnesses, victims or just fellow cops but automatically pick up my own call-sign or any incident of note. Listening to the police radio was like tuning into another piece of yourself. Once you find the right channel, you're all set; right now I was still finding that channel and only picking up some of the words that were coming through.

They were rushed. With only two cops guarding the scene and an unexpected angry mob turning up they had their hands full. Yes, they were guarding the scene and they had to protect themselves, but it seemed they had a mob to deal with outside the supermarket and also a group that were advancing inside the store, so now the most immediate issue was saving life and limb, the innocent lives of the supermarket staff.

Enough people had died.

As well as the voices of the two cops there were rushed updates from colleagues speeding to their aid with two-tones providing a soundtrack over the whole incident.

I could also hear the angry horde chanting, shouting and the sound of missiles landing at their destinations.

I imagined the destruction being caused.

'How long ...' panting, crackling, '... back-up?'

The calm voice of the control room operator responded, 'three minutes out.' But I knew the calm was a working façade. Like us he would be glued to his screen, watching for the caller ID to pop up, his earpiece, waiting for more. To know everyone was safe. His heart in his throat, swallowing hard to clear it so he could work and support his colleagues.

'CS spray disseminated ... Need to stop them all going into the store.' Martin blew out a deep breath. Still we didn't move.

'Charlie Tango two one to NH.' NH being Nottinghamshire's control room call sign.

It was quieter now, less crowd shouting coming through, but a definite sole voice screaming out. The recipient of the CS I imagined. Its effects short-term but effective.

'Go head, Charlie Tango two one.'

'We have one under arrest and the staff have all made it out safely through the rear loading doors. Repeat, all staff are safe but this crowd are angry so we'd appreciate that back-up as soon as.'

'Good to know, Charlie Tango two one. Back-up should be with you shortly.'

I stood up from the desk, the corner having dug a deep wedge into my thigh. I was stiff and uncomfortable but I was relieved that the officers and supermarket staff were safe.

'I'll put the kettle on. Make us all a cuppa. Then we've got work to do.'

'Charlie Tango two one to NH. The offenders are back and there are more of them. We need that back-up and we need it now.'

85

I stopped moving and listened. My hearing tuned in only to the sound of the radio and nothing else.

'NH, the supermarket staff are in the police vehicle. There is nowhere else safe to put them. There is quite a crowd gathered around the front of the building and more keep coming. We seriously need that back-up. They're loud, leery and definitely looking for trouble. Lots of shouting about killer goods and—'

There was a loud thud that sounded as though it was close to the mic of the user. I moved back to my spot on Aaron's desk where the radio was and turned the volume button up. Aaron flinched. The space around his desk felt claustrophobic as the rest of the team closed in to listen to unfolding events. Martin and Ross had both pulled their chairs up either side of Aaron, and a few others were gathered behind them, while others spanned out from the sides. Ross's face was a closed mask. Cold and hard.

Aaron was ramrod straight and was making sure his tie was on properly and evenly. He looked uncomfortable, but I knew we were crowding him.

'Charlie Tango two one?'

'They're throwing bricks. Requesting PSU.'

The Police Support Unit would be better placed to deal with public order of this magnitude. I felt impotent.

'NH to Charlie Tango two one?'

There was silence in return. And silence in the incident room.

The silence dragged out for what seemed like an eternity but what must have realistically only been a couple of minutes. In that time the control room kept trying to make contact with the officers at the supermarket. A couple of marked cars and PSU vans were barrelling their way towards the two officers needing assistance. Two-tones punctured the air as the assisting officers updated control as they sped through the night to support their colleagues and protect the members of the public who were trapped inside a police vehicle, which didn't seem to be a very safe place to be right now.

'Charlie Tango two one to NH.'

'Thank fuck,' said Ross.

'Go ahead, Charlie Tango two one.'

'There's been a lot of damage; bricks are being thrown at the vehicle the supermarket staff are in. It's bedlam here. Back-up is pulling in now. I don't know if it'll be enough. We need to get these members of the public out of here urgently.'

'There are more units on the way to you, Charlie Tango two one.'

There was a loud roar, then the sound of smashing glass then the radio went silent again.

The mic opened up with the PSU van saying they were about a minute out. But a lot could happen in a minute.

All was quiet, broken only with the occasional whispered comment. I was itching to get out and help but that was the job for the uniform staff; our job was to work the murder case behind it all because that was what would stop this escalation of events. Not that we were doing that right now. Now we wanted to make sure our colleagues were safe. And finding out that information meant sitting here listening to the police radio.

It crackled to life with a start after several minutes of deathly silence.

'getting bottles and bricks thrown ...'

'Papa Sierra Uniform zero one to NH. Show us at location please.'

The serious back-up was now there. I hoped things would calm down.

'Offenders running.'

'Request dogs and Papa zero eight.' The helicopter.

'Running towards the main road. They're scattering.' Heavy footsteps were falling as the commentary continued. The foot chase was on and a dog officer was requested as well as the helicopter. Officers and supermarket workers were safe. They needed to round up the ringleaders of the night and try to contain the public panic.

86

Papa zero eight and the dogs were unable to round up any of the offenders of the supermarket incident. They must have had vehicles close by that we didn't know about and had no way of tracking. It had been a long drawn-out affair attempting to trace the group but in the end everyone had had to walk away.

The man responsible for driving the car that had mowed into the mother and child, killing the child, was still in custody at the Bridewell. A remand application was currently being worked on, ready for the morning courts.

And I had six missed calls from Youens. I went to my office and called him back. It was a tense and uncomfortable conversation. He was obviously unhappy about the public order events he now had to police on his area and he knew full well that they were connected to my case. He wanted to know how it was going and what we were going to do. To hear that we were still working on the digoxin case and that it was slow going was not what he wanted to hear, at all. The fact that I was a couple of ranks below him made it so much easier for him to get that point across in a much firmer manner than he might otherwise have had if I was the same rank as him. I bit my lip. There was nothing I could do. And that was the point. Not that there was nothing I could do about Youens giving me grief, but that there was nothing I could do about this case. The offender was calling all the shots until we got a good lead.

The headline for the *Today* was an extension on the online article and was highly emotive and was bound to be pulling in readers for the paper.

Four-Year-Old Killed In Supermarket Rage Car Incident

I finished reading the article.

Following the incident, a crowd gathered outside during the hours it was closed and threw a couple of bricks through the doors and within the store after gaining partial access. There was no loss of life or injury. The extent of the damage has yet to be assessed. No offenders were arrested during this incident. One man is currently in custody for the murder and attempted murder of the York family earlier in the day

I put the newspaper down and leaned back in my chair. The byline was Ethan Gale. I had been avoiding Ethan since that night. It had been a mistake, great as it was, but we were never going to make a relationship work so having great sex with him and tangling my emotions up into a mess that I was unable to sort through was going to do neither of us any favours.

Though the headline grabbed your attention, the article was a straightforward piece of reporting of the incidents yesterday. No over-dramatising of events or criticism of the police, which made a change, but there was a lot to report and there probably wasn't that much room for conjecture in it. No matter how much I hoped that the news reports would lessen over coming days, I wasn't banking on it. We had our hands full.

I'd had a few hours' sleep and had been back in the office at six-thirty a.m., only popping out for a few minutes to grab the paper to see what the situation was. The morning briefing had gone smoothly enough. I'd tasked Evie with keeping an eye on social media as well as the other actions she was working on. Ross was still keeping a tight rein on exhibits, but as we didn't have any searches ongoing he was also freed up to help out with the vast digoxin enquiries. Claire was preparing another media statement in light of yesterday's incidents. Catherine wanted to try and calm the public. She had been involved in a lengthy conversation with Chief Superintendent Youens last night after he'd yelled at me for a while and was in agreement with him that we needed to address the issue head on. There were even discussions about having a television appeal for calm in the wake of the murder. Claire had the dubious pleasure of being holed away with Catherine in her office hashing that one out with her; then they would come back to me to let me know what the best approach was. I didn't mind having this taken out of my hands. Claire knew what she was doing in terms of working with the media, and if it all went pear-shaped on TV then I was more than happy for it to be Catherine who had made that decision. I wanted to be boots on the ground, not worrying about the right thing to say to the baying media – even though sometimes an investigation could be led entirely by the media. That didn't sit well with me. Their job was to report facts, events that had occurred, not indulge in conjecture or to rile up the public into a frenzy and cause an outpouring of emotion and feeling that couldn't be contained within a page any longer. That's how I felt about it, anyway. If I had the same conversation with Ethan, I'm sure I would get a different point of view.

I browsed down the list of emails in my inbox looking for any of significance among the 100 plus that were still sitting there, unopened. Scanning email headers, I saw there were several in from CSU as more results came back from seized items that had been examined. The same results were coming in. The poison used was digoxin, which matched what had been found on the PM. I forwarded the emails on to Aaron who would create actions to contact the families so we could identify where food items had been purchased. Because our earlier enquiries hadn't proved fruitful I suggested we keep going follow this one to the end.

We were progressing, but at the same time we were getting nowhere. It was frustrating. And it was this loop of frustration that was going round in my head when Evie walked in with a worried look on her face. As per usual she was carrying her laptop under her arm, which meant she was going to show me something. However, whether I understood what Evie showed me on the computer was debatable as she was a genius with technology.

'What is it?'

She pulled up a chair and opened the lid of her portable workstation. 'We have a problem.'

'Really? I hadn't noticed.'

'Okay. We have another problem.'

'Can it wait? The problem we're dealing with already is giving us enough trouble.' I gave her my most hopeful look.

'If you think the disorder from last night being spread about on Facebook can wait?'

I looked at her. 'Well, it's kind of expected isn't it? In today's age?'

She tapped at her keyboard, 'I don't just mean the obvious chatter about it, which of course is what started it, but it's growing, Hannah. It's spreading – and rapidly. So much so, it has its own hashtag.'

'Wonderful. And what is that?' All I had so far were questions.

She spun the screen around to show me. There was a Facebook screen of comments under the hashtag #NottsCopsAreShit. Bloody wonderful and imaginative as it was. I read down some of the comments and it didn't take many of them to get the gist of what was happening.

Notts Neil; Good on em for last nights trouble. #NottsCopsAreShit and deserve the fuckin runaround.

Paul Treycott; Fucking #NottsCopsAreShit alright. They should hav bin battered with those bricks.

Fiona MacKay; #NottsCopsAreShit so let's fuck em.

Dean Mallard; #NottsCopsAreShit so let's give em some shit alright!

Evie was right, this didn't look good. Not good at all.

I looked at her. 'How long, Evie?'

'They've been rumbling since it happened last night, but it's building momentum. The more it's posted, the more people are seeing it and the more it's posted again. An ever-increasing circle.'

'Fucking hell. How did we end up on the tail end of this?'

'I don't know, but we need to be on the final end of it, don't we?'

'We do. Thanks, Evie. Can you keep an eye on it and also on Twitter please? I know they do hashtags a hell of a lot more on there and if it gets on there then, well, I don't even want to think about it.'

She nodded and closed her laptop.

'And for now, I'd better update Youens. He's going to be one happy chap.'

'Rather you than me. I've heard he's going through a tough divorce and it's not one he wanted.'

'Ah. That explains a bit more then. I'll try and tread a bit lighter, no matter what he throws at me.'

'You, tread lightly? I've seen you on a night out, don't forget.'

And with that, Evie disappeared out the door.

87

The day went from the clichéd bad to worse. I had a meeting with Catherine so she could update the chief constable, then I went out to see Youens.

As I was shown into his office, I saw the photograph of his family on his desk. He was sitting in front of the Major Oak in Sherwood Forest, the large oak tree that folklore said that Robin Hood and his Merry Men used to hide out in. He had his wife at his side, with two young boys behind them, about eight and ten years of age, pulling faces. It was a photograph I had seen on my many visits to his office, but it would have been background noise. Not visible, even though seen. But now I saw it properly for the first time and it held a different meaning than many other family photographs on desks. The whole image in front of me was of a man clinging to something he no longer had and while he was trying to throw himself into his job, his division was slipping into disarray around him as well. It was no wonder that he was stern and curt when all he wanted was a part of his life to run as it should. I knew cops who threw themselves into work to numb the pain of disintegrating home lives and it worked to a degree, but not if work was falling in on itself, as Youens' was. I'd make an effort today. I'd do what I could to make this man's job as easy as I possible, though in the circumstances, we had our work cut out for us.

'Good morning, Hannah, can I get you anything to drink?'

I knew from previous visits that Youens didn't have green tea. 'A black coffee would be good, thanks.'

He sighed. Something I would have previously taken as a sign of annoyance at what I'd said, but now I looked more closely at him I could see it was tiredness. He was tired. Lines ran from the corners of his eyes and dark shadows underlined them.

He walked to his door, stuck his head outside and spoke to his personal assistant. When he walked back into his office he indicated we should sit on the chairs away from his desk.

'What can you tell me?' he asked.

This time I was more than happy to go over it all with him. Strange how perceptions of people warp our interactions with them. He was already well aware of the incident at the supermarket and I updated him on the escalating threat we were facing with the online mob that was building momentum. And where I would have previously taken comments and sighs as sounds of annoyance, I saw frustration and, what? Fatigue, in a job that was tiring him? When his family was crumbling?

My meeting with Youens was one of the better ones we'd had. We'd agreed that having a more visible presence was a way forward. It would help reassure the people who were frightened by what was happening and it would also help us get a heads up before, rather than after, an incident happened.

I was typing up my notes when Aaron walked into the office.

'Hey. You'll be surprised to hear I had a good meeting with Youens.'

He didn't answer me so I looked up from my keyboard. 'What's wrong now?'

'Evie came to see me while you were out.'

'Shit.'

'Yep.'

'How bad?'

'It's bad, Hannah. This needs to go all the way up.'

'Tell me.'

'There's a Twitter hashtag that's trending, whatever that means, Notts cops are shit? And along with the hashtag, trouble is being stirred up against us. People are saying that cops can't protect people and are arresting everyone but the killer.'

'Christ, Aaron.' I rubbed at my arm where an ache was starting up.

'Ross has also found a couple of low-key public order jobs on the box. A couple of shops have had items thrown around and one has had its windows smashed in. Tie them together and we have the start of a real problem, I'm told.' He pulled his tie tighter. 'I really don't understand what trending hashtags are or how relevant they are to this.'

'They're pretty damn relevant if they're trending and they're being used by Notts residents.' I dug the pad of my thumb deep into the scar tissue on my arm and kneaded it.

'Oh yeah, another one is,' he stopped and looked at the notebook in his hand, '"The everyday people of the county are left at the mercy of the poison killer because hashtag Notts cops are shit".'

88

It had been a long day and there were still many hours in front of us. Cops were out there taking the brunt of the public's anger on our lack of progress. We needed to find this killer – and fast. Cop cars had had bricks and bottles thrown at them. Cops themselves had been targeted with missiles and force support had been activated; vans with protective bars over the windshield and specialist equipment for the staff. They were to attend any and all public order incidents. There was full on Gold, Silver and Bronze command structure set up, which is a single command structure, for incidents such as this, where officers knew who was in charge, rather than having too many cooks and all that. One officer of a high rank at Gold and was in overall charge, another officer of reasonable rank was Silver and was tactical and the Bronze officer implemented it all, deciding where the staff were needed to make it all work.

There were local news stations buzzing around with cameras out on the streets.

I needed a break; I was too tense up here in the incident room and my office was crackling with the pressure. There was a deep dark throbbing in my scar. I picked up the blister pack of pain medication that I kept stashed in my top drawer and took a walk down the stairs to the Ladies on the floor below. It might not be more private, but at least I wouldn't be interrupted by any of my own staff.

It was quieter downstairs as some of the staff had left for the day, though there were a lot more still here than usual because of the extra pressure on resources. People had been asked to stay on. I went into the Ladies and was pleased to see it empty. I leaned my back against the wall and took a deep breath, pressing the back of my skull against the firm concrete wall. Breathing in the silence, the quiet that my body felt it hadn't been able to get near for so long. This job had been running along like rapids down a rocky river bed and it felt as though we were hurtling towards something dark. That something was waiting for us as we lurched headlong with little direction, pulled by the current of events.

I grabbed the top of my arm fully with my opposite hand and squeezed tightly. The deep throbbing inside felt like a ticking time bomb. Like a warning signal. It felt connected to everything that was happening. The more events spiralled, the more my arm throbbed. I squeezed again and then took the pills I had in my pocket, washing them down with water from the tap. Allowing the cold stream to flow over my face as I bent over the sink. The cool rush relaxing my muscles.

I couldn't stay down here in the Ladies forever. I had a job to do. I had to help Ross regain his presence of mind and I simply had to keep going.

I pulled the door to the corridor open and saw people running. I stood for a brief moment and wondered if there was another public order offence happening – or another murder. Something to get everyone running to their desks, or to phones, or out of the building. But as I stood there I heard ... no, I *smelled* it.

Fire.

The front of the building was on fire.

89

It was the smell that hit me first. A deep, dark, nasty smell that caught in the back of my throat. I coughed, clearing it from where it clung like a vice with teeth. Sharp and nasty.

Then the drama unfolded like a slow motion reel as I watched people running from the front end of the building with wide panicked eyes. And others running towards it. The ones running away were front counter and other staff that came in to do a nine to five job behind a desk, not risk life and limb while they were at it.

The sound was the next thing to hit me. A rushing, like wind, with a crackle inside of it. All with a building momentum. Taking on a life of its own. Raised shouts over the top of it. Screams and instructions mingled together.

The slow motion reel slowed further as I took in the sound, sight and smell before me and it hit me at maximum volume. All of it.

I ran out of the Ladies, into the corridor. The heat punched me full in the face. It felt as though someone had jammed the heating up in the middle of summer. Screaming assaulted my ears and my nose and throat constricted as the acrid particles from the smoke grabbed hold and clung on, smothering. I coughed again. Hard. Bending over double trying to clear my airway so I could move and help.

Quickly I turned towards the front of the building to see what had happened. It was roaring. Bright orange flames danced, licking their way up the walls towards the ceiling. Searching their way across by means of pictures and posters, finding their next meal to consume and feast on. Some cops had fire extinguishers but they were all but useless.

'Fuck.'

I turned around. 'Check the offices as you move backwards. Make sure we don't leave anyone behind.'

'Okay.' The young officer opened the door to our right and went in, bellowing. As he did I heard something else. I looked back at the fire. Then heard it again. Someone was shouting from the other side of the fire.

90

I looked back but the officer who was just here had gone, and was now sweeping the offices looking for people left in this corridor. He moved fast. Through the roar of the fire, the squeal of the alarm and the air gushing out of the extinguishers being used by the cops next to me, I could hear faint shouts.

I tapped the two guys on their shoulders, which were pulled up tight and tense. Their shirts damp. One was only young, his face straining with concentration. The other was older, gut fighting with his waistband, his hair all but gone. I saw recognition of my rank when they looked at me but their focus was on the flames and the heat that was engulfing our station.

Leaning in close, I yelled, 'I can hear shouting.' Indicating with my arms in front of us, 'Through the fire.'

Their eyes widened, then their grips tightened on the red canisters in their hands.

I looked around for another fire extinguisher but there wasn't one. They were being used.

And they were now empty.

The two cops turned to me. We were moving back as the flames pushed forward, the corridor not much wider than my arm span. 'Go,' I shouted. 'Make sure people are getting out further back.'

'But Ma'am?'

He meant the people on the other side.

'Go. Help others get out. Now.'

This was a big station.

They dropped the empty shells with a clatter and ran.

I stood. I listened.

What the hell?

I was further away now. Pushed back by the fire. I could hear … I didn't know what I could hear any more. The sound of the fire and the building creaking. The screaming of the fire alarm and the noise all crashing inside my head.

The heat was stifling me. But there were people, cops, and civilian staff, trapped on the other side.

Suddenly, it seemed to jump forward, towards me. The heat a solid brick wall and the flames were an angry barricade. I turned to run but hadn't realised how far back I'd been pushed. I was now at the end of the corridor where the stairs were. I crashed straight into the corner of the wall, my head and upper arm slamming directly into the sharp corner.

Pain lit up my synapses. I stumbled back.

The heat lapped at my back.

My arm throbbed deep and my brain slowed.

Vision became narrowed, tunnelled. Greying at the sides.

I sucked in air. Gasping for it to fill my lungs, to fill my head.

Grabbing hold of my arm, I forced my feet forward, towards the stairs. With my good arm I reached forward for the banister, letting go of my arm, letting the pain slice into my brain. I needed to haul myself up the stairs. In the incident room they might not be aware this screeching sound of the fire alarm was the real thing. Often we ignored alarms while someone went to check out whether it was real or not. Now, as I clung to the rail at the bottom of the stairs I realised how stupid this was.

But it didn't matter now. I needed to get them out.

My chest hurt.

The greying in my vision became worse.

I sucked in more air.

I clutched the handrail tighter and pulled with everything I had. One slow step at a time.

My feet felt sluggish, heavy, my head like cotton wool.

I pulled harder on the handrail. I had to keep going. The ringing of the alarm was so loud here in the stairwell. The air was clear in here but my head was not. I figured I was feeling the effects of inhaling too much smoke now as my brain felt fuzzy and sluggish.

Just a few more steps.

My knee slammed hard onto the concrete slab of the step as I struggled to pull myself upwards. The pain shot through and up to my brain, piercing the fog that was threatening to close me down altogether. With the palms of my hands on the cool step, I pushed up. I was nearly there.

As I looked at the door at the top, it opened. Ross walked through, his phone to his ear, chatting animatedly. It took him a second or two before he noticed me pulling myself to my feet. I couldn't catch my breath to shout him.

'Ma'am!' He nearly dropped his phone, hands bouncing in front of him as he juggled to keep hold of it, eventually shoving it in his pocket. A look of shock registered on his face. He moved quickly and was at the side of me in seconds. His arms under mine, lifting me upright.

Now, we had to get everyone out of the building before our killer managed to take the lives of police officers.

91

We stood in the car park, freezing. The heat from the fire made the evening air feel even cooler than it probably was. Several staff members had been taken to the hospital for smoke inhalation. The people I had heard shouting were actually trying to make sure people at the other side were okay and were in fact not in any more danger than I was myself. That wasn't saying much, considering I had nearly given out to the effects of smoke inhalation myself. A couple of ambulances were in attendance, treating people.

There was still a lot of work to be done and what had happened showed that it was more urgent that we got on with the task at hand. The city was losing its mind.

Perched inside the ambulance with the oxygen mask over my face, I tried to process what we knew and watched as another marked car lit up its blues and sped out into the darkening day. A day where people were panicking and were hurting each other, when what they were afraid of was being hurt.

The ambulance dipped slightly as Aaron climbed in and sat opposite me. 'The fire service has it all out now.'

I pulled at the clear plastic covering my nose and mouth. Not holding on properly and letting the elastic that kept it in place pull it back with a slap. 'humph.'

'What was that?'

I pulled again, this time with a firmer grip, sliding it up over my head, depositing the hissing mask at my side. 'Go on.'

'They said, though it looks bad, it's not actually that structurally serious. Part of the front of the building is damaged and there is a lot of smoke and water damage, but the building itself is sound.'

'Great. So, we can go back in?'

'The building's been cleared; I didn't say *you* had.'

'Oh for God's sake. Aaron.'

'They're going to put a couple of uniforms on the front to protect the building for the rest of the evening. Mutual Aid has been requested and is on its way over to help with the public order that's taking over, not just in the city but spreading county wide.'

Mutual Aid was us asking for policing assistance from other forces in the face of this public order outbreak we were dealing with. It was common practice and we provided assistance to our colleagues whenever needed. 'How long before we can get back in?'

'How long before you get cleared by the paramedic?'

'What are you, my father?'

'Are you going to let him know? He's bound to have seen this on the news.'

I sighed. 'Yes, I'll do that now.' I picked up my phone. Aaron was right. Dad would be worried. He would have seen it on the news. I tapped out a brief text. Aaron glared at me. 'What?'

'Not a phone call?'

'We're busy. Have you seen what's happening around us? We need to get a move on, Aaron. If I phone him, we'll get into an awkward and uncomfortable discussion that'll last twice as long as it would need to.'

'So why don't you go see her?'

'You really are channelling him today aren't you?' I snapped. I'd been through enough today without talking with Aaron or my father about my sister.

'I don't understand why you don't talk to your dad about it, Hannah. He's your dad and she's your sister. He wants to talk to you about it, but you avoid it and then you avoid him. Avoiding doesn't help you.'

'It's helping me just fine.'

'It looks like it.'

'Can we get on with the job we have here?'

The paramedic treating me had insisted I be checked out at A&E for the effects of smoke inhalation. Apparently it could be pretty lethal.

It took another couple of hours for the fire service to allow everyone back into the building and by then light really wasn't available. The rest of the staff who had stayed had stomped round in circles to stave off the cold that the dwindling light brought with it as they'd waited to gain entry.

The ambulances had long gone and so, after several hours of being assessed, I'd made it back inside.

The lower part of the station was not in any state to be used. Everything was sodden, and that included computers. Luckily, everything was backed up on the force server, so was still accessible by those computers that were still working.

Once inside, I made a beeline for the kettle. No work was going to get done until I had a warm drink in my hand. Then we had to get our heads together for a few hours before I sent everyone home for a few hours' sleep. The frustration was rattling around inside me, making me twitchy. Not only could we not bring in this offender but he was also setting off a chain reaction within the city. If it wasn't contained soon, it could very easily spread out to the rest of the country, as we had seen happen on past occasions with the London riots being a prime example. Nottingham had felt more than a ripple from those. This was already a disaster but had the potential to scale up and that was a sight I really didn't want to see. This killer was responsible for enough already. We had to stop him and we had to stop him now.

92

Isaac sat at home, watching the television, shocked by what he was seeing. This wasn't what he wanted.

The television flashed images of flickering orange and angry sounds. Newscasters shouting to be heard over crowds who were screaming about police incompetence and loss of life. Missiles thrown indiscriminately. Bottles filled with petrol, with their instantaneous effect, bricks, and empty bottles; shearing glass, shards meant to slice.

He looked at the screen.

Shocked.

Mouth ajar.

Isaac listened to the reporter talking about the growing discord. How social media was a tool in spreading the word and growing the numbers of people out on the streets. She used words he didn't understand. Hashtags. Twitter and Facebook. He barely used his mobile phone for texting and he'd only done that so he could keep in touch with Em. She'd preferred to text rather than talk. It was something she could do when time was short and he would rather have that contact than none at all. She'd been the one to talk him into buying a mobile phone. When she was a child she'd wheedled at him for her own phone because everyone at school was getting them. Although he didn't believe in getting things for that reason, a phone seemed sensible when she sat him down that evening and talked to him about the pros of having it. Of being able to keep in touch with her when she went out. Of having that constant link with her. If he was ever worried, he could phone or text her. Looking back now, Isaac could see she had played on his fears for her safety. Like any typical teenager, she was not infallible to being manipulative but he could see the sense in the argument and had bought her one. After giving in to her, he'd had to buy himself one so he could text her if needed. It was easier than phoning her. Especially when she was younger. When she didn't want to be hanging out on phone calls with her dad all the time. She could throw a text back out at him and she knew he would be happy she was there.

Now, he looked at the screen and didn't understand how technology meant to progress and help lives was causing so much destruction.

'It's his fault you know.' Connie was stood in the doorway behind him. Always behind him.

'What?'

'This. It's his fault.' She walked into the room. Watching events unfold on the television as she moved. The flashing images reflecting in her eyes. More life mirrored in her eyes from the television screen than actually being lived through them, he thought as he studied her.

'Whose fault?'

'The killer who's poisoning everyone. That's where this started. All this. It's his fault.'

Isaac felt those words like a physical body blow.

93

This wasn't what he had wanted. It was supposed to go as planned – but this was as far outside the plan as you could get. The mirroring in Connie's eyes struck him as ironic and he couldn't turn away from her. All the action was on the screen in front of him but it was his petite and withdrawn wife who was mesmerising him now as the carnage that played out on the streets outside seemed to dance on within her.

Connie on the other hand, could not look away from the local news. The ticker tape at the bottom of the screen constantly updated the new events that were occurring, when the reporter could not keep up. Her eyes simply shone. Her mouth set in a grim, angry line. Anger mirroring that of the people on the screen. She was visibly vibrating with it.

He rubbed his jawline. Felt the bristles from his chin against his palm.

Connie stretched her arms out, fists clenched. 'Can he not see what he is doing? Is this what he wants? Complete breakdown.' She sat on the edge of the seat at the side of him and the spell he'd been wrapped in as he watched her was broken.

'Maybe he didn't intend for this to happen. It looks pretty independent to me.'

She railed on him. 'How can you say that? How?' She stood again and turned to face him. Isaac hoped his guilt didn't show. 'Look at the television, will you? Look what is happening. How can you terrify people and not expect them to react?'

'Connie?'

She grabbed the television remote control from the arm of his chair and turned the volume right up. He wanted to cover his ears. The shouting of the people, the shop alarms going off, the reporter shouting above it all to be heard, all in the confines of their small living room. Closed in.

'Look at it. Really look, you foolish old man.' She was yelling at him. More words than they'd spoken in so long and yet they were words of anger.

The sounds were bouncing and oscillating in his head.

'What if Em were still alive? What then? Would you still be so indifferent then, if her safety were in question, would you? What if Em were out there?'

94

It had been an incredibly long shift. I had lost track of how many hours had been spent at the office today but it still wasn't long enough. However, my batteries weren't charged sufficiently and neither were the rest of the team's. I had to let them go and get some rest before they collapsed of exhaustion.

The emotion of the death of Bridgette York and added stress of the subsequent ongoing riots, the risk of their own lives with the firebombing of the station on top of the workload of the case was too much to ask a person to deal with. I'd sent them all home for some much-needed sleep.

I plumped up the cushion on the sofa a couple of times and leaned back on it, my feet up. A glass of red wine sat on the table beside me, already half drunk, along with the painkillers I'd taken for the pounding that was going on within the scar in my arm. It didn't feel healed. There shouldn't still be this much pain. I was lucky that my GP was understanding and prescribed me the pain pills, knowing that it troubled me so much and that I had an occupation that required my full concentration and not the amount of distraction the arm injury gave me. Slamming into the corner of the wall hadn't helped.

The pills weren't taking the edge off the pain, so I was hoping a glass or two of wine was going to help me sleep.

I pulled the newspapers from the table and spread the first one across my knee. It was easy to find Ethan's byline, as his article was front page. Where he always wanted to be.

I reread it. Then reread it again.

Although it was one of his more balanced reports, and he hadn't directly attributed the death of Bridgette to the police, it didn't stop clear of hinting where the blame might lie.

I slugged the rest of the wine and topped up the glass again with the bottle I'd brought into the living room with me and dragged the next newspaper to my knee.

I reread all of Ethan's bylines from the start of the investigation.

How could he do this, knowing I was heading up this case? Knowing what I'd been through. What *we'd* been through as a team.

I knew Catherine had been reading these and she hated every word, as much as I did, and even though she didn't know about our relationship she still held me to account for not closing this case and for allowing this witch-hunt to continue. Catherine was protecting herself. I could almost feel her scrutinising me. Eyeing me up for the kill if this case went any further wrong.

I drank more.

My head felt fuzzy. My brain, now tired.

There were rules on relationships with reporters. It was my responsibility at the time to have informed the job that I was in a relationship with Ethan, but it had imploded last year after the Manders case was closed and Sally was killed under my supervision.

I reread the articles. The article of the opening of Sally's inquest, articles in which the police were made to look like a bunch of Keystone Cops.

Like *I* was a Keystone Cop.

Now, I didn't need to fill in any forms. Not for that one night that we had spent together.

I picked up my phone and looked at Ethan's number. Hovered over the dial icon. That night had been great. He'd been hungry for me, he'd been sensitive. He'd made it feel as though we'd never been apart. Then work had phoned and it had been my wake-up call. How could I manage a relationship with him?

Damn it to hell.

I dropped my mobile down to the floor. I couldn't do it. It was too messed up.

I finished the bottle.

There was no more pain.

Not in my arm.

95

4 weeks ago

There were multiple bottles and strips of medicines. All prescribed in the name of Emma Knight. All with the purpose of keeping her life going. He tipped the crate onto its side and sat on it. A disturbed spider scurried off in the opposite direction, wanting another dark corner. The medicine was laid out in front of him on the old kitchen worktop he had fitted in the garden shed some twenty-odd years ago. It was now worn, battered, scarred and chipped. He rubbed his eye with the heel of his hand, now feeling like the worktop he had fitted with love so many years ago.

So many medicines. Such a waste. At the side of the medicine was Connie's laptop. She wouldn't miss it. She didn't miss anything now. Well anything other than … Nothing was worth a damn. And if she did miss it, she wouldn't think Isaac had it with him in the garden. She always said he had two left thumbs. What that meant, he wasn't sure. No matter how his thumbs worked, his mind was still capable of using an Internet search engine. He opened the lid with his two left thumbs and clicked on the home icon. There was no need for a password in this house. There was love and trust. And what could they do on the laptop anyway?

The machine was slow. They hadn't been bothered about getting a state-of-the-art piece of equipment, just something to keep them connected to Em as she dipped her toes out into the world. To be her safety net, should she need one. And she had. She really had. But this damn laptop couldn't catch her and neither had Isaac.

Or anyone else.

The screen lit and he opened a browser, which was even slower to load. Too far away from the house. Even he knew that, but as long as he could do what he needed to, it didn't matter how much time it took. He had all the time in the world now. He worked methodically, using laptop and notebook and pen to write down what he found out. After each search, the pile of medicines gradually changed from his left side to the right, and when he finally closed the lid on the laptop the entire pile had moved. He had what he wanted. All he had to do now was move it to the allotment – further away from his home, away from Connie.

96

The light that filtered through my eyelids was brighter than I expected. My phone alarm was set for six a.m. I wanted to move but everything felt stiff. And cold. Freezing, in fact. Then I realised I was still on the sofa. That would be why it was so light; I didn't have blackout lining in the living room and the summer sun rises at an ungodly hour. Rolling my neck with as much care as I could, I reached down to the floor where I knew my phone would be. My head; throbbing. My arm; protesting.

I needed some painkillers. And I needed a shower.

Blinking sleep out of my eyes and pushing myself up, I tried to focus through the pain that enveloped my fragile body. The room was bathed in sunlight.

I looked at my phone and checked the time.

'Fuck.'

It was dead. I hadn't charged it and I had no idea what time it was. There wasn't a single clock in my apartment. I lived and breathed by the phone in my pocket.

Fuck, fuck, fuck.

Painkillers and a quick shower helped to wake me up. My phone had also had time to wake. It told me in no uncertain terms that I'd slept in, and I'd done a bloody good job of it. It was nine-thirty a.m. and there were seven missed calls and five messages. I slipped on my shoes, grabbed the in-car charger from the drawer and started to listen to the messages as I made my way into work.

The first one was Aaron, wanting to know where I was.

The second one was Aaron, wanting to know what time I was going to be in.

The third one was Aaron, now sounding annoyed. Catherine was chasing him up, looking for me. He told me the city was in meltdown and I needed to be in work.

The fourth message told me Aaron couldn't cover for me any more and Catherine was on the warpath.

I slammed on my brakes as the car in front hit his for the red lights at the Shakespeare Street/Mansfield Road junction. The driver's eyes glinted at me in the rear-view mirror as by some minor miracle I missed hitting him, though he could easily have driven through the amber light safely because stopping so suddenly really was more of an issue and driving through would not have been the cause of any accident. He couldn't see that I was on my phone, as I had my hands-free on through the speakers in the car. I was safe. He was an idiot.

The next message was from Catherine.

She wanted to know where the hell I was. Was I supposed to be leading this team, this investigation?

Oh, fuck.

The lights changed, and we moved off. Not before the guy in the Prius glared at me again in his mirror and threw his left hand up in the middle of the car, showing his frustration.

The last message on my phone, I'm not sure I wanted to hear. The painkillers didn't seem to be doing their thing. The day had got off to a bad start. I wanted it to start again. Or miss it altogether. I felt like shit. Catherine was on my back. I wasn't getting anywhere with the investigation and the inquest was looming like a huge dark tidal wave, waiting to drown us all in its surging waters.

It was Catherine again, telling me that if I wanted to keep control of this investigation – or any investigation in the future – I needed to get into her office right away.

97

The kettle whistled to announce its arrival at boiling point. Switching the kettle on was the first thing I had done after arriving at work. I'd driven into the rear staff car park, having seen the fire damage done to the front. Two uniform officers were standing by the door, showing we were still here – not to be moved or intimidated.

I tipped the water over the teabag and walked towards the incident room. As I pushed the door open with my spare hand a couple of heads turned to look. Aaron stood, straightened his tie and made a beeline for me, determination in his step, as I walked towards him.

'Where have you been?' His voice was low. If he didn't want this conversation to be heard, then I probably didn't either.

'Hey, look I'm sorry, I know I'm late, I forgot to plug my phone in last night and it died so my alarm didn't go off.'

'And you only just woke up?'

'Yes, I only just woke up.'

'Everyone else managed to make it in.'

'I know.' I pushed the door again, this time moving towards my office.

'Even Ross.' Could I take any more painkillers yet? I doubted it. Bloody hell. This was going to be a long day. I needed to tough it out.

'I'm sorry. Catherine's left me a couple of messages as well. I need to go and see her.' I turned to look at him as we neared my office door. 'How bad is it?'

Aaron touched the knot on his tie but it was straight, even. Nothing for him to do. His hand dropped back to his side. Always so calm, so organised. 'Well, she's far from happy, Hannah. She expected you in early with everyone else. I tried to cover for you for a while but she was like a dog with a bone and wanted to talk to you after events yesterday. Eventually she figured out you weren't even in.'

'Did you help her?' I couldn't help it.

'Help her what?' He looked confused. This irritated me more.

'Figure out I wasn't in.'

'No, why would I?'

'I don't know, Aaron, why would you?' I wanted to put my mug down, to rub both my arms, but we were still standing in the corridor outside my office.

'Hannah, what are you getting at? You're late. I don't understand the rest of it.'

'Don't you, Aaron?' I raised my voice at him. Goddamn it, I wanted this bloody mug out of my hands and I wanted this pain to stop. All of this pain.

'Hannah?'

'It's all about the work with you, Aaron. Just the work. It's been six months since Sally was killed and not once have we sat down and talked about how you feel. Not once have I seen you get stressed in the job. You've breezed through this. I'd say, dispassionately, almost. Very together. Ross has nearly imploded. Martin is living his life differently, spending time with Sharon and their dogs. Christ, Grey is turning into a ghost. Yet you, you, I see no change.' I was aware my voice had gone up several octaves, but right at this moment in time I didn't care. What I cared about was my team and it didn't feel as though Aaron was a part of that team. He stood there, stock still. Voiceless.

'So, what I'm thinking is that you didn't cover for me quite as well as you could have done because this is a job and I wasn't here where I was supposed to be – and why should you cover for me? It's not as though we're a team for you, is it? Where is your heart, Aaron? I see no evidence of it.' I was practically screaming in his face; my pain, fears, hurt and anger driving me on. The mug in my hand was shaking so much the tea was slopping over the sides, burning my hand, the sting hitting my nerve endings and resulting in an increase in my emotional outburst.

Aaron kept his voice low, but stepped closer so I could hear him, a look of sadness on his face. 'I did try to cover for you, Hannah. I tried. Catherine is on a mission. You know how bad it is right now.' He paused while I took a breath. I looked behind him and saw I was drawing an audience. Ross.

'The reason I don't talk to you about my feelings is because I have Asperger's. I *am* upset about Sally. I am upset that the team isn't coping well and I want to do the best that I can to support you and to help you support them. The simplest way I can think to do that is to work as hard as I can, so that's why you see me the way that you do. I will always support you as long as we work together, Hannah.'

And with that, he walked away.

98

Evie took the mug I was still holding and set it down on her desk. She pulled open her top drawer, fished out a pack of chocolate biscuits and handed them to me. There were only a few left.

My life was spiralling. 'How could I do this to him?' I paced to the end of her office and turned on my heel.

'You weren't to know.'

'I wasn't to know he has Asperger's, but I am supposed to know how to treat my staff, Evie.' I turned again as I reached the opposite end of her small office. 'There's no way I should have yelled at him in the corridor like that. There's no way I should have yelled at him like that, full stop.'

'You're stressed, you know that, right?'

The biscuit tasted sweet in my mouth, the melted chocolate sticking like glue, and I struggled to answer. Evie passed me my mug and I slurped down a mouthful of now-cool green tea.

'Yes. I do. But what can I do? There's nowhere to run, with this investigation going on, and Sally's inquest about to start up again soon.' A sigh escaped from me. 'What have I done to Aaron?'

I paced back to the other end of her office. Evie watched me from her chair, her stunning curls piled on top of her head today. Strands had escaped from where grips and bobbles were trying to restrain them. 'I doubt you have done anything to him. It's likely he told you so you'd understand. From what you said, he's trying to support you and the team. Let him.'

I twisted myself round again as I made to walk another stretch of her office. 'He's right though. Things are falling apart. Or rather, I'm falling apart and I've needed him. I'm losing focus.'

I looked at my friend.

'Do you know why I was late in today?'

'No, why?'

She grabbed the biscuit packet from me as I made my way to the last one and pulled it out of the pack for herself.

'Because I was busy getting drunk on my own last night, on a bottle of red, while I reread articles Ethan had written about the investigation and the initial one about the inquest, and I forgot to plug in my phone and fell asleep on the sofa. Drowning in my own sorrows.'

Evie held out the half biscuit she had left. I ate it.

'I need to refocus on my team and on the investigation, and not on the past. Not on Ethan. Not on what I may or may not have done. I need to pull them through this and they won't get through it if I fall by the wayside first.'

I walked back to Evie's desk and finished my green tea.

'That article I reread last night.'

'Which one?'

'About Sally's inquest. Her death. Her murder. It felt too much.'

'I know, sweetie. But you seem to be on the right track at the minute.'

I paused. *Death.*

Death.

Murder.

What was it about those things?

Death, it was so final.

Painful.

'Shit!'

'What?'

'Death.'

'I don't follow.'

'The digoxin. We've not thought about it widely enough. Well, we thought we were … but what if the patient who is prescribed the digoxin is actually dead now and someone *else* is using their prescription?'

'Now, I follow.'

'That is a list of patients I need.'

99

Connie dropped the paper on his knee. It landed heavily. Smacking down flat.

'I thought I'd bring it to you this morning, rather than have you dashing to the door for it.'

Isaac hadn't even heard it arrive today. His mood was dark. Unlike the sunlight which was already streaming through the window with a warmth to it that hinted at a searing day.

'Thanks.'

She was already gone, her footsteps fading up the staircase towards Em's room.

The *Today* was face down. He didn't move. He was afraid. For the first time since this started, not since it all started, because that involved Emma and there was no fear like the fear of losing a child, but since he started his plan of action for her, since then, he was afraid.

His hand shook as he turned the newspaper over and laid it out flat so he could read it. The headlines clamouring for every pixel of space, their sensationalised words fighting against the images taken during the previous night. Isaac's heart hammered against his chest. He

couldn't breathe.

City Hit By Riots

The city of Nottingham is recovering from the worst night of violence in its recent memory after riots broke out in several suburbs as well as the city centre.

Events took an alarming turn as St Ann's police station was firebombed while officers were still inside the building. The Today *has been informed that there are three civilian staff in hospital with minor smoke inhalation. Carol Timpson, 54, Keeley Bond, 23, and Mike Gott, 31.*

Fire crews were quick to the scene and to put the fire out. The building is structurally secure and officers are back at work today.

The disorder started after the sudden and violent death of 4-year-old Bridgette York, the previous day, who was shopping with her mother at Tesco on Carlton Hill, when a car ploughed into the store, killing her instantly.

As the driver of the vehicle was arrested, anger erupted around the lack of identification of the so-called 'poison killer'.

Rioting first broke out at the supermarket where Bridgette died when a group of people targeted the store to display their outrage at the turn of events.

Police attempted to quell the unrest but it soon became apparent they were outmanned as the protesters turned on officers, throwing projectiles; bottles, bricks and any other items they could get their hands on.

This was a catalyst for social media-led hysteria as a strongly-worded hashtag #nottscopsare**** flooded Facebook and Twitter and the police found themselves the target rather than the law enforcement.

This quickly escalated to widespread disorder and emergency services were stretched to the limit as the fire service and medical personnel battled to gain control, save lives and bring order again.

DCI Anthony Grey said, 'This was an act of disorder that put the lives of Nottinghamshire police officers and staff at risk.

'They showed great courage in the face of adversity last night and they will continue to serve and protect the people of Nottinghamshire. We ask for calm and control today and for your help if we are to resolve this situation as quickly as possible. I would urge anyone who has any knowledge of the 'poison killer' to come forward; your information will be treated in the utmost confidence.'

The 'poison killer' may not have expected this level of disruption but we have to wonder if this plays into his longer-term game plan.

Longer-term game plan? Is that how they were seeing him? As a man, with a longer-term game plan? Isaac's chest was really hurting now. What had he done? Connie was right. It could have been Em out there. If she had still been alive and some father decided this was a good idea, then she could have been in the middle of this.

He was poison. Look what he had turned into. He had to get out of the house. Away from Connie. He was sure she could see right through him. Before all this – when they were a real couple, before they were just Emma's bereaved parents, she could see him and see through him.

He had to get away.

The allotment.

Isaac dropped the paper on the floor and picked up his car keys.

100

The updated list was obtained from HEAD with relative speed as we narrowed down the parameters to just outside the timeframe the murders started. Giving time allowance for shock to wear off. Because we knew what we wanted and we knew where to go this time, it was all so much easier.

Martin had worked efficiently on this as I had gone to Catherine's office.

Thanks to Evie, I was in a much better frame of mind to see her than I had been when I'd first arrived at work. Had I gone straight in to see her while my emotions were still all over, my job could have been in a very tenuous position. As it was, Evie had allowed me to talk things through, combined with a lot of pacing and consuming of chocolate biscuits, but now I felt clearer, more level-headed. More focused on the job at hand. On my team.

Detective Superintendent Catherine Walker on the other hand, could have done with sharing a few chocolate biscuits with Evie. She was in a foul mood and was not shy in letting me know. I was shown into her office as soon as I arrived. It was still early but her office was already starting to warm up. There were two walls of windows, creating an impressive greenhouse effect. One of the windows was pushed open but it was doing little to ease the heat that was accumulating in the room.

I pushed my fringe back off my face and closed the door before taking a seat in front of Catherine's desk. A single bead of sweat slid down my spine. I arched my back so it wouldn't stick to my shirt. Catherine didn't seem fazed by the heat. She looked cool, if somewhat annoyed.

'Where the hell have you been, Hannah? Do you think you have the time to slope off and have a lie-in when we have all hell breaking loose outside our doors?'

She didn't give me time to explain before she continued, 'Let me answer that for you, if you are not up to task, then tell me now and I shall reassign the investigation to someone who feels the case is within their capabilities.'

She gave me an icy glare. I just wished it did something to cool the room down. She then picked up her phone and demanded Grey join us. We waited it out. Both silent. She'd made her point, I didn't think she was expecting me to wade into this with her.

As soon as he arrived, shirt collar looking loose around his neck, Catherine erupted again. Grey paused where he was, obviously unsure what he was walking into. I didn't have the words to get into this with her. I'd had my own meltdown; I wasn't prepared to share in hers. I gave her the silence to blow off some steam.

'Bloody hell, Anthony, we need a strong team on this, with strong leadership. Do we really think this is the right case for Hannah to be running?'

Several more beads of sweat slithered down the same path as the first, collecting in a damp patch in the waistband of my trousers. No amount of fidgeting was going to stop this happening. I could barely focus on Catherine's words for the discomfort of her office.

Grey looked at me. 'I think she can cope. We've given her the resources. No one could have predicted the public order problems we've seen erupt this past few days. This would have happened, whomever was running this case.'

He was supporting me. Grey was actually backing me up to Catherine. This was a first.

She didn't look pleased.

'And you, Hannah, do you think this is the right case for you before the inquest is heard in full and then finalised?'

Grey had actually backed me up.

'I don't think any job is the right one, because that means someone has died,' I leaned forward in my chair, 'but I do think it's an investigation I am wholly capable of leading.'

She pursed her lips. 'I'm getting a lot of pressure from the Chief on this one. The cost to the force has gone up prohibitively with the need for Mutual Aid assistance and the surge in negative publicity for the county does not please him, especially when it's crime related. He's not happy. Not happy at all.'

I wished she'd opened another window. The hair at my scalp clung to my head. I wanted out of there. 'Well, I can't speak for the chief's mood, Ma'am, but I can speak for my own and that of my team, and we are good. We're determined and we're putting in the hours we need to. The extra staff that have been provided are fitting in well and are being utilised. And I think we may have a pretty good lead going this morning.'

Both Catherine and Grey gave me a questioning look.

'I'll know more when I get back to the incident room,' I clarified, 'but we're requesting the list of patients prescribed digoxin who are actually deceased.'

'What?' Her tone was incredulous.

'I was thinking about it – and what if the poisoner is not the person who is being prescribed digoxin or a distributor who has accidentally put digoxin out as something more innocuous, but a family member or friend of a deceased patient? I mean, why would you be using your own medicine? The very medicine that is keeping you alive? This makes more sense. A family member with digoxin left over.'

'That does make sense. Good move, Hannah. Do some work on it and let me know as soon as you have results.'

Martin had no trouble getting the updated HEAD list with the deceased patients on it. There were only three patients who had previously been taking digoxin who had died in the short timeframe we were looking at, which made our job a whole lot easier. *If* this was the right track. It was a long shot but it was a lot more than we'd had to go on than at any other point during the investigation.

We shared the three names out and the intelligence tasks involved and discovered that one of the families of the patients had actually taken the left-over medication in to the pharmacy to be disposed of after their death. That left two patients with medication still in the hands of grieving family members.

I sent Ross and Martin to visit the GP surgeries of the two remaining patients and they came back with some surprising results. Though patient confidentiality still existed for patients who were dead, the GP of one of the patients in particular felt that in the current circumstances, it was necessary to share certain information with us and for us to use that information as we saw fit within our investigation. And having the awareness of the situation that we now did, thanks to the GP, I felt for what we were about to do.

I realised we'd been looking in the wrong place all along.

101

Aaron and I stood in front of the white uPVC door and waited to see if anyone would answer. The search team was parked up in a van a couple of doors down. We didn't want to spook anyone here. If we were right, which I believed we were, then this couple, though responsible for utter carnage, had been through quite enough. Rampaging through their front door was not going to resolve the issues we had and I had no intention of screwing up as I had done last year.

I believed we were at the correct address, but I wasn't taking chances with this so I'd sent Martin and Ross and another search team to the other address to cover our bases.

Aaron was quiet, hands firmly in his trouser pockets. He wasn't expecting trouble either.

How did I resolve this with him? He'd taken me into his confidence but in the most awkward of circumstances. With, I imagine, little way out. I didn't want him to be in distress and definitely not with me.

The door opened.

The woman stood before me was pale and slender. Her skin tight to her face.

'Mrs Knight?'

'Yes.'

'Can we come in please?' I held up my warrant card so she could see it. 'We need to speak with you and your husband and it's better if we don't do it on your doorstep.'

The woman sighed. Not annoyance. Or fear. More resignation. Had she expected this day?

We followed her in to a living room that was clean but lacking. In what exactly, I couldn't quite put my finger on.

'Is Mr Knight at home? This conversation needs to involve both of you.'

'No, he's not.' She seated herself on one of the two chairs in the room and indicated with a hand for us to do the same. 'Can I ask why you're here?'

'Before I answer any questions,' I took the other chair and Aaron took up position on the two-seater sofa, 'can I ask you about your daughter, Emma?'

She sucked in a breath and her hand went up to her mouth.

'I'm sorry, Mrs Knight, we need to talk about this. We are aware of your loss and don't want to be insensitive but we need to ask where her medications are, the ones she was taking for her heart failure?'

She nodded and stood.

'This way. I'll show you.'

We walked through to a large square airy kitchen. A circular family table was placed in the centre of the room. Connie Knight opened an upper level cupboard door and started moving mugs, boxes of paracetamol, ibuprofen and antacid. She moved them from one side of the cupboard to the other and back again. Her arm movements became more and more frantic.

'Mrs Knight?'

She turned around.

A single tear slipped down her face.

'It's not here.'

102

The tears kept falling silently. Aaron fiddled with his tie; a sign I was now beginning to understand. So many things were slipping into place.

'Connie,' I looked at her, at her soundless distress. 'Can I call you Connie?'

She nodded.

'We need to know where your husband is. Where has Isaac gone?'

One hand gripped tight hold of the kitchen worktop. Her skin, taut and white over her knuckles.

'He left. You've only just missed him,' her voice was barely a whisper. She didn't ask why we needed to speak to him. The tears told me all I needed to know. They kept falling. A silent trail of her agony.

'Where? Where has he gone? It's important we get to him as quickly as possible.'

'He has an allotment. The one on Bessell Lane at the other side of Stapleford. He spends a lot of time there. I don't see much of him. He says he's going there. We hurt each other with our grief. He goes to the allotment so he doesn't have to face me.' Her fingers gripped harder.

'And the drugs?' Aaron asked.

She nodded and tears fell from her face to the floor. 'Yes. If he's taken them. Then yes.'

103

We were too far away and too many lives had already been lost for me to be precious about who got to Isaac Knight first, so I phoned Ross and told him and Martin, as they were closer, to get to the allotment and we'd meet them there.

The support van started up and pulled off behind us. Getting off this housing estate wasn't going to be a problem but we'd seen how snarled the traffic was on the main roads as we drove in. People were trying to get home from work now. It had taken us several hours to get the list, make the enquiries and get the search warrant.

Aaron was quiet behind the wheel. Focused.

'I'm sorry, Aaron.'

'Don't be.' He didn't flinch.

'But I am.' I hated myself sometimes. 'I lashed out and it was wrong. I took it out on you and I shouldn't have. I'm sorry.'

'It doesn't matter.'

Derby Road was slow going. Painful.

'But it does. I rely on you and you know that – and I repay you how? By shouting at you in the corridor.'

Silence.

'I didn't mean to put you in a place where you felt you didn't have a choice but to make that disclosure.'

'I know you didn't.'

Dammit. I wanted a conversation. To be let off, I suppose.

'Do they know?'

'Who know, what?' His focus was firmly on the road and progressing as quickly as he could to our destination.

'Work. About … about the Asperger's.'

'Yes, I disclosed it on my application form, then went through the rest of the application process and passed it in the same way as any other person.'

'Okay.'

'I just choose not to keep telling every single set of supervisors every time I changed department within the organisation, Hannah.'

'I get that. Again, I'm sorry I put you in that position.'

'Don't worry about it. I won't.'

'Okay.'

I picked up my phone to call Ross to see if they were there yet. He'd had it rough. I was worried about how this was going to turn out. It was a volatile and sensitive situation. Was Ross really the right person for this job? To be talking to the poison killer? I'd been supportive as I should be, but that didn't mean I thought he was in quite the right place yet. He had Martin with him, though.

'Thank you,' I said.

'For?'

'Telling me.'

I pressed Ross's number. There was no answer.

104

It was warm outside, but inside the confines of the small, dark shed it was cooler. He liked that about the allotment. The coolness it offered in the face of blazing heat, as well as the obvious privacy. The weather report said that it would be dry and sunny all week. Another week for him to spend his time here. It had been a long time since he used the allotment for the purpose it was intended. He couldn't remember the last time he had planted or tended a vegetable or green salad. Many people came to their allotments for time out as well as for growing, but time out was all he came for now.

The knock on the wooden door made him jump. No one came here. Connie didn't visit and he gave her no reason to. He hadn't spoken to his allotment neighbours in such a long time, other than a passing 'good morning'. Before he lost Emma, at weekends they would sit outside and drink whiskey out of old jars until late in the day and wander home after a good day planting and putting the world to rights. But now, he wouldn't know who would be knocking on his small part of the world. Isaac didn't move, his thoughts lost in the past.

Then a voice broke through.

'Mr Knight, it's the police, can you open up please so we can have a word?'

So this was it, then.

Isaac had never wanted it to go this far. He hadn't wanted that small girl to die. He didn't want the city to crumble and break. He simply wanted people to notice his girl was gone and to pay attention as to why, to do something about it.

What would happen to him now?

His hands shook in his lap where he was seated.

He never wanted this hell to break loose.

'Mr Knight? We really need you to open the door. It'd be much better if we could come in and talk to you, rather than talk to you through the door where others might hear your business.'

Isaac Knight stood and opened the door.

105

There were two men standing in front of him. One younger than the other. Both looked very serious. They asked to come in and he moved aside so they could enter. The shed might have been small but there was room to move as he kept it tidy. Underneath the running kitchen worktop was a cupboard where he was storing all Em's leftover medications.

Two three-legged stools fit neatly into the space and propped in the far corner were his spade, fork and trowel.

They looked at him a moment and he looked back. The time had come.

Then the older of the two men broke the silence. He introduced them, though Isaac instantly forgot their names as his mind whirled with the mental overload of what he'd done and what was to come. The older officer then told him that officers had been to his house. That they'd spoken to Connie.

His Connie.

His darling, Connie.

His wife. The woman he loved. The woman he had pushed away for so long. Police turning up at their door because of him. How do you cope with more pain when you already have more than the world should ever throw at a person? How does one deal with the grief when a child has been so savagely taken from you – slowly and painfully?

The older one spoke again, breaking through the fog and pain of swirling thoughts. He said they were looking for something and that Connie found it wasn't where she expected it to be, became upset and directed them here. Maybe Isaac could help?

His mind stuck on the words that she had become upset. *He* had done this to her. How could he have not known this would have hurt her?

A small voice emerged from Isaac. 'She has been grieving so much. She lost so much. I never wanted to cause her any pain.'

106

David cleaned out the bucket and tidied it away into the cupboard. Mrs Rudyard wasn't well today and had vomited all over herself and the floor in the dining hall, much to the shock and disgust of some of the others. They were a funny old bunch. Set in their ways. Crotchety and bad tempered at times, but he loved working here. He'd cleaned up the floor and chatted to the residents to calm them down while Cressida had taken Mrs Rudyard back to her room to get cleaned up.

He wasn't worried about her. She was old now, ninety-two years of age and still going strong. But they would keep an eye on her.

He opened her door and found her sitting up in her chair. A spot of colour, one on each cheek, glowing on her face. He adored this woman. Nothing ever stopped her. He fully expected her to get her letter from the Queen and he'd be here to open it with her. She smiled that cheeky smile at him as he walked in.

'So, David, did I upset Vernon and Pauline just now? I can imagine their faces.' Mrs Rudyard laughed, which changed into a cough.

'Hey, take it easy.' David sat in the other chair. 'You did get a few tuts and funny looks as you were leaving, but you also had some concerned looks, Lois. Give them some credit, you have some friends out there.'

She made a shooing motion with her hand. 'I know, I know. I'm fine. It must have been something I ate this morning. I feel better now it's out. I'm going to sit in here for a little while and listen to my audiobook before I come out to the rec room. Okay?'

'Okay. You want me to pass you your CD player from the bedside table?'

'Yes please, David.'

He handed her the small machine. 'What're you listening to?'

'*I Know Why The Caged Bird Sings.*'

'Any good?'

'Yes. You should read more, young man.'

He laughed. 'I read plenty, Lois.'

'I don't mean the sports pages.'

'You'll convert me one day, but I spend so many hours here I don't have much time left. I do enjoy hearing about the stories through you, so let me know all about *The Caged Birds* when you're done.'

'Okay.' She put her skeletal hand over his. 'Thank you, David. You make this place so much more bearable.'

He smiled down at her and patted her hand with his free one. 'You know you're my favourite and you're the person who makes working here a complete pleasure.' He stood and moved towards the door.

'Press the buzzer when you want help to come back out to the rec room.'

107

They asked him if he had any medications in the shed that he wanted to hand over before they did a search of the entire area. Shed and allotment.

Isaac only took a moment to think about his answer. He had been thinking of nothing else but the consequences of his actions the past few days, even if he hadn't considered this particular scenario. He knew what the right thing to do was.

He sat with a thud down on the stool he had recently vacated. It was cooler now, the air in the allotment shed chilling the plastic seat. He welcomed the freshness. It was starting to feel stuffy and claustrophobic in this space, where the single strip light overhead cast a weird amber sheen on everything in the wooden hut.

'I did it for Emma, you know,' he said as he twisted to collect the last of her medication from one of the cupboards on the floor. 'The medical profession failed her. Let her down.' Upright again now, bottles in hand. 'They let her die.' He could feel his heart contract in his chest as he talked about her. His baby. His precious baby. 'I wanted them to know, to feel some pain, to notice.' He looked the older of the two officers in the eye and sneered. 'To look down from their ivory towers and see that their prized drug was killing people, that it was in the press and for all the wrong reasons, that people were talking badly about it, that they needed to do something about it and quickly before anyone else died. Their drugs were faulty, they didn't save lives at all, they needed to know that and what better way than to show them, to show it as harmful. They would look at it then. Assess it again. How long is it since it was assessed?' He could feel the cold sharp blade of anger cut through the grief as he talked.

The medication was quietly taken out of his hand and placed into a clear plastic bag with an orange stripe around the top and sealed.

The older officer looked at him, 'Mr Knight ... Isaac.' He paused, took a breath then started again, 'Emma stopped taking the drugs of her own accord because they made her feel ill. We've seen the medical records. She informed her GP she was going to do this and she didn't want it disclosing to either you or her mother because it would upset you so much.'

Isaac looked at him. Silent.

'Isaac, she stopped taking the digoxin herself. It was helping her, but she chose not to take it.'

His chest contracted again and he felt a heat rush through him. How could they try and blame Emma? And when she wasn't here to defend what they said? She would never do that. She wouldn't give up on life, on the life she had planned, the white picket fence, the 2.4 family, wanting to be a barrister. She wouldn't give up on herself like that. And she wouldn't give up on them. Him. Her mother. Good God, her mother.

He stood with such force the stool flew back and crashed into the spade and fork in the corner, making them topple over. There was a moment of metallic noise and the three men regarded each other.

Then he hissed, 'How dare you? She would never do that. She loved her family too much. She would never abandon us without a fight. You think you've won,' he laughed, 'you have the last of the medication, but I put products back on the shelves yesterday.' More laughter and this time he seemed genuinely happy. Gleeful.

The older one queried him, 'What are you saying?'

'There are contaminated products still in the shops.'

108

Ross stepped forward. His heart was in his mouth. He couldn't stand back and watch from the sidelines any more. This man was hurting. The grief was palpable in the small space. The anger combustible. He could feel the stirrings of recognition, of the feelings, in the pit of his stomach. Ross could see these emotions were eating at Isaac. Raw and savage. Here was a man who was lashing out because he couldn't cope with what was going on inside of him. Ross needed to reach him if they were to save lives – instead of watching more be snuffed out.

Space in the shed was tight but Ross shifted his weight past Martin so he could be seen by Isaac Knight properly. He wanted to create eye contact. He wanted to create a bond of honesty.

But could he do that? Could he go there? Face his own grief?

Martin's arm went out to the side, blocking his path as he tried to step past him. Ross put his hand onto Martin's arm, looked him in the eye and nodded. He was okay to do this. Martin hesitated, keeping his arm in the way, but Ross knew they didn't have time for this.

'Isaac … is it okay to call you Isaac?'

'Do what you will, it doesn't matter now'

'Ross?' Martin interjected, but Ross continued to speak.

'Let's grab these seats and get a bit more comfortable. It's not the best place I've ever had to have a conversation.' He grabbed the toppled stool, handed it to Isaac and pulled up the other one for himself. 'But, then again, it's not the worst.' He smiled.

Isaac seated himself but didn't respond.

'Look, I have to caution you before I go on, because it's procedural stuff, but I want to talk to you, Isaac, it's really important. Okay?'

He nodded, mutely, and Ross quietly cautioned him.

'Look, Isaac, I can hear your pain. Really, I can. And believe it or not, I understand it.'

Martin leaned back on the worktop and listened. Isaac glared at him.

'I had a colleague last year; you may have read about her. She died. On duty.'

Isaac looked up at Ross then.

'Her name was Sally. She was wonderful, you know. Funny, serious, hard-working, kind, self-conscious, annoying, frustrating, everything a person can be, should be and I looked up to her. I thought we'd work together for a long time and she'd teach me everything she knew and we'd laugh about the jobs we'd worked and support each other when times got tough ...'

He rubbed his face and Isaac's stance relaxed somewhat. His shoulders slumped forward.

'But, guess what? She didn't want supporting. When it came down to the crunch, she didn't want me.

'I was there. I was sat opposite her every day, but she didn't reach out. She held onto her secret and she didn't reach out. And because of that, I lost her.' He looked at Martin now. '*We* lost her.' Martin nodded.

A tear slipped down Isaac's face and he brushed it away with the back of his hand.

'It's been six months now and I've screwed up because I've not been able to come to terms with that, but day by day it gets easier. And the one thing I've had to learn is that Sally made her own decisions because she was her own person. This was the person I had chosen to love as a friend – so how can I then go and challenge her in death for the very decision that made her who she was?'

Martin cleared his throat and looked away towards the allotment shed door, which was ajar.

'If you ask me, Isaac, the decisions Emma made are the decisions that made her who she was. The grown woman you loved. The girl you nurtured into a woman. How can you challenge her now? How can you continue with this fight?'

109

After the brightness of the day, the inside of the shed looked dark. For a minute I couldn't make out who was who, but I could hear what was going on. I stood in the doorway and listened. It was Ross I could hear talking.

I followed the sound of his voice to two figures on stools facing each other at the end of the shed, and figured out he was the one on my right. He was leaning forward, elbows on his knees, face up to the man in front of him. Isaac Knight was slumped, his shoulders curled over. A man defeated. Martin was leaning against a kitchen work counter; relaxed, but aware of the scene in front of him.

Aaron was eager to go inside and make the arrest, but I wanted to listen and understand what was happening first, rather than going in all guns blazing. What I heard, from Ross, about his feelings towards Sally and how he had struggled to deal with it had moved me close to tears. His honesty to this man he had only just met and who had been killing innocent people was brave. I was so very proud of Ross, not just in his honesty but in assessing the situation, sensing just how to get the right reaction from Isaac, knowing that using his own personal experience, something so deeply personal, would help this volatile and emotional man. He'd changed, turned himself around since the incident at court. It had served as a wake-up call. A costly one, but one that had worked. He was looking like the officer I knew him to be. Competent and articulate. Intelligent and resourceful.

Martin must have sensed us or heard us approach, as he turned his head and saw me in the doorway. I offered him a smile. They had this in hand. I wasn't worried. It looked as though we were about to close this job, bar all the paperwork.

Then Isaac Knight spoke.

And what he said chilled me to the core. On the warm spring day, stood in the glow of the sun, on the threshold of the shed, with the rays warming my skin, I shivered.

Isaac Knight told Ross where he had placed the last of the products.

I hadn't heard the start of this conversation. I didn't know we had more products out there.

We needed to find them before they killed anyone else.

I hoped we weren't too late.

110

David had expected to hear the buzzer from Lois's room by now. Time passed so quickly here in Ruby House, with all the chores and all the demands the elderly residents made. He adored working with them and he loved working here. Two great things about his job were the residents and how quickly time did pass.

There were your normal day-to-day chores that needed attention but there were also the small things, the joyful things, playing cards, singing songs, playing peacekeeper. He didn't know many of his friends who were as happy to go to work.

His thoughts turned again to Lois. He'd become distracted by a fight between a couple of the residents after he left her in her room and it had escalated when Milly put her false teeth in Edward's cup of tea and he exploded on her, waving his walking stick in the air, only just missing her head. It had taken him a good half hour or more to talk them both down. Milly had been furious at the way Edward had bitched about Lois after she had vomited in the dining hall. Another feisty one. David only hoped he'd have half as much life in him at their age as they had.

Now he had everyone settled, he walked up the flight of stairs to Lois's room, knocked and waited.

There was no reply.

He knocked again.

Still no reply.

She'd probably nodded off while listening to her audiobook. He could hear it quietly playing away in her room. David turned the handle and crept in.

'Lois?'

She was still in the chair where he left her, but there was something not quite right. And he'd worked here long enough to know what that was.

'Oh my God, Lois, no.'

111

It was seven weeks following the arrest of Isaac Knight and I was with Aaron in my office. We'd closed down the shop where Knight had stated he had left another contaminated product, on the day we arrested him. He said he'd injected an orange and placed it in the store container. We couldn't find any products with digoxin in and no further suspicious deaths were reported.

'I wonder how many deaths went undetected as suspicious?' I mused aloud.

'I don't know. It's a strange one. Digoxin can kill you and look like the very thing it's supposed to be preventing you from dying from. A heart problem.'

'Grief ... a strong emotion. Strong enough to drive a man to do something like that.' I fiddled with a pen in my fingers.

'Losing a child has to be one of the hardest losses to come back from because you never ever expect to outlive your children.'

'Do we know how Connie is doing?'

'Martin spoke to her yesterday and she's doing okay. Still at her sister's in Durham and will be for the foreseeable future. The fact that she's the wife of the Nottinghamshire poisoner is hard on her. Not just emotionally, but in her day-to-day life. She gets trouble when anyone recognises her. She's torn about selling the house because of the memories it holds of Emma, but other than that she'd sell it in a heartbeat.'

I looked at him but he hadn't realised what he'd said. I was glad I had Aaron. He'd always been the level head in comparison to my sometimes-emotional one, and now I understood why. I was glad he'd told me about the Asperger's, but still wished it hadn't been under such stressful circumstances, that it didn't feel as though I'd forced him into a corner. I wished he'd felt he'd been able to candidly tell me, but that was my problem to live with, not his.

'And the local force in Durham are aware she's there, in case there are problems?'

'Yes, that's all in place.'

'Great. She's had a lot to deal with. We don't want her to have to put up with any more.'

Aaron stood to leave.

'Aaron?'

'Yeah.'

'I know it was a couple of weeks ago, but are you doing okay after the inquest?'

He paused and considered me before answering. I put my pen down and waited on him.

'It's the natural order of our processes. I'm fine.'

112

I closed the door behind me and turned to face Detective Superintendent Catherine Walker. Her face was closed off. A few more lines around the eyes, maybe, than there had been a few weeks ago. Her organised desk, acting as a barrier between us, took on a more ominous feel, as I had no idea why I had been called in. The Isaac Knight case had been a tough investigation, both in terms of the crimes and consequences, and the emotions involved, but it was over. We'd stopped further deaths, identified the offender and pacified the public. However, EMSOU had been hauled over the coals by the press on a few occasions during the investigation. We'd been made to look like incompetent fools – and Catherine wasn't a fan of looking like a fool. I needed to brace myself. I steeled myself for what I thought was coming; the barrage of complaints, the list of errors we'd committed during the investigation.

'Have a seat, Hannah.'

'Ma'am.' I pulled down the jacket I was wearing, straightening it. Catherine didn't move. She continued to look at me. Watchful. Studying. I ran my fingers through my fringe, then sat on my hands.

'You might be wondering why I've called you in.' She leaned forward, resting her arms on the desk. 'I want to talk to you about the internal impact of the completion hearing of Sally's inquest,' she paused, allowing me to digest this. It wasn't at all what I was expecting and Catherine knew that. A cold trickle ran down the length of my spine. 'As you know, it's not complimentary of Nottinghamshire police, specifically the supervision of the detective constables on the enquiry.' The cold trickle that had run down my spine sprinted back up, grabbed hold of my head and squeezed. I bit my lip. Hard.

'Hannah, we knew this was coming. We've been preparing for it – or for something like it.'

Who had? What had they prepared? 'Okay.'

'Because the report found that there was a neglect of supervisory duty of care towards Sally which led indirectly to her death. Although it was her own actions that placed her in harm's way, had a supervisor paid more attention or checked in with her at the hospital after the explosion involving the car, then certain circumstances could have been avoided.'

I didn't know which was hurting more now, the icy grip on my head or my arm that had started to throb as it tended to do at inopportune moments. What was going to happen to me? Was this it? My job? My career? I couldn't speak. I let Catherine continue.

'Are you okay, Hannah?' My bloody arm. But I couldn't move my hands from under my legs as I wouldn't be able to control them.

'Hannah?'

'What? Sorry, Ma'am. Yes, yes, I'm fine. So you say that preparations have been made for this eventuality?' That final question.

'As you'd expect with a death on duty. The coroner wants us to recognise what has happened, though she has no further jurisdiction, and the command team want a scapegoat, I'm afraid.' She clasped her hands together in front of her as though in prayer.

Fuck.

'You were hospitalised at the same time as Sally was, and I'm talking about the time you both survived when you were in the car during the gas explosion.' She nodded at me, as if this was a question.

'Okay.' It was about all I could say.

'And supervisory duty was passed over to the DCI on duty at that time, which was Anthony Grey. He was the line manager in charge of the investigation. The buck, I'm afraid, stops with him. Therefore, he is being moved onto divisional CID with immediate effect. He's been informed.'

Grey? *Divisional CID?* It sucked you in and squished you up like a black hole. Not enough officers and permanent overtime. Dealing with anything and everything that no one else could or would take on. I knew he had worried about the repercussions of the inquest and the IPCC investigation and what that could potentially mean for him. As supervisors we all did. We hadn't needed to say it out loud, it was an unwritten rule that if it goes to shit on your watch, then there's a chance a move's afoot.

I felt for him but I was also relieved for myself. What kind of person did that make me? My arm wouldn't stop nagging at me. I needed some painkillers.

We'd lost Anthony.

'So,' Catherine carried on as though another part of our team fracturing off was nothing, 'his replacement will be arriving as soon as Anthony clears out his office. I don't know if you know him? DCI Kevin Baxter? He's coming from the Mansfield office. Golden boy, by all accounts. Isn't scared about ruffling feathers and wants things doing his way. Won't put up with slackers or those who think they can do what they want, regardless of policy. The command team feel he's what is needed here and is a nod to the coroner that we have taken this seriously.

'Have you heard of him yourself, Hannah?'

'Me? No, Ma'am. I'm a little shocked, to be honest. It's a lot to take in.' So, the folder I had in my desk, containing a copy of Sally's murder file, was resulting in the loss of yet another one of our own. A clear up, but in an unexpected and unwanted way.

'I know. But don't worry. Baxter may have his ways, but he still answers to me. We all want what's best for the unit and the people we serve, don't we?'

'Absolutely.' I needed to get out of here and I needed to see Grey. But what would I say to him? How do I say I'm sorry he's leaving when he'll know damn well that I'm relieved to be staying in role? What kind of friend did that make me? Could I really face him or would he see through me?

And what was in store for me in Grey's replacement, what would I be facing in Kevin Baxter?

What I needed after today, were my painkillers.

About the Author

Rebecca Bradley is a retired police detective who lives in Nottinghamshire with her family and her two Cockerpoos Alfie and Lola. They keep her company while she writes. Rebecca needs to drink copious amounts of tea to function throughout the day and if she could, she would survive on a diet of tea and cake.

She lives with the genetic disorder Hypermobile Ehlers-Danlos Syndrome and secondary disorder to that, Postural Orthostatic Tachycardia Syndrome. These are a part of her daily life and she has to adjust her days accordingly, but she still manages to commit murder and will continue to for a long time to come.

If you enjoyed Made to be Broken and would be happy to leave a review online that would be much appreciated, as word of mouth is often how other readers find new books to read.

DI Hannah Robbins will return. Sign up to the newsletter on the blog to make sure you don't miss the launch date. There will also be regular giveaways to members of the newsletter list, as well as early previews and exclusives that won't be available on the blog.

You can find Rebecca on her blog: http://Rebeccabradleycrime.com

On Twitter: http://Twitter.com/RebeccaJBradley

And on Facebook: http://Facebook.com/RebeccaBradleyCrime

Please look her up, as she would love to chat.

Acknowledgements

My name is the one attached to Made to be Broken, but it takes so many more people than just the author to create a novel and this one has been no different.

I may know my police procedure, but I certainly don't know my poisons or how they affect the body and I don't know how to write a newspaper article and I don't know the real world that high functioning Aspergers people have to contend with. So, it is with my deepest thanks and heartfelt gratitude that I acknowledge the following people for their help, expertise and guidance and ask for their understanding with any liberties I may have taken.

I am indebted to Denyse Kirkby, who helped me not only with Aaron during Made to be Broken, but who knew from the very off, as I wrote Shallow Waters, that Aaron was living with Aspergers and as a writer who lives with Aspergers herself, Denyse has been instrumental in making sure he is not a comedy version, but a genuine, functioning member of the team. This was important to both of us.

With thanks again to Lauren Turner for her expertise with Ethan. I found out just how different writing fiction and writing articles were during Made to be Broken and I'm sure Lauren must have laughed hysterically when I sent her my first attempt at an article. Any errors, as always, are my own.

Now, poisoning someone. It's not something you have to think about every day and asking the difficult questions of a pathologist can be quite unnerving. You never know quite what they're going to think of you, but Dr Mark Stephens answered everything very calmly and without getting worried. So, thank you.

Thank you to the book club, Bookit!, at Mansfield in Nottinghamshire, run by Sadie Booth, for advice on labelling Isaac's chapters after a meeting where I queried how to run two timelines for one character.

To Jane Isaac and Dave Sivers for trudging through an early draft that was making me want to give up writing all together. It made it to completion!

Thank you Jane, Lisa Cutts and Susi Holliday for providing me with such fabulous quotes. I adore you.

There are so many other people who have offered words of encouragement, they are too many to name for fear of leaving someone out and offending, but to you all, I am truly grateful. To those who make me laugh when I want to cry at the mess I'm making of the manuscript, you know who you are, I thank you for being there, every single time!

Without Keshini Naidoo, I would not have turned this from scrambled mess into something resembling a novel. I owe you so much gratitude. Thank you. And Helen Baggott, thank you for the finishing touches, without which, it all falls down.

Finally, to Pete and our children, who always put up with me. Thank you.

Printed in Great Britain
by Amazon

46586674R00218